CROSSING LIVE

Andrew Bowie was born in Scotland. He grew up in Australia and now lives in Oxfordshire in the UK. *Crossing Live* is his second novel. His first, *Peloton of Two*, was published in 2016.

For more information about Andrew and his books, visit: www.andrewbowie.net

CROSSING LIVE

Andrew Bowie

AUGMONT BOOKS

First published in 2017
by Augmont Books

Copyright © Andrew Bowie 2017

The right of Andrew Bowie to be identified as the author of this work has been asserted in accordance with the Copyright, Designs and Patents Act 1998. All rights reserved.

All characters and events in this publication are fictitious and any resemblance to real persons, living or dead, is purely coincidental.

ISBN 9780995649019

1

'Taxi for Kendall.'

Roland had arrived home from work to find the white Commodore sitting in his driveway. The engine was idling and the air conditioning was working overtime. The driver had reluctantly lowered the window to give the booking name. With the late-afternoon temperature still in the high thirties, Roland could hardly blame him. 'My name's Kendall,' he replied. 'But there must be some sort of mistake. I didn't order a taxi.'

The driver checked his notebook and shook his head. 'It says here I'm to collect a Roland Kendall from this address.'

Roland could think of only one person who would book a taxi without bothering to let him know. But he needed to be sure before sending it away. 'Did they happen to say who requested it?'

'Someone by the name of Porter. The instructions are to drop you at the Channel 5 studios on Mt Coot-tha, if possible by 5.30.'

'Okay. Thanks, but I won't be needing you after all.'

The driver stared at him, exasperated. 'Look, mate. I've been waiting here a good 20 minutes already. Someone will have to pay for the call-out even if you're not going.'

‘I’m going, all right. But not by car. I’ve been sitting at a desk all day and feel like taking my bike out for a spin. Don’t worry, Channel 5 will stump up for the fare. Phil Porter runs the place.’

‘Suit yourself, then.’ The driver eased his head through the window and studied the ominous line of cloud drifting in from the west. ‘You’d better get your skates on if you don’t want to get wet.’

Roland nodded. The odds of getting to Channel 5 before the rain came on looked slim. But he was determined to make his own way there. Every tiny act of independence from Phil was a victory. It made giving in, when he had to, so much easier. As the taxi departed, he hurried into the house to change.

The Mt Coot-tha climb never seemed to get easier, no matter how many times Roland tackled it. The long, low ridge on the edge of Brisbane’s western suburbs was barely high enough to qualify as a mountain. But the scenic drive leading to the summit rose steadily for more than two kilometres. Roland was still climbing when the storm broke. He struggled on through heavy rain but, when it hardened into hail, he realised it was pointless to continue. He turned into the summit car park and raced for the safety of the lookout.

Standing in the open-sided shelter, he unclipped his cycle helmet, wiped the water from his eyes, and watched the storm batter the city. The unexpected summons from Phil worried him. They had been friends for more than a decade, since the beginning of their respective university courses. After graduation, they had both joined Porter Corp, where Phil, the youngest son of Sir Adrian Porter, had risen effortlessly through his father’s business empire. Roland still floundered in the organisation’s murkiest depths and survived by virtue of occasional lifelines sent down from above. The invitation by taxi, a new tactic from Phil, could only mean that his career was, once again, on life support.

The storm gradually spent itself and moved out into Moreton Bay, leaving the western suburbs bathed in a brilliant, rain-filtered sunlight. A bus nosed into the car park and began to offload a tour group of Japanese honeymooners. As they streamed towards the lookout, Canons, Nikons, and Minoltas at the ready, Roland decided it was time to move on. He freewheeled onto the road and continued around the mountain drive, passing the other commercial television studios before reaching the entrance to Channel 5.

He locked his cycle outside and walked into the building, shivering as he passed into the deep chill of the air conditioning. In his hard-soled cycling shoes, he clicked across the foyer's spotless floor tiles. The tap-dance attracted the attention of a grey-haired security guard, who stared with evident alarm at the new arrival's skintight cycling gear and storm-battered appearance. Roland imagined his description being stored away in case of trouble: Suspect's height: *1.8m*. Build: *lean*. Eyes: *hazel*. Hair: *light brown, wavy, windswept*. Other distinguishing features: *loud harlequin-patterned shirt, muddy legs*.

He tried to lighten the mood with a friendly smile. When that failed, he played his only trump card. 'I have an appointment to see Phil Porter.'

The mention of Channel 5's senior executive changed everything. The guard looked down at his clipboard, then back at Roland with a grudging respect. 'You're Mr Kendall?'

'That's me.'

'Mr Porter left a message for you. He's delayed in an overrunning meeting and asked that you wait for him in his office.' He paused to hand Roland a preprinted visitor's pass. 'If you'd like to take a seat, I'll find someone to show you the way.'

Phil's office was the largest and most expensively appointed room in the building's administration wing. It featured a full-length picture window that looked across the landscaped grounds behind the studios. A large silky oak desk, which was littered with paperwork, sat just inside the window. Two enormous white leather sofas dominated the remaining floorspace. They faced each other across a glass-topped coffee table.

A grid of nine television screens was mounted on the wall near the sofas. The top three were switched off. The rest were tuned silently to the six channels broadcasting in the Brisbane area. It was just before 6 p.m. and, even for an occasional viewer like Roland, identifying them was easy. A subtitled soap opera in the lower right corner pinpointed the Special Broadcasting Service. Next to it, the ABC was rerunning a faded Roger Ramjet cartoon. On the remaining screens, the commercial channels were playing self-promotional videos featuring helicopters and news cars decorated with their network logos.

Channel 5 was on a larger screen in the centre of the matrix. Four of its current stars, dressed in white flares and wide-lapelled jackets, were performing a thinly disguised imitation of an ABBA video. They had squeezed themselves *Arrival*-style into the front seat of a helicopter, and were lip-synching to the station's latest jingle: *Watching us, Watching you – Uhuh!*

The meme wormed its way into Roland's brain and he was humming the chorus when the news bulletin started. He scanned the room for a remote control to turn on the sound and was still looking when Phil Porter steered himself through the half-open door.

'Roly,' he said, grinning. 'Glad you managed to get yourself here at last. It might have been quicker and a whole lot drier if you'd used the taxi I sent for you.'

Roland tugged at his still-sodden cycling shirt and laughed. 'I thought some exercise would be a good idea. But it looks like I picked the wrong day for it.'

Phil was a fraction taller than Roland and a good 20 kilos

heavier. His longish fair hair was pulled back into a tidy ponytail and he had a neatly trimmed goatee that tried and failed to add some maturity to his broad, childlike face. He paused just inside the door, flicked it shut with his leg, and took a substantial bite from the Lebanese pocket bread he had in his hand.

'Damn,' he said through a mouthful of shredded vegetable, 'I missed the headlines. Did you catch the lead story?'

Roland shrugged. 'Without the sound it's impossible to tell.'

'With ratings like ours, it mostly doesn't matter what anyone is actually saying. But I suppose we should have a listen. As my father likes to remind me, I am responsible for everything that goes to air.'

He took a remote control from his jacket pocket and aimed it at the centre monitor. The measured, reassuring voice of newsreader David Burton filled the room:

> *We'll be looking at the impact of this afternoon's storm in a special report after the break. Lauren.*

The camera cut to Lauren D'Aussey, Burton's co-reader. They were an attractive on-screen couple. Burton, fair and tanned with a dimpled chin, was a perfect match for the elegant, fine-featured D'Aussey. She pronounced her name Doh-zay, but after a recent article labelling Channel 5 the ratings dwarfs, she was now widely referred to as Dozy. Burton, by extension, had been rechristened Snow White.

The letters EJA appeared over Lauren's shoulder as she introduced the next item:

> *A previously unknown green group calling itself the Environmental Justice Army issued threats today against land developers in the south-east corner of Queensland.*

In a videotaped statement the EJA declared a one-week deadline before it begins a campaign of violence against companies and individuals it says are guilty of crimes against the environment.

Our environment correspondent Suzanne Denning has more ...

'I think we've pretty much got the gist,' Phil said. He pressed the red button on the remote and the screen faded to black. After taking another bite from the pocket bread, he began to sift through the paperwork on his desk. 'I know your file is here somewhere.'

'My file? Do you keep one on all of your friends?'

'Only the ones who require regular record keeping.'

He located the worryingly thick folder in a drawer and heaved it onto the desktop. With his reading glasses on, he skimmed down the first page, tugging absent-mindedly on his beard as he read. Roland watched for a clue to the contents but was soon distracted by a fragment of carrot that had somehow lodged under Phil's chin.

'First the bad news,' Phil said as he turned the page. 'You, my friend, are fired.'

Roland struggled to take the news in. For most of his decade with Porter Corp, he had known that this day would eventually come. A part of him welcomed it, relishing the freedom and sense of expanding possibilities it would bring. But the realist in him was alarmed at the prospect of being suddenly cut adrift. It triggered inevitable feelings of disbelief and injustice. 'I wasn't aware that I'd done anything wrong.'

'Let's not get into the grisly details, mate. It's enough to know that this is the end of the line. Porter Corp has run out of subsidiaries to transfer you to.' He paused and looked directly at Roland. 'I know this is difficult, but none of us can hide the fact that you'll never be the corporate type. If it helps, you're not the only one going. Things are tight in the economy right now. Porter Corp is slimming down, reconfiguring as a lean, mean and hungry operation.'

The image of austerity fell apart when Phil picked up the pocket bread and took another substantial bite. As he munched his way through it, he casually asked, 'Any thoughts on what you might do next?'

'It's a bit early for that, isn't it? I'm still getting used to the idea that it's all over. When exactly do I finish?'

'You already have. The people at Porter Vaults don't want you back. I've got a notice of termination here, along with your final pay and a surprisingly generous reference.' He paused to prise the lid from a Styrofoam cup. It resisted doggedly, then suddenly came free, dribbling coffee across the reference Roland would need for his next job. 'Shit! Sorry, mate.'

Phil dabbed at the worst of the stain with a tissue, but the damage was done. He folded the letter and tucked it into its envelope. Casually, he added, 'If you don't have any immediate plans, there might be a temporary position going here at Channel 5.'

Roland was instantly suspicious. 'Are you sure you want to take on someone with a track record like mine? Someone so careless his only work reference has a massive coffee stain on it?'

'I need someone I can trust. It doesn't take a reference to tell me you're top of that list.'

Roland and Phil knew everything there was to know about each other. They had shared a house during university days and for a while after. It was Phil's first property, bought for him by his father as an investment. Roland had stayed on when Phil and the other tenants moved on. He still paid token rent, an arrangement Phil used to minimise his tax.

'I don't know the first thing about television,' Roland insisted.

'I don't even watch it much.'

'Mate, I'm not offering you a job on air. The truth is, Channel 5 is in deep trouble. Dad has lost confidence in my ability to turn things around. The final straw was that ratings dwarfs article in the bloody *Courier Mail* last month. He's decided to bring in a consultant from America.

'Nominally, I'll still be in charge. But Hinsley, that's the American, will make the decisions. Dad may be a bit of a bastard, but he wouldn't sack his own son. At least, I don't think he would.'

Roland shrugged. He knew that Sir Adrian Porter would happily dispense with the services of any family member if the business situation demanded it. Phil had to know this too, but wouldn't thank Roland for mentioning it. 'What exactly would I have to do here?'

'Hinsley is bringing a close colleague with him, but he's asked for a local person to join their team. That's the job I want you to take. You'll be something called an engagement strategist.'

'I can't see how I'll be any use in a role like that. I don't even know what it means.'

'You're not supposed to be useful. I need someone in his inner circle who can keep me fully informed on what he's up to. Just do what he tells you, get so close you're practically touching, and tell me everything he says and does.'

If anyone else had asked him to do it, Roland would have told them to get lost. But Phil was his closest friend as well as his employer and landlord. The alternative was changing everything in his life, all at once. Despite a vague desire for this, he wasn't ready to tackle it yet. 'I don't know, Phil. I'm not the kind of person people confide in. And he's bound to suspect me as soon as it gets around that we're friends.'

'It's only for a couple of months at most. You'll be paid good money, double what you get now. The contract is watertight for six months, regardless of how long you're actually with us. Work for two months, get paid for six. That's an offer you can't possibly refuse.'

It was obvious now that Phil had engineered the whole thing – the crisis meeting, the loss of one job and the irresistible offer of something better. Roland could have objected, pushed for a return to the status quo. But the lure of the extra money and the cushion of six months to find that elusive new direction in life had him hooked. 'It looks like I don't have anything to lose. When do I start?'

'Tomorrow. Hinsley arrives in Brisbane on Saturday and takes over on Monday morning. We've got to be ready for him when he walks in the door. He'll be using this office. You'll be sharing a room next door with his assistant, B.B. Olsen.'

'Bee? As in the little buzzy things that make honey?'

'Times two, Roly. She spells it B dot B dot. It's all she has for names. She and Hinsley operate telepathically, so you'll need to get close to her too.'

'B.B. Olsen,' Roland repeated, wondering if he was up to the task.

'Come and see me tomorrow morning when you arrive. 8.30 okay with you?'

'Fine.'

'Thanks, Roly. You're a real mate.'

Phil pointed the remote control at the central screen and the room filled with the husky tones of Lauren D'Aussey. He was instantly lost in one of his favourite pastimes. Watching television. His eyes locked on the screen and his mouth fell slightly open as he gulped down everything the box on the far side of the room was willing to send his way.

With the meeting so obviously over, Roland muttered a goodbye and made for the door.

2

On Monday morning Roland lay in bed until the last possible moment, savouring thoughts of a surprise resignation from his new job. He kicked the covers onto the floor, spread himself across the sheets and tried to convince himself that this was his big moment, the point where he took back control, the first day of the rest of his life.

As he watched the ceiling fan oscillate directly overhead, he imagined his way through a dramatic phone call to Channel 5. The scene unfolded perfectly and reached peak satisfaction when he told Phil to find another patsy for his dirty work. Then it all turned sour when the imaginary Phil retaliated with a volley of big life questions: *What would you do next? Where would you live? How would you eat?*

The resignation fantasy faded and Roland was left with the realisation that, not only did he have to go to work, he had to be there before the Americans arrived. Phil wanted a copy of the day's meeting schedule waiting on Hinsley's desk when he arrived, and Roland had forgotten to do this before leaving early on Friday. He wondered if it really mattered but, in the end, decided that a good first impression was essential for anyone starting a new career in the industrial espionage business.

Reluctantly, he got up, snatched a quick breakfast and hurried up the mountain to Channel 5.

Two days' acquaintance and a staff building pass had defrosted Roland's relations with the security guard. But he still felt a disapproving stare on the back of his neck as he wheeled his bicycle along the recently polished corridor to the building's executive wing. Reaching his office, he carefully manoeuvred the cycle's titanium handlebar-ends through the doorway. Then he stopped dead, thinking for a moment he must have walked into the wrong room.

On Friday his desk and chair had been the only furniture in the room. He had positioned them for the best view through the full-length window to the landscaped gardens behind the studios. Now they were squeezed into the corner behind the door and a newer larger desk had taken prime position. Surrounding this interloper was an array of packing boxes containing an Apple Macintosh, a printer, a fax machine and a filter-coffee maker. On the desk sat a slim camel-coloured leather briefcase. The lid was open and Roland was tempted to take a quick look inside, but he was in too much of a hurry.

He leaned his cycle against the wall and bent down to retrieve the only copy of the day's schedule. This had somehow been pinned under the leg of his desk and was now permanently scarred. With no time to make a fresh copy, he slipped the creased document into a new manila folder and hurried down the corridor to Phil's old office.

As he opened the door he half-expected to see a cleaner shampooing the last coffee stains from the carpet, or Phil dumping the contents of the filing cabinets into a wheelie bin. He was still surprised to find the room occupied. Sitting behind the desk was a broad-shouldered man of about forty. He had neat dark hair and a healthy tanned complexion. A pair of rimless reading glasses was balanced low on the bridge of his nose.

He looked up as Roland walked in and, in an unmistakably American accent, asked, 'Is there something I can help you with?'

Roland realised this was probably his new boss. Taking in the American's scarlet bow-tie and matching braces, he suddenly felt uncomfortably underdressed in his own sweat-stained T-shirt and lycra shorts. Cautiously, he asked, 'Are you Mr Hinsley?'

'That's what the sign says.' The American pointed to a foot-long plastic prism on the front of the desk. To Roland it was nothing more than a block of clear plastic. He looked doubtfully back at the man sitting confidently behind it.

'Try moving round in front of it.'

When Roland did this, the name *H. Dalton Hinsley* projected from a silver background in a three-dimensional hologram.

'Neat, isn't it. A present from a friend when I left the States.' Hinsley took his reading glasses off and looked Roland up and down. 'Are you some kind of courier?'

'No, I work here. My name's Kendall.'

'Roland Kendall?' Hinsley glanced at the open folder in front of him. As he read, he added, 'Do you always go around dressed like that, Roland Kendall?'

'Well, I cycle to work and change when I get here.' Holding out the folder in his hand, he added, 'I just wanted to put this on your desk before you arrived, but it looks like I'm too late.'

'You're about 24 hours too late. I started yesterday. Sunday is the best day to get things done. And a great way to find out who else is putting in extra hours on their own time.'

Roland, who was unlikely ever to be caught at work on a Sunday, nodded with a purely academic interest.

'Sit down,' Hinsley said, as he turned a page in what appeared to be Roland's personnel folder. 'It says here that you work for me? Is that a fact?'

'It is,' Roland replied. 'I'm your new engagement strategist.'

'It also says you started here just a couple of days ago.'

'On Friday morning.'

'Tell me, Roland Kendall, exactly how much do you know about the wonderful world of television?'

'Absolutely nothing. I don't even watch it much. I'd rather listen to the radio.'

Hinsley chuckled. 'Well at least I don't have to worry about you having preconceived ideas. And I admire your honesty. Look, I know you got this job because you're a close personal friend of Phil Porter.'

Here it comes, Roland thought, wondering how long it would take to clean out his new desk.

'There's nothing wrong with a little honest nepotism,' Hinsley continued. 'That's the free enterprise way. It's also the free enterprise way that people who don't perform don't last. Channel 5 is about to move into the fast lane of life and there are going to be some pretty dramatic changes around here. You can be one of those changes or you can help me make them. Which would you like it to be?'

Roland suspected he would never be a fast-lane person, even when someone else was doing the driving. But he'd given a commitment to Phil and had to see it through. He tried to think of a compelling reason for Hinsley to keep him on, but could only manage, 'I very much want to stay, Mr Hinsley. I think you'll find me surprisingly useful.'

'I'm sure I will. Now you wanted to give me this?' He picked up the folder and glanced sceptically at the crumpled schedule. 'Looks like I'm late for my first appointment. You'd better show me to Porter's office.'

Roland had no idea where Phil's new office was, or if Phil was even in it. 'He's probably waiting in the reception area. You were supposed to be arriving about now.'

'I know, but I always like to take the offensive early. Roland, you and I will talk again later today. Until then, I want you to work through this schedule and cancel everything.' He handed back the creased document. 'I need to leave plenty of time for some first-day hiring and firing. You made the right decision a moment ago. It was hanging in the balance whether you would be number one on my list of leavers. Oh, and spread the word around: the next person to call me Mr Hinsley definitely goes on that list. It's Dalton. Okay?'

'Okay, Dalton.' Roland glanced again at the plastic name tag on the American's desk and wondered what the H. stood for. He could tell that Dalton knew exactly what he was thinking, but the question remained unasked and unanswered.

'It's time I started to make my presence felt,' Dalton said as he headed for the door. 'Let's go find your old buddy Phil.'

They found Roland's *old buddy* in the foyer. After the introductions, Roland slipped away to shower and change. With both his official and unofficial managers scheduled to be together for some time, he was looking forward to at least an hour's peace.

Returning to his own office, he opened the door and caught a woman searching through the drawers of his desk. A flicker of embarrassment showed in her face, but it was gone in a moment. 'Hi there,' she said airily, in an accent very much like Dalton's.

'I think you might be at the wrong desk.'

'Do you just think that? Or do you know it?'

Roland stared at her while he worked out a response. She was about his height and slim with short, tightly curled jet-black hair. Her face, now that she had recovered her poise, had an open, friendly expression. But her eyes were dark and laser-like and they put Roland instantly on guard. 'It *was* mine an hour ago,' he replied. 'But it's turning into one of those days when nothing has any real certainty.'

'You must be Roland,' she said, crossing the room to offer her hand. 'I'm B.B. Olsen. And I'm sure we're going to enjoy working together.'

B.B. gripped his hand tightly and parted her highly glossed red lips into a corporate smile. She was wearing a black skirt and cream blouse under a collarless, oversized scarlet jacket. Roland noted that the colour matched exactly with Dalton's bow-tie and braces. He wondered if he too would soon be coordinating his wardrobe with them on early-morning phone calls.

Sensing submission, she released his hand. 'You caught me going through your drawers, but I'm cool with that. It was well worth the risk. I can tell a lot about a person just by analysing the contents of their desk.'

'What have you worked out about me?' he asked, hoping it wasn't much.

'I haven't finished yet, but this is the story so far. You chew your pencil. Which could be evidence of insecurity, or maybe something a little more Freudian. You eat a lot of Mars Bars, suggesting a lack of a balanced diet. And you do cryptic crosswords, but you're not much good at them. Six across, by the way, is ESCAPADE.

'I got all of that from the top drawer. The rest were mostly empty, except for the bottom one where I found several pairs of clean underwear and a T-shirt. I still haven't figured out what's happening there.' She paused, waiting for an explanation, but he refused to be drawn. 'It's not much, I admit, but there's plenty of time to get to know each other better. In fact, let's do coffee together now. I can't focus before the third cup of the day and you look like you could use a boost too.'

Over the next half-hour Roland learned that B.B. was 38 years old and came from Baltimore. She had a masters degree in psychology, and had recently completed her doctorate in media science. She told him that people issues were both her job and her passion and that she had worked with Dalton for more than five years. B.B. just loved Australia, or at least she loved Australian accents, marsupials, and especially Olivia Noot'n'jawn. Her friends called her Beeb and she insisted that Roland consider himself one of these. Under cross-examination, he let slip that he lived alone, and enjoyed cycling, books, movies and classical music. And that his friends called him Roly. Beeb decided she was now one of those too.

Shortly after returning to their office they had their first test of wills. Roland was making phone calls to cancel the scheduled staff gatherings with Dalton, while B.B. unpacked the large quantity of paperwork she had brought with her from America. With an armful of files, she crossed to the recessed corner of the office where he had left his bike. For no apparent reason, she stumbled and brushed her leg against the chain. To Roland it looked quite deliberate.

As she wiped an oily smudge from her leg, she stared coldly at him. 'You don't regularly park your cycle in the office, right?'

'Well, I thought it was pretty much out of the way over there.' Seeing that she disagreed, he added, 'It's a very expensive bike, Beeb. A hand-built frame.'

The value of this was totally lost on her. 'I don't see any way we can ever agree on this.'

'I'll make sure it's not in your way.'

'Roly, I need you to take the cycle outside. Right now.'

The tone told him they had reached a critical moment in their embryonic relationship. He could argue and inevitably lose. Or he could let her have the early win she seemed to think was necessary. He smiled pointedly and wheeled the bike outside.

He felt like staying outside with it and would have done, except for the heat. It was one of those mid-January days when Brisbane was almost too hot to touch, when the heat bounced off the concrete walkways and seared the soles of your shoes. The

Channel 5 building was a stunning piece of architecture, but its highly reflective glass cladding and the absence of shade made its environs a nightmare in the hottest months of the year.

In ten minutes Roland needed the chill of air conditioning again. Rather than return to his own office, he went looking for Phil. He found him in a smaller and, so far, more Spartan version of the room he had given up for Dalton. His feet were resting on the desk and he was leaning back in his chair as he watched the *Kutie Koala Kids Klub*, Channel 5's half-hearted answer to *Play School.* Kutie Koala, a silent, slightly scruffy marsupial with an alarmingly low IQ, was pretending to be an elephant by bending over and swinging one arm in front and one behind. Miss Jane, Kutie Koala's long-suffering sidekick, was doing her best to convince four sceptical preschoolers that an overweight, middle-aged man in a koala suit, pretending to be an elephant, was helping to make sense of their tiny worlds.

Phil, as usual, was riveted by anything broadcast through the medium of television. 'Morning, Roly,' he said without taking his eyes away from Kutie Koala. 'Got the sack yet?'

'I think it's more a question of me resigning. I don't know how long I can stay in the same room as B.B. Olsen.'

'Dalton just spent half an hour telling me how good she is.'

'And he's on to us already. He knows we're friends.'

'He told me all of that. He thinks it's a good idea, that you'll keep him and me on the same page.' Phil dipped his hand into a plastic container and dug out a handful of dried fruit and nuts. 'Want some trail mix?'

Roland could see he wasn't getting his point across. He walked into the centre of the room and stood between Phil and the television screen. 'Phil, it's a waste of time. I'll never fit in around people like that.'

Reluctantly, Phil lifted the remote control and switched the television off. 'Give it a couple of weeks, Roland. Please. I'm working flat out on a major new project. I don't have time to concentrate on what Dalton is doing to the place. If you help me out, I'll find you something else as soon as I can. Okay?'

'Okay,' Roland replied, brightening at the prospect. 'But only if you get me out of lunch with Beeb. She wants to analyse my underwear, or something.'

'Sorry, mate. I'm meeting Dad for lunch. You and your underwear are on your own.'

3

When Roland returned to his own office he found a technician installing the fax machine in the corner he had imagined for his bike.

Beeb had left a note on his desk:

> *Roly,*
>
> *Sorry to let you down so soon, but we'll have to take a rain-check on lunch. Dalton and I are now eating with Sir Adrian Porter and Phil.*
>
> *Don't let the technician go until the Macintosh, the printer and the scanner are all working. By which I mean tested and verified by you, not just switched on. I'm holding you responsible for this.*
>
> *Beeb.*

Buoyed by the thought that Phil's lunch and not his own would now be ruined, Roland screwed up the note and threw it across the room. With extraordinary precision it hit the lid of Beeb's briefcase and deflected inside. He smiled in satisfaction, took a book from his daypack, and settled down for some much-needed quiet time. Sensing that his freedom around Dalton and

Beeb would be limited, he read through lunch, sustaining himself on a Mars Bar and an apple. He left the wrapper and apple core in his top drawer for Beeb to find.

The peace ended around 2.30 when Dalton phoned and called him through to his office. When he arrived, B.B. and Dalton were huddled together behind the desk. Their heads were almost touching as they peered at the tiny screen on Dalton's laptop computer.

'I have to confess,' Dalton said, 'I forgot about you. But Beeb recommended that you be here for this. Take a seat.'

Roland started to sit in the visitor's chair facing them, but Dalton stopped him. 'Not there. Over here with us.'

He pointed to a spare seat next to Beeb, who was now wearing a pair of large-framed glasses. The red frames matched exactly with the colour of her lip gloss and jacket. Roland wondered, as he sat beside her, if they were a fashion accessory.

With the dynamics apparently right, they sat and waited. Dalton closed his eyes and held his index fingers to his temples in some form of private meditation. B.B. doodled idly on her clipboard. And Roland squinted sideways at her glasses as he tried to decide if the lenses had any optical value. After a while he gave up, stifled a yawn, and wondered what they were waiting for. It took him several minutes to realise he could actually ask, but the question was still forming when a visitor knocked on the door.

Dalton exhaled slowly and opened his eyes. 'Come in.'

Lauren D'Aussey entered the room, looking cool and elegant in a floral-print summer dress. The ex-model was an expert in first impressions and she glided confidently towards them with her loose dark hair rippling in perfect waves and her lips carefully contoured into a professional smile.

'Lauren,' Dalton said, after returning the smile. 'Glad to meet you in person. Sit down.'

She paused beside the chair as though it was a prop on a catwalk, then slipped into it and tidily crossed her legs.

'You haven't met my team yet,' Dalton continued. 'B.B. Olsen and Roland Kendall.'

B.B. nodded coldly. Sensing the sudden drop in temperature, Roland overcompensated with an idiot grin.

Dalton came straight to the point. 'Lauren, I have a proposition for you. Something we're all extremely excited about. We think you will be too. I'm offering you your own show.'

Lauren was stunned. She leaned back in her seat and, in her low, husky voice, asked, 'You want me to read the news solo?'

'I'm talking about something way better for you than the news. I want you to front a new weekday morning magazine-style show. The details are still being ironed out but the focus will be on social and cultural issues. We think you're a perfect fit as the host. It means leaving the news, of course, but ...'

'I wouldn't want to do that,' Lauren broke in, suspicious. 'I'm happy with what I do now.'

'You might be, Lauren, but no one else is.'

Roland began to see that he'd taken the last spot on a firing squad. He wanted to rebel, to shout: *What's this we? I'm not unhappy with her work. I don't even watch it.*

Unaware of the dissent brewing on his team, Dalton continued, 'You know the score, Lauren. When a team is in trouble someone has to make the supreme sacrifice. For Channel 5 News, that someone is you.

'Our research identifies you as the weak link in the team. No one can beat you when it comes to good diction and good looks. But this is 1990. Viewers want a news team staffed entirely by professional journalists. For you the choice is clear: take over as host of my new *Morning Lite* programme or we terminate your contract. You've got until the start of business tomorrow to think about it.'

Lauren looked as cool as ever but, when she spoke, her voice was noticeably thinner. 'You can't take me off the news. You can't just walk in here and do a thing like that.'

'Honey,' Beeb said, 'that's exactly what he's been brought in to do.'

'Phil won't let this happen to me.'

'Phil Porter is out of the loop,' Dalton told her. 'I'm in charge now, and I alone make the decisions.'

'Then I'll go directly to Sir Adrian. He's a personal friend of my family. I have connections.'

'I know all about your connections. That's why you're perfect for *Morning Lite*. Listen, Lauren. Go to Sir Adrian and you lose *Morning Lite* too. Your only chance of an on-air job in this town will be as holiday back-up to Miss Jane on the *Kutie Koala Kids Klub*.'

'Maybe even inside the Koala costume,' Beeb added acidly.

During the long silence that followed, Lauren stared intently at Dalton. Dalton, B.B. and Roland stared back at her. Lauren crumbled first. In a move that indicated she was resigned to the inevitable, she asked, 'Who's taking my place?'

Dalton smiled enigmatically and turned to the newest member of his team. 'Roland, do you want to field that one?'

Caught off guard, Roland searched Dalton's face for a clue. Seeing nothing, he was about to pass the buck to B.B. when he realised it was a test he couldn't afford to fail.

'Lauren,' he said, thinking as he spoke, 'we can't tell you that right now. The first job was to give you the good news about *Morning Lite*. Now we're all on the same page about that, we can speak to the right people about stepping into your news-reading shoes.' Turning to Beeb, he added, 'Anything you'd like to add, Beeb?'

B.B. took over without hesitation. 'We don't make a move like this without extensive market research. I have a stack of data three feet high pointing us to the ideal replacement. You'll know later today once the announcement has been made.'

'It's Lisa Demchek, isn't it? She's been angling for this ever since she set foot in the place.'

'Think it over till tomorrow, Lauren,' Dalton said, closing down the discussion. 'Unless I hear otherwise, I'll assume you're saying yes to *Morning Lite*. You can arrange a meeting through Roland. He'll be here early. Thank you, that's all.'

The ex-model and now ex-newsreader sat stiffly for a moment. She recovered her poise and left the room. As the door closed, Dalton said, 'Roland, when she calls you tomorrow, I don't want to speak to her. Let me know her answer but don't put her through. Beeb, what's your reading on this?'

'She'll take it, Dalton. It's in the bag.'

'I agree. And how about Roland here, with his: *Lauren, we can't tell you that right now. The first job was to give you the good news about Morning Lite.*'

'He was okay. I could use him on my staff interview sessions later this week. I don't feel good about those things unless they're at least two on one.'

'He's all yours. Now let's deal with the next one on the list. Roland, go find Suzanne Denning and bring her here. Don't tell her anything about what we just did to Lauren.'

Roland ignored Dalton's instruction and went instead to Phil's office. Finding it empty, he scribbled a note:

> *Lauren D'Aussey has just been sacked from the news team. Possible replacement is Lisa Demchek. Next head on the chopping block belongs to Suzanne Denning. I'll fill you in later.*

He continued to the newsroom, a vast open-plan office about

30 metres long and 20 wide. Inside its double doors, he stopped and took in the sea of chest-high partitions and the huge picture window that ran the length of one wall. The window looked out onto the helipad where the sleek charcoal-grey Channel 5 chopper was just touching down.

Completely lost, he asked a passer-by for help and was given a complicated set of twists and turns that would deliver him to Denning's workstation. He had navigated about halfway through the maze when the newsroom doors crashed open. He turned and saw Lauren D'Aussey weave between the partitions and disappear into the glass-walled office belonging to the Head of News. Roland and everyone else in the newsroom watched as Lauren paced around the tiny space, gesturing wildly with both arms as she offloaded the breaking news about her future. Kevin Hardy, the unfortunate occupant of the office, stared open-mouthed at her. A moment later the entire newsroom was caught when D'Aussey turned and saw them all looking her way. She snatched at the cord for the vertical blinds and whipped them shut, cutting off the transmission at what seemed to be a critical moment.

Roland remembered his mission and crossed to Denning's cubicle. When he arrived she was sitting with her back to him, punching words onto a computer keyboard at a manic pace. He cleared his throat and said, 'Excuse me, Suzanne.'

'I'm busy. Come back later.'

'Suzanne.'

'I said I was busy. Find someone else to bother.'

Realising that the voice belonged to a stranger, she turned and leaned back in her seat. She flicked her long ash-blonde hair over her shoulder and smiled brightly. 'You're Roland, aren't you?'

Roland had seen her work her charms a hundred times on air, using her wide-set blue eyes, a wrinkle of the lips, or an inquiring tilt of her perfect chin to trap even the most hardened politician into a confession. Close to her for the first time, he felt an emotional charge that television could never convey. He urgently wanted to confess something. All he could think of was, 'Yes, I'm Roland Kendall.'

He knew he was staring at her, but couldn't stop. She realised this eventually and asked, 'Is there something in particular you wanted, Roland Kendall? Or did you just want to watch an ace reporter hard at work?'

He reddened and shook himself free from her spell. 'Dalton Hinsley asked me to come and find you. He needs to speak with you right away.'

'Can't it wait? I'm working to a deadline.'

'This is urgent. You really need to come with me now.'

As they crossed the newsroom to the door, she leaned conspiratorially towards him. 'What's this all about?'

He felt her eyes on him again and wanted to warn her that it was bad news. But he couldn't bear to be the one to tell her. 'Sorry, I have absolutely no idea.'

'But I heard you were his right-hand man, his engagement strategist.'

'From what I can tell so far, that means I have to go and find the people he wants to engage with.'

'You must know something, surely. You can't engage if you don't know the strategy.'

He thought she was making fun of him but, when he glanced sideways, she was smiling warmly. He couldn't help grinning back. 'Honestly, there's nothing I can tell you.'

She continued to probe as they walked along the corridor to the executive wing and he was relieved when they reached Dalton's office. When they walked in, Roland saw that Dalton and B.B. had relocated to one of the leather sofas. Dalton was stretched out along three of the four cushions. His eyes were covered by a sleeping mask and he was chanting tunelessly under his breath. Beeb had squeezed herself onto the end of the sofa at his feet. She was humming in time with him. Startled, Roland stopped in the doorway causing Suzanne to collide with him.

B.B. heard them and held up her hand. She whispered, 'Just give us a moment.'

Suzanne raised her eyebrows at Roland. He managed to shrug casually as though he'd seen it all before. After a few seconds, Dalton removed the mask, sat up and breathed deeply. Acknowledging their presence, he smiled and gestured towards the other sofa.

'We often take a little time out during difficult moments in the day,' he explained as they sat down. 'It's so relaxing, and it makes us feel more focused as a team. Maybe you'd like to try it with us. I could take both of you through the basic steps right now if you like.'

When neither of them showed an interest, he shrugged and turned to business. 'Suzanne, I'm glad Roland was able to find you. I want to put a proposition to you.'

Roland couldn't bear to watch her face when the axe fell. He switched his attention to Dalton and was surprised that the smile was warmer now than it had been with Lauren.

'You may have heard by now,' Dalton said, 'that I've decided to make some changes to the news team.'

Suzanne sat forward, interested. 'I hadn't heard, but it doesn't surprise me. We obviously need them.'

'I just spoke with Lauren and told her she's out of the line-up. That creates a space for a woman in the co-anchor role. I'd like to hear your ideas on how we should go about filling it.'

'The way I see it, your choice is obvious. There's only one woman on the team who can do the job the way it needs to be done. My advice is: don't look any further than this sofa.'

'Lauren seemed to think we might go with Lisa Demchek instead.'

'Frankly, that tells me more about Lauren's judgement than Lisa's qualifications for the job. Lisa's good, but she doesn't have my experience yet. And it's too early to tell if she'll ever develop the extra something you need for an anchor role. I think I have that something, and I'm pretty sure you think so too. Why else would I be sitting here right now?'

Roland was amazed by her assertiveness. It wasn't how the Suzanne Denning of his imagination, the woman he was more than ready to be smitten with, was supposed to behave. He listened with a mixture of envy and slight distaste as she outlined why she was perfect for the role. 'For this to work, Dalton, you need a professional journalist in the anchor's chair. She has to be dynamic, confident and capable. And, above all, she needs to be someone the viewers feel they can trust. You also have to find her quickly and without any fuss. I have all those qualities, and I'm ready to hit the ground running.'

Dalton smacked his hands together in delight. 'I'm also looking for someone who is frank and forthright. You seem to have those qualities sewn up too. I mostly like to trust my instincts on a thing like this, but I took the precaution of engaging in extensive market research before we flew in. I don't suppose it surprises you that you score well with our target audience. Everything you said a moment ago was right on the money. I have to move fast and I don't see the need to look any further. Will you take the job?'

'With pleasure.'

'You'll want to discuss details, haggle over contracts, but I'm going to let you and Beeb sort that out. Okay?'

'Just show me the dotted line and I'll sign it now.'

'Suzanne, I want you to stop celebrating for a moment and listen very carefully. You need to understand what you're getting into here. Once that contract is signed we will own every little inch of you. From the moment you wake up in the morning till the moment you crawl exhausted back into bed at night, we are going to tell you how to live your life. And when I say we, I mean Beeb here.'

B.B. leaned forward to drive the point home. 'Dalton's not kidding, honey. I'll be that loving, caring bigger sister you'll wish you never had. She's always going to know what's best for you. And she never ever takes a vacation. Dalton misspoke a moment ago and I need to clear that up right now: it doesn't stop when you crawl into bed at night, not if you plan on doing anything other than sleeping when you get there. Your new big sister will be signing off on anyone who might want to stop by and share that happy little nest with you.'

Chastened and a little rattled, Suzanne let the mask of confidence slip. She leaned back and tucked a strand of hair behind one ear. Her face hardened, losing most of its puppy-dog glee. 'I'll do whatever it takes. When do I start?'

Dalton smiled and the moment of darkness was forgotten. 'Not until the debut of *Newscentre 5*. That's the name of the new format I'm launching. David Burton can read the news on his own until then. Now if you'll excuse me, I have to tell your manager about this. Roland, go back to the newsroom and ask Kevin Hardy to drop by. Then wait in your office till I need you.'

To Suzanne, he added, 'I'm counting on you to keep this quiet until I've spoken to everyone who matters. I should have told them first, so there will be a lot of ruffled feathers to deal with.'

'Dalton, I think I can keep this to myself for maybe 30 minutes at most. After that, who knows. So please, try to be quick.'

As she walked down the corridor with Roland, Suzanne let out a yelp and punched the air. She took him by the arm and said, 'I can't believe it! I can't believe it! I was so afraid I'd blown it with that massive overconfidence act. You didn't think I was too pushy, did you? I did my research on him, just in case, and I thought he'd want me to take the opportunity by the throat. Roly – I can call you Roly, can't I? – this is my lucky day. I didn't expect anything like this for a couple of years, if ever.'

'Don't these people scare you, even just a little?'

'You mean the part about selling my soul to them? I've come across that hard-as-nails act before. It's all show. Just part of the game we all have to play in this business. God, I still can't believe it!'

It went on like that until they reached the newsroom, when she forced herself to settle down. They parted and she went back to her workstation and did a silent war dance. Roland delivered his message to Hardy, then went outside for some fresh air. His first day in the fast lane had left him short of oxygen and more than a little giddy.

4

Roland knew by the middle of his first week at Channel 5 that he would be of almost no use to Phil as a spy.

He was never directly excluded from events in Dalton's office, but the Americans operated without the need for verbal communication. A gesture, sometimes little more than the twitch of an eyebrow or half-dip of the head, was all it usually took for them to reach an understanding. On the few occasions when words were necessary they spoke in a code entirely of their own. It wasn't helped by Roland's own tendency to let his mind wander, especially when the television monitors in Dalton's office were turned on or a breeze was stirring in the gum trees on the other side of the picture window. After the first day he had nothing more of substance to report and doubted he ever would.

Dalton worked alone in his office for long stretches of every day. This left Roland entirely at B.B.'s disposal. At first she kept him busy with a constant stream of questions on the Australian way of life, from the intricacies of spelling and pronunciation to detailed statistical queries. *What does the average Queenslander eat for breakfast? What's their favourite tipple? How many years of schooling do they have on average?* He was continually found wanting and it was a relief when she gave up and sought more reliable answers from an electronic encyclopaedia on a CD-ROM.

With his role as Aussie oracle supplanted by a computer, Roland was reduced to playing a waiting game until B.B. was ready to schedule her getting-to-know-you sessions with the news team. He made it clear he was reluctant to sit in on them, but Beeb was insistent. 'If you want to be part of our inner circle, you have to start identifying strongly with our agenda. Dalton and I know what we're doing. We've done this in local stations all the way across America. Our model works every time and, more important, it works fast.'

'Perhaps if I knew a little more about your plan for Channel 5.'

Beeb hesitated while she decided how much to tell him. She began in generalities. 'Our turnaround model is built around a strong local news team. Everything else follows from that. Our job, and yours, for the next weeks and months is to deliver a compelling, exciting news product.'

'So Kutie Koala and Miss Jane can breathe easy.'

'For now, anyway. We'll have our hands full dealing with the news team. The first step was to perform surgery. You saw that happen Monday. We had to cut the cancer out and we chose Lauren as the manifestation of the tumour. The next step is to assert our total authority over the rest of the group. We'll do that by putting pressure on its weaker members. That's where I want you involved.'

'Me! I'm more the sort of person who is put under pressure. I wouldn't know how to do it to anyone else.'

'You don't know what you're capable of until you try. We checked around and people in the newsroom see you as Phil Porter's man. They also know you're close to Sir Adrian Porter – Dalton started that rumour personally – and that means your presence is a constant reminder that we act with the owner's complete authority.' She leaned forward and lowered her voice. 'People round here are real nervous and they'll stay that way till we allow them to relax. That invests us, you included, with a lot of power.'

Conscious of Phil's voice inside his head egging him on, Roland asked, 'And what are your plans for the rest of the news team?'

Beeb smiled slyly. 'Now Roly, if I told you that, you wouldn't stick around and be part of my interviews, would you?'

They both knew she was right. Softening her smile, she added, 'Dalton doesn't enjoy firing people – it's not his style – which is why we needed to be there to support him. We were never going to let Lauren go entirely, you know.'

'You weren't?'

'It just had to look that way. She's a talented woman, but she isn't right for the *Newscentre 5* concept. Lauren will be a constant reminder to the rest of the team about what can happen to them.' She chuckled and added, 'TV is a Darwinian world, Roly. Only a few make it to the top, and it's a constant fight to stay there.'

Aware that he would avoid taking part if he could, B.B. gave him no advance warning of the first interview. Minutes before the Channel 5 sportscaster, Malcolm McDarrow, was due to arrive for his session, Beeb called Roland over to sit beside her and handed him a black clipboard. At first he thought she wanted him to check the attached papers for spelling and style. As he scanned the first page, he realised it was the script for an interview and that his name was highlighted where he was expected to ask a question.

'Beeb, I don't think I can do this.'

'Roly, you're going to take part, so get used to it. Just look interested, ask your questions when I prompt you and make an occasional mark on the clipboard. Don't depart from the script, and don't worry about the answers. I have a voice-activated tape recorder in my top drawer. Remember, it's all about putting people under a little gentle pressure.'

He had no time to protest further. Malcolm McDarrow thumped a balled fist against the open door and ambled into the room. He was a bull of a man, still thick with muscle from neck to thigh even though his playing days were long gone. His wide head grew in a solid block out of his shoulders and his small hawk-like eyes clung close to the sides of his twice-broken nose. McDarrow was going prematurely bald and it accentuated the worry lines above his heavy brow ridge. He looked like a man who was thinking hard even when he was simply walking across a room.

B.B. sat him down and asked him to write a short summary of his accomplishments and life goals. The task took McDarrow a surprisingly long time, largely because he sucked noisily on his pen between each thought. After his own first encounter with Beeb, Roland saw activities like this in a new light. To show that he was paying attention, he ostentatiously wrote *Freudian?* on his clipboard. When Beeb saw this, she leaned over and added *You, or him?* followed by a smiley face. He followed her gaze and realised that the tip of his own biro had telltale tooth marks of its own.

'What's this all for anyway?' McDarrow asked when he had written almost a page.

'We just want to get to know you better, Malcolm,' Beeb replied. Curiously, she had sounded out both *l*'s in his name.

Roland already knew the truth about the handwriting sample. It would soon be faxed to a graphologist for analysis. He had been shocked by this, but Beeb had assured him it was now standard practice throughout corporate America. As he watched Mal's hairy hand awkwardly sketching out his life story, he couldn't help wondering what conclusions the handwriting expert would reach about the rugby league legend.

Eventually McDarrow handed over his two pages. Beeb made a show of being interested in the contents. 'This Broncos you keep mentioning. That's some kind of sports team, right?'

McDarrow chuckled at what he thought was an ice-breaking joke. Then he glanced at Roland and realised that no one else was laughing. He started to explain, but after a polite delay, Beeb cut him off. 'Maybe you can tell me all about it some other time, Malcolm.'

She slipped the two pages of handwriting into an envelope. 'What you've written here is extremely useful. It tells us all the good things, the positives we can use to promote you. But now, I want you to go a step further and tell me the things you'd rather we didn't know, the failures and vices of Malcolm McDarrow. Come on Malcolm, tell us your darkest secret.'

McDarrow was used to hard tackles, but this one winded him a little. 'There's nothing much to tell,' he replied with a shrug. 'I'm just your typical red-blooded Aussie male.'

'Let's get specific then. Let's talk about alcohol. You like to drink a little, I hear.'

McDarrow shifted uncomfortably in his seat. He creased his eyebrows until his eyes almost disappeared. 'Yeah, I reckon I like a beer as much as the next man. Don't see the problem with that.'

'We're worried you might like it a little too much. That you're spending all your free time within strolling distance of a bar. Face it, people are beginning to talk.'

'Bullshit!'

'You're an important part of our news team, Malcolm. That's why we're concerned. We don't want to lose you, but we have to be sure you can commit to us one hundred and ten per cent. We're going to promote you pretty heavily when we launch *Newscentre 5* and we don't want any nasty little negatives working their way into the equation.'

'I don't drink too much,' McDarrow said slowly, emphasising each word. 'I can handle myself.'

'From what we've heard, we just don't agree.' Turning to Roland, she said, 'You have the next question, I think.'

Roland, who had been a reluctant spectator, found his first question on the script and became an even more reluctant participant. 'Malcolm,' he read, ignoring the bracketed instruction to pronounce the second *l*, 'we're a little worried about the image women viewers have of you. Audience research shows that females in the 18-to-54-year-old age groups see you as broadcasting only to men. How do you see us solving this problem?'

'I don't see it as a problem. Sports news *is* for men. Everyone knows that. I don't give a stuff what 18-to-54-year-old women think.'

'Malcolm,' Beeb broke in, her mispronunciation of the name beginning to really irritate both Roland and McDarrow, 'women are more than fifty per cent of our audience. Do you expect them to just go away and make their man's dinner while you anchor the sports news?'

'Why not! At that time of night there's always plenty to do in the kitchen.'

Sensing victory, Beeb turned to Roland. 'You have a follow-up question, I think.'

Roland looked at the script and saw that she was right. He read it and baulked. 'Beeb, is this really necessary?'

'I think it is.'

Roland still hesitated and it took a sharp kick under the desk to make him begin. 'Mal, mate,' he said, trying to soften the blow, 'we know all about those regular overnight stays at that Gold Coast gentleman's club. Every sordid little detail. How do you think your wife will react when she finds out what you've been up to?'

In his playing days Mal had acquired a string of nicknames. The first, when he burst onto the scene as a gifted teenager, was Magic Mal. A string of mainly alliterative variations had followed, but the one that stuck, the one that seemed most appropriate now, was Arrow McDarrow. Roland had just enough time to consider this as he watched Mal explode out of his seat and launch himself with try-scoring speed around the table. Fixing a hand on Roland's throat, Mal hauled him out of his seat and slammed him against the wall. 'You little bastard,' he growled. 'Mention one word of that to her and I'll do you.'

Beeb somehow managed to insert herself between them at this point. In a cool, sharp voice, she said, 'Chill out, Malcolm! Roland asked you a simple question. He was only doing his job.'

Surprisingly this worked. The red mist lifted and McDarrow slowly brought his emotions under control. After a moment, Beeb said, 'Let's take a break and finish this later.'

As Mal disappeared through the door, Roland slumped back into his seat. He brought his breathing under control again and felt the adrenalin wash from his body.

'Good job, Roly,' Beeb said, grinning wildly. 'It was a textbook reaction, exactly what I expected.'

'Then why did you make me do it?'

'Because now I have him where I want him. Even better, he'll tell everyone what a hard-faced bitch I am.'

'It's me he grabbed by the throat, Beeb. Not you. And it's me he'll bear the grudge against.' Roland wanted to throw something at her. Only the thought that she might also be expecting this stopped him.

'He knows I pushed you to do it. I'm going to go find him now and follow it through. We're going to remake Malcolm into a kinder, gentler late-20th-century man and he's going to thank us when we're through with him.' In the doorway, she said, 'By the way, Dalton wants to see you urgently. I didn't tell you earlier because I thought you'd try to skip out on our session with Mal.'

She went off to continue her persecution of McDarrow, leaving Roland to wonder how he could take his own revenge on her. Only petty things came to mind, but the thought of restoring the factory defaults on her cherished fax machine or loosening the screws on the back of her chair was enough to bring a smile to his face. Afraid she might soon return with Mal, he aborted the plans for vengeance and hurried down the corridor to Dalton's office.

An open door was usually a signal that Dalton was in and free for visitors but, when Roland walked into the office, it appeared at first to be empty. As he turned to leave, he saw two red-socked feet protruding from behind one of the sofas. He crept far enough across the room to confirm that it was Dalton. The American was lying on the carpet with his hands clasped together over his stomach as if laid out for burial. Roland began to edge back towards the door, but as he did so the coffee maker on the far side of the room let out a violent gasp. It gurgled again, and this was the signal for Dalton to turn over, do a dozen push-ups and spring to his feet.

'Roland,' he said, acknowledging his assistant's presence for the first time. 'You look a little stressed. We're not working you too hard, are we?'

Roland considered giving his account of the McDarrow incident, but decided that B.B. was likely to tell it better. 'I'll survive. I've just been helping Beeb with one of her staff interviews.'

'First one, huh?'

Roland nodded.

'She gave you some tough questions to ask, I bet. She likes to put people under pressure. That includes you too, you know.'

Dalton picked up his shoes and walked over to the desk. The aroma of fresh coffee filled the room and Roland hoped he would be offered a cup. 'Beeb wanted to run polygraph tests as well,' Dalton added as he laced up his shoes. 'But I thought that was overkill. Besides, it's hard to quickly find someone skilful enough with lie detectors when you're working outside your normal time zone.'

Seeing the startled look on Roland's face, Dalton added, 'Lie detectors are an invaluable personnel tool. But don't worry. We won't be needing them here.'

He crossed to the coffee maker and poured two cups. 'Sit down and I'll let you in on a little secret. Beeb and I are playing a classic management double act. I'm the one in the white hat, the doer of good deeds, and she's the one in the black hat, the evil one, the managerial Darth Vader. We decided it's the best strategy for fast results at Channel 5. She had to establish her persona quickly, so she picked out McDarrow to come down hard on. His profile suggested he would react the strongest. You know – a great athlete, a popular man, but not a happening guy in the head department.'

Remembering Mal's head hurtling towards him a few minutes earlier, Roland wondered just what had been happening in that particular department.

'I'm telling you this,' Dalton continued, 'so you'll know to expect a tough time around Beeb. But it's nothing personal. Now, the reason I wanted to see you is this: I've tied up a deal with a major advertiser and I need you to do some quick research for me. We're going to give away $50,000 in cash or gold to a lucky viewer of our new prime-time news show. What do you think?'

Roland was stunned. 'You're going to bribe people to watch the news?'

'I prefer the word enticement, and I need you to start calling it that too. We need as many viewers as possible to switch channels in the first ratings period, and it seems to me that $50,000 should be enough to help make that possible. What I want you to do is find out the kind of viewer competitions that have been done before in the Brisbane area. I want a complete list, everything you and anyone else at the station can think of.'

'How long have I got?' He reached for the mug of coffee Dalton had put in front of him.

'I want the list tomorrow lunchtime. So get going, Roland. Forget the coffee and snap to it.'

5

Roland at last had hard information to share with Phil. But when he tried to do so, his friend was curiously uninterested.

'I'm really busy right now, Roly,' Phil said. The television in his office was tuned to the American CNN news channel and his eyes were glued to it. 'I won't be around much for the next few days. Let me know what Dalton decides to do about the competition.'

As Roland was leaving, Phil added, 'You should be careful you don't get too closely involved with Dalton and Beeb. People are already talking about the three of you in one breath.'

'I thought that's what you wanted, mate.'

'Yeah, I suppose so. Sorry, Roly. I was just worried you might be crossing to the dark side. I don't want to lose you to them.'

Confused by this exchange, and disappointed by the lack of interest, Roland left Phil with CNN. He spent the afternoon talking to staff at Channel 5 about promotional competitions. By 5 o'clock he had come up with a depressingly short list of competition types, mostly variations on bingo or lucky numbers. As he left the office, B.B. told him she needed his help to interview Suzanne Denning in the morning. He cycled home wondering how he could possibly avoid it.

The twin problems of the gold and B.B. kept him awake for much of the night. He couldn't decide if it was childish to avoid her as much as possible, or if it was just plain common sense. When the next morning dawned clear and cool, he opted for the avoidance route. He rang the station early and left a message on Beeb's answering machine telling her he was doing urgent research for Dalton. He ate a leisurely breakfast then rode along the riverside cycleway to the city, crossed the river and arrived at the State Library a little after its 10 a.m. opening time.

He browsed for a while through the periodicals display, then tried a number of keyword searches in the computerised catalogue. On the way down to the cafe for morning tea, he remembered a book he had once read about a competition in England for a prize in gold. He found it on the shelves and spent an hour reading and making notes, then left the library and cycled back to Channel 5.

Dalton's office was empty, a conclusion Roland reached only after checking behind the sofas and under the desk. Reluctantly, he returned to his own office, where he was surprised to find Suzanne Denning still with Beeb.

'I'm glad you're back, Roly,' B.B. said. 'Suzanne had to postpone for a couple of hours, so we're just getting the session under way.'

'I can't stay,' he said hastily. 'I have to find Dalton. Any idea where he is?'

'Out of the office. He's calling in on me when he gets back, so why not talk with Suzanne while we wait.'

He was trapped, somewhat willingly this time. It was an opportunity to find out more about Suzanne Denning, who was smiling warmly at him and looking physically a lot less dangerous than McDarrow.

'Suzanne has already given us a handwritten summary of her achievements,' Beeb said.

She passed the two pages to him as he sat down beside her. While she asked a few follow-up questions, Roland read that Suzanne came from Sydney, was 28 years old and had been with Channel 5 for almost two years. She had gone to university in Sydney, then worked in country television in New South Wales before moving to Brisbane.

'Let me know if you find anything interesting in there?' Suzanne said as he turned the page.

He looked up, embarrassed that she had caught him reading for his own interest. Luckily, B.B. chose this moment to turn serious. 'Suzanne, Channel 5 will be marketing you and David Burton very heavily in the coming weeks. We'll obviously be pushing a number of positive stories about you in the press. We need to know now if there's anything negative that could find its way into print.'

'Negative? I don't think so.'

'Come on, honey. We've all got things we'd rather keep under wraps. What I'm basically asking is: have you ever stolen the collection money at church, been convicted of any felonies, that sort of thing?'

'Sorry to disappoint you, but I lead a pretty normal lifestyle. About the worst thing I do is smoke and drink more than my mother would like, but so does everyone in the newsroom.'

'You don't do other drugs?'

Worried about what might come next, Roland edged across his seat to put a little distance between him and Beeb.

'Definitely not,' Suzanne replied, distracted by Roland's slow-motion traverse. 'Anyone who knows me will tell you that.'

'Okay, okay,' Beeb said, backing off. 'I just had to ask. Would it surprise you to know that David Burton has smoked dope?'

'David is one of the good guys. About the only serious mistake you're likely to dig up from his recent past is the Kevin Keegan perm he had a couple of years ago. Look, I know I have to start playing the image game and I don't have a problem with it. I can assure you there's nothing about me that could possibly harm Channel 5. I don't do drugs and I'm not a granny-basher. My only problem is that I'm a workaholic. I live right now for my career in news. Some people might find that a little dull.'

'You won't object, then, if we take a few liberties with your backstory. Shape it a little to appeal to our viewers?'

'Do whatever you like, so long as you leave a little of my self-respect intact. I'll do the charity events, visit retirement homes, anything you like. If you want an action woman, I'll read the news while bungee-jumping. Whatever it takes.'

'I'm glad to hear that, Suzanne,' Dalton said from the doorway. 'It's why I chose you for the job. The trouble is, what will you want in return?'

'That's easy, Dalton. I want to host a regular environmental news programme. And the first report I want to do is on this Environmental Justice Army threat.'

'I'm not on top of your local news yet.'

'No one is on top of the EJA story. They came out of the blue a week ago and we know nothing about them. The point is that Channel 5 has an opportunity here to take a lead on serious reporting of environmental issues. My idea is for a regular prime time segment devoted to green reporting. It's important to me and I think you'll find it's important to your target audience.'

'We should talk more about this concept,' Dalton said, his eyes lighting up as he realised the potential of her idea. 'Beeb will set up some time for us later today. But I really came to find Roland. He's been looking at promotional competitions.'

Roland crossed to his own desk and returned with the list he had compiled the day before. 'Most of it is a variation on bingo or lucky numbers – scratch and win, that sort of thing. There's nothing there that would inspire me to tune in.'

Dalton finished with the sheet and dropped it in front of

Beeb. 'I hoped you might come up with something a little more exciting than this.'

'Well, I did find a book at the library this morning which gave me an idea. You said something about the $50,000 being in gold.'

'Sure. But it can be any way we want it.'

'Gold is perfect. It occurred to me that the obvious thing to do with gold is bury it and start a treasure hunt.'

Dalton cocked an eyebrow at B.B. who nodded briskly. 'We're interested,' he said. 'Tell us more.'

'I don't think anything like this has been done on live television before. My idea is that we bury the gold somewhere in the viewing area. Then we provide viewers with a new clue each night until someone solves the puzzle and locates the prize. Everyone likes a challenge like that, even those who wouldn't bother with bingo cards. All they would have to do is tune in every night for the next clue. We can make it last as long as you want by making the clues simple or hard.'

'I like it. I want you to start work right away on a set of clues.'

Roland hesitated. 'That's not exactly my line. There must be someone else who could do it better.'

'Roland, this is your baby. The fewer people involved, the less chance there is of the details leaking out. I need a location for the prize and 20 clues, one each week night for four weeks. If there's no winner by then, we'll sky-write the answer across the city from a biplane and start an old-fashioned gold rush. From now on, you talk only to me about this. Got that?'

'Okay, Dalton.'

'You too, Suzanne. Keep your lips sealed.'

'I won't tell a soul,' she replied. 'But I want it on the record that I don't agree with inducements to make people tune in. Shouldn't we stand or fall by the quality of our programming?'

'Quality! Let's not kid ourselves here. *Newscentre 5* is aimed squarely at Mr and Ms Average and their 2.4 children. They are just the kind of people who need $50,000 plenty bad.' He grinned and turned to Beeb. 'Tell her our motto, Beeb.'

'Do you remember Marshall McLuhan's famous maxim about broadcasting?'

'Of course. It's straight out of Journalism 101. *The medium is the message.*'

'Well, we think he almost got it right. It should actually read *Medium is the message.* Bad programming is easy, good quality is a little harder, but it's super-hard to be medium. Medium is what Mr and Ms Average out there want, and that's what we'll give them with *Newscentre 5.*'

While a nonplussed Denning absorbed this, Dalton turned back to Roland. 'The clock's ticking, Roland. Check in with me at regular intervals.'

6

Deciding what to do with the gold was harder than Roland imagined. His first instinct was to bury it but, as Friday afternoon wore on, he toyed with more complex possibilities. It occurred to him that he could sink it in the Brisbane River or further out into Moreton Bay. When that idea came to nothing, he detoured for a while into the possibility of having the gold cast into the shape of a common object, then painted and left in plain sight in a public space.

He realised eventually that he was overcomplicating the task and next morning returned to the original concept of buried treasure. He went shopping and bought maps, a notebook and a compass, and spent the rest of the weekend pacing around city landmarks. By Sunday night, he had a notebook full of potential burial sites, complete with intricate sketches and calculations.

Early on Monday he rang Channel 5 and left another message on Beeb's answering machine, telling her he would be working at home. He then worked methodically through the possibilities in his notes. During a coffee break he found an old hardback copy of *Treasure Island* and quickly lost himself in the adventures of Jim Hawkins. He convinced himself that the story would somehow provide a useful clue for his own treasure hunt and wasted most of the afternoon rereading it.

He returned to Channel 5 the next morning, certain that Dalton would expect him to have made a decision. When he reached his office, he found B.B. poring over a thick printout of audience research statistics.

'Well this is a surprise,' she said, taking off her glasses to look at him. Today the frames were emerald green, a perfect match for the silk scarf she was wearing with her wide-shouldered pin-striped suit. 'I was beginning to think you were avoiding us.'

'I've been working flat out on finding the perfect location for the treasure.'

'And it's going well?'

'Yes,' he lied. 'I think so, anyway.'

'Dalton will like that. I'm going through to him now. Drop by on us around ten.'

Alone, he pored over his notes again, using a fresh sheet on his blotter to summarise the pros and cons of each possible location. With time running out, he decided to wing it. He walked down the corridor to Dalton's office a few minutes early.

B.B. and Dalton were on the sofa watching one of the monitors. 'Long time no see,' Dalton said, in a tone of obvious reproof. Nodding at the screen, he added, 'Take a look at our secret weapon.'

The monitor displayed the prototype for the redesigned news studio. It looked to Roland like a cross between a game show set and the low-budget bridge of a sci-fi spacecraft. Every panel was charcoal-grey, all of it highlighted with scarlet and blue striping. At the rear of the set were three giant television screens. Projected onto each of them was the news team's new logo, the word *Newscenter* beside a 5, all of it written in scarlet lettering. It was the first time Roland had seen the logo in writing. He wondered if it was part of his job description to advise Dalton and Beeb on Australian spelling conventions. He quickly decided he wouldn't be the one to tell them they had got it wrong.

The rest of the set was empty until B.B. pressed the play button on the remote control. David Burton and Suzanne Denning appeared from opposite sides of the screen, trundling across the set behind sleek motorised desks. The lower halves of their bodies were completely hidden behind sloping grey panels. Slimline microphones and tiny monitors were just visible on the surface of each desk. Projecting at chest level out to each side were Perspex teleprompter screens.

They met in front of the giant *Newscenter5* screen and turned jerkily to face the cameras. Burton and Denning grinned uncomfortably as their vehicles bumped together, then reversed until they were a few metres apart.

'What do you think, Roly?' Dalton asked without taking his eyes from the screen.

Roland bit his lip and tried to look thoughtful. When McDarrow joined the others on the set, it was too much. Mal's low-slung sports desk was several sizes too small. He looked like a child who had stolen his little brother's pedal car. Roland burst out laughing.

Thinking that McDarrow alone had caused the outburst, Dalton said, 'Obviously, we'll scale Malcolm's unit up for a better fit.'

Roland realised what Suzanne and David reminded him of. 'They look just like Davros, the Leader of the Daleks.'

'Who are the Daleks, for Christ's sake?'

'I don't think I can explain. It's a sort of a sci-fi programme.'

'If you mean it looks futuristic, you're right on the money. Every element is computer-controlled and independently mobile. That includes the anchor buggies David and Suzanne are riding. This, Roland, is the future of news broadcasting. And we alone have access to it.'

Seeing the smirk on Roland's face, Dalton flushed. 'Kill the tape, Beeb. You know, Roland, I'm worried you and I are not bonding properly. If we don't find a way of connecting real quick, our relationship could be heading for trouble.'

Roland doubted that he and Dalton would ever bond, not without the liberal use of superglue. But it wasn't a moment for honesty. 'I don't quite understand what you're getting at, Dalton.'

'I have a meeting I need to be at,' Beeb said, getting out of her seat and heading for the door.

'Sure,' Dalton replied, still staring darkly at Roland. 'One thing, Beeb,' he called after her. 'Find out about this Dalek angle. Maybe it's something we can use.'

To Roland's surprise, the anger evaporated as soon as Beeb closed the door. Dalton smiled, a little half-heartedly. 'Maybe we're all getting a little too emotional. It's only to be expected when things are moving so fast. Instead, how about you tell me where you're at with the treasure hunt.'

'I had no idea how much research would be needed. Selecting the site, designing the puzzle, not to mention the clues.'

'Uh-huh,' Dalton replied, only half-listening. He reached for a zippered overnight bag at his feet and lifted it onto the coffee table. It contained a metal strongbox about 30 centimetres square. The new *Newscenter5* logo was stamped onto the upper surface of the lid. Dalton opened it, unfolded the velvet lining and slid the box across the glass table top to Roland. Recessed into the padded lining were a half-dozen slender gold bars.

'The sponsor dropped it off this morning,' Dalton said as Roland fingered one of the bars. 'I want you to bury it tonight.'

'Tonight? Dalton, I'm a little worried about messing this up. Don't you think it should be in the hands of a professional?'

'Trust me, it's better done by one person quickly than bringing in a whole team of experts. Secrecy and speed, Roland. Secrecy and speed. Do you have a problem with that?'

Roland could see quite a few problems, none of which would interest Dalton. 'Okay,' he replied, surrendering to the absurdity of it. 'I'll do it tonight.'

Back in his own office, he sat with the gold in front of him, hoping for inspiration. He needed help, at the very least from someone with a car. Phil was the obvious choice and, for once, he was in his office and answering his phone.

'I can't tonight, Roly,' he said, when Roland had explained the situation. 'There's something big happening that I can't postpone.'

'Phil, you have to get me out of this mess. I can't carry the gold and tools on my bike. I need you to drive me there.'

'Drive you where?'

'I don't know yet. I haven't decided.'

'Leave it with me. I'll think of someone. Stay in your office.'

'Where else am I likely to go when I'm babysitting a couple of kilos of gold.'

He was afraid of letting the treasure out of his sight. After an hour he carried it with him to the toilet, and then to the kitchen for coffee. Each time he put the package down he felt the need to check the contents of the box afterwards. Back in his office he sat it on the corner of the desk and tried to make progress on selecting a site. But he couldn't concentrate until he knew that Phil had found someone.

After a while he started pacing around the room and found that it eased the tension. Passing Beeb's desk for the twentieth time, he noticed that she had left her glasses on top of a computer printout. He held the large round glasses up to his eyes and saw perfectly through them, then slipped them on and tried reading the screen of her Apple Mac.

'Roland, honey,' a familiar voice said from the doorway, 'those just don't do anything at all for you.'

He tensed, then relaxed when he saw that it was Suzanne and not B.B. at the door. 'You shouldn't do that to people. You sounded just like her.'

'I've spent so much time with her in the last week, I've almost perfected the accent. But at least I haven't started wearing her glasses yet.'

'They're fake, you know. I've been sure of it all week.'

'They're not the only fakes around here. The place is crawling with them: audience research analysts, set designers, mass media psychologists. Beeb is locked in the conference room with some of them now. There's even a choreographer from the Queensland Ballet working with the computer programmers on the *Newscenter5* set dynamics. By the way, what do you think of the new me?'

He had been doing his best not to let his jaw drop since she had walked into the room. Her hair had been chopped into a lopsided bob. Chin-length on one side, it hung edgily against her collarbone on the other. It looked as though multiple stylists had been involved and they had argued violently about the outcome.

'I love it,' he said, praying she would believe him.

'You'd better be telling the truth. I was hijacked by a coven of image consultants an hour ago and they hassled me into it. I can't go back into the newsroom until I'm sure no one will laugh.' She shook her hair over her face. 'Be honest with me. It's freakish, isn't it.'

She pushed her hair back into place, bit her lip and looked at him, demanding another compliment.

'Suzanne, I think you look great.'

'Thanks,' she replied, clearly struggling to believe him.

‘Anyway, I just passed Phil Porter in the corridor. He said something about you wanting to ask me out tonight, but being too shy to do it yourself.’

‘That’s not true.’

‘You mean you aren’t too shy?’

‘No. That is ...’

‘Roland, you’re behaving suddenly like someone who’s more than a little shy.’

Flustered, he wished the whole conversation could begin again. ‘Look, the idea of going out with you tonight hadn’t even occurred to me. Phil’s been having a bit of a joke at our expense.’

‘Shit. He’s always doing that to me. You’d think I’d learn after a while.’

‘After the first decade you’ll probably get used to it. You can’t help liking him in the end.’

He realised this was all the assistance he was likely to get from Phil and decided to take matters into his own hands. ‘I really do need your help. I’ve got a problem that has to be dealt with tonight and you’re the only person I can trust.’

She stopped playing with her hair. ‘I might be willing to help, but only if you stop calling me Suzanne. It’s Suzie. I’ve had a gutful of consultants Suzanning this and Suzanning that at me all week. What do you want me to do?’

He showed her the gold and explained that he needed a driver.

‘Count me in. It sounds like fun. But I’m reading the hourly news updates tonight. I can’t leave here before quarter to 11.’

‘The later the better. I can’t let anyone see me bury the prize. I’ll wait here for you.’

‘Okay. I’ve got to get back to work. I think I feel brave enough now to walk into the newsroom looking like the new me. Thanks for saying nice things, even if they weren’t true.’

‘I meant it.’

'Roly, you're a terrible liar.' At the doorway, she added, 'I'll collect you here around 11. Where are we going to bury the stuff?'

'I have absolutely no idea. And I don't much care, so long as it's in the ground tonight.'

7

When Suzanne returned at 11 p.m., Roland was still making shorthand notes on the angles and measurements he would use at the burial site.

'Have you got all the gear?' he asked. On a mid-afternoon progress call, she had offered to borrow a range of gardening tools from the Channel 5 groundsman.

'That I 'ave, Cap'n,' she replied, tugging an imaginary forelock. 'Shovel an' pick are in t'car, an' yer favret parrot's outside waitin' t'hop on yer shoulder.'

Roland was edgy after an entire day with the gold. He could barely muster a tired smile at her pirate's lackey routine. 'I'm sorry, but there's nothing about this whole thing that seems funny any more.'

'Sorry, Cap'n,' she persisted. ''Tis all that speech coachin' I've 'ad this week. That and the smell o' that there treasure. Gets to ordinary folk's minds, it does. Gold fever, I calls it!'

He rolled his eyeballs and she finally took the hint. He followed her to the foyer and down the steps to the staff car park. In plain English, she asked, 'Do you want to put the loot in the boot?'

'I'll feel better if it's in the front with us.'

He felt dangerously exposed in the open-topped Mazda as they sped out of the car park and hurtled down the mountain. Suzie took an aggressive line through every corner and flattened the throttle down the long straight descent past the Botanical Gardens. As they approached the roundabout at the end of the Western Freeway, she asked, 'Isn't it about time you told me where we're going?'

He shook his head. Superstition prevented him from speaking the exact location aloud. Instead he gave her a simple set of left and right instructions until they arrived at the park he had chosen.

She pulled in to the side of the road and switched off the ignition. 'What now?'

After the hair-raising ride it felt good to be stationary again. He sat silently for a moment, savouring the cool evening breeze. Everything had seemed much simpler back at the office, but with plenty of traffic and an occasional pedestrian still passing, the prospect of burying the box in the park across the road was extremely uninviting. 'I think we should wait for a while. It's busier than I imagined.'

'Sounds like a good idea. But I'd better put the roof up – we don't want to get arrested for loitering.'

She raised the car's soft-top, then collected a thermos and two plastic cups from the boot. The coffee was stale and lukewarm but it was something to do and they drank in silence for a while. Eventually she started to fish in her bag for her cigarettes. 'Do you mind if I smoke?'

He did mind very much. But because it was her car and because she was helping him, he said, 'Go ahead.'

His voice gave him away and when she lit up she exhaled through the open window. Between puffs she pulled at a stunted strand of hair while he tapped his plastic mug nervously against the dashboard. Alone with her, he felt an excitement that wasn't in any way connected with the treasure hunt. He had hoped for an opportunity like this since they had first met in the newsroom, but now it was here he was too agitated to enjoy it. The voice of reason told him she was a complete stranger, who was probably thinking about stock market fluctuations or growing tensions in the Middle East. And yet, all he wanted to do was find a way of looking at her without her knowing.

The longer the silence went on, the harder it was to start a conversation, and the more irritated they became with the other's smoking or tapping. Finally, with his mind on the dig again, he found a way to break the ice. 'If you'd rather stay in the car while I bury the box, I won't mind.'

'There is no way I'm going to miss out on the fun part. Wherever you go, I'm coming too.'

It was exactly the response he'd hoped for. If he was about to commit a crime – which he realised he probably was – having an accomplice would steady his nerves. Having Suzie Denning as his accomplice seemed particularly soothing. She radiated self-assurance, more than enough for both of them. He realised he was looking at her and started to turn away, but she caught him and smiled.

'You're enjoying this, aren't you?' he said.

'Why not? I've never buried treasure before and I don't suppose I'll have the chance to do it again.'

'I still can't believe Dalton asked me to do this.'

'You didn't think he and Beeb would actually get their hands dirty with it, did you? Can you imagine it? He'd have a team of dig consultants flown in from America, and she'd oversee it like a military operation.'

They both laughed. Then Suzie turned serious. 'The thing I object to is having a competition in the first place. Channel 5 has a good news team. We shouldn't be hiding behind a gimmick like this.'

'It could have been worse. Dalton might have gone for a scratch-card lottery. This way, at least, the viewers will have to exercise their minds if they want the gold.'

'And that's why it won't work. People aren't interested in thinking deeply at six o'clock in the evening. They've had a hard day at work and they just want to relax and be told what went on in their corner of the world. We'll end up having to give them the answers too.'

Roland was surprised she was so cynical about the audience she seemingly connected with so well. 'I don't understand, Suzanne. If you don't think it will work, then why are you here?'

'I told you. I've never buried treasure before. And don't call me Suzanne. I can't stand it.'

'Sorry.'

The cabin of the little Mazda seemed too small again. She took a last draw on her cigarette and stubbed it out. Then she turned and smiled. 'Don't apologise, Roly. I'm the one who's sorry. The stress of the last week is getting to me. I really do think this is a bit of a lark. And I've got another reason for coming tonight too – I wanted to find out what Roland Kendall was like. Last week I thought you were some sort of junior Dalton. But when I caught you wearing Beeb's glasses today, I knew there was something else going on. Now that I see how uncomfortable you are around the gold, I'm more intrigued by why you're here, than why I am.'

'I can't really explain it. The last ten days have just sort of happened to me. One minute I'm recoiling in horror at what they're doing. The next, I'm drawn in and realising that a little bit of me is enjoying the ride. I've never been so confused in my life.'

Suzie was a professional listener, and she looked intently at him as though she knew there was more to tell. He wanted to say something about what he was doing for Phil, would have welcomed the therapy of letting it all out. But he held back. The moment passed and they lapsed into another silence.

After a while she put her head out the window and looked around. 'It's getting late. Shall we give it a go?'

'Okay. You carry the gold. I'll bring the tools and the parrot.'

It was the first light-hearted thing he'd said all night and she responded with a mock salute. 'Aye, aye, Cap'n Kendall. I'm right behind thee.'

The park's memorial gates were closed and locked, but there had never been a boundary fence. Roland led Suzie into the park, where they skirted a football oval and climbed through a stand of trees to the top of the hill. His target was the Ionic column of the war memorial on the crest of the hill. It sat on a square base that had been inscribed with the names of the fallen from the local area. Surrounding the whole structure was a decorative fence comprising a square of stone posts and a long chain linking them.

In the distance Roland saw the dark silhouette of Mt Coot-tha. Strung out along its length were the winking red lights of the television transmission towers. When Suzie came up beside him, he asked, 'Which one's Channel 5?'

'There,' she said, pointing to the tallest. 'The gold will be right under our noses the whole time.'

'Give or take a kilometre or two. I might even work that into a clue.'

With Suzie at his side calling out the instructions from his notebook, he made an elaborately choreographed series of steps and turns away from the war memorial and away from the winking red lights. When she had read out the final instruction, he stopped and spread a sack on the ground at his feet. With the spade he cut a small square of turf, lifted it out and placed it carefully onto the sack.

As he did this they heard the jangling of a chain and the thud of multiple feet pounding up the slope. Roland dropped the spade and froze, but Suzie stepped forward and put her arms around him. 'Relax,' she whispered. 'Put your arms around me. You've wanted to all night, haven't you?'

He didn't have to be asked twice. It felt awkward at first, as though they were strangers forced together on the dance floor. But as the seconds ticked by, Roland relaxed and began to enjoy it. Her eyes were bright in the moonlight and she was smiling broadly. It was infectious and he started to laugh.

'Shh!' she whispered. 'You'll spoil the moment.'

Her words were a confirmation that this was a moment, perhaps something more. They both turned serious and stared deeply into each other's eyes.

They stayed like this until a jogger, accompanied by a Dobermann, appeared on the crest of the hill. He ran towards them, then veered towards the war memorial, where he stopped to reset the timer on his watch. Aware that he was staring at them, Suzie gripped Roland by the neck and kissed him.

The Dobermann seemed to find this objectionable. It growled and strained on its lead, but the jogger settled it and jerked it after him as he started down the slope to the other side of the park. If he saw the garden tools or the box at the feet of the two lovers, he thought nothing of it. Man and dog dropped out of sight as quickly as they had appeared.

Roland and Suzie clung together a little longer than necessary. When the sound of the dog's chain had faded completely, she finally pushed him away. Still smiling, she said, 'We have work to do.'

He lifted the pick and smacked it into the ground. With the top soil loosened, he dug for ten minutes until the hole was deep enough to take the box. He hefted it into the hole, resisted the temptation to check the gold one last time, and shovelled earth over it. Suzie held the torch over the hole while he worked.

He finished by replacing the square of turf and tamping it down with his feet. He took the torch from Suzie to inspect his handiwork. When the light caught her face he saw a huge grin. He realised he was doing the same thing. 'What do you think?' he asked, prodding at the turf with the toe of his shoe.

'It looks good in the dark.'

'I'll come back at first light and check it.'

The last task was to dispose of the excess earth. They carried it on the sack along the crest of the hill and tipped it over a fence onto the railway embankment. Satisfied, they retrieved the pick and shovel and walked back to the car.

As she started the engine, Suzie broke the silence. 'That was fantastic. And what about that jogger?'

'If it wasn't for you, I'd still be standing there with the spade in my hands. We should do that again sometime.'

He'd meant the kiss, but she seemed to think he was talking about the gold. 'No thanks. It was fun, but I won't be giving up the day job just yet.'

Minutes later, when they turned into his street, he invited her in for a drink. She checked her watch and shook her head. 'Sorry, I have to get home. There's some late news from the US I need to catch up with.' As he got out of the car, she added, 'Some other time, though.'

8

Suzie's abrupt departure left Roland feeling empty and alone. In the lounge, he sifted through a stack of records and picked out an old recording of Bach's Goldberg Variations, his go-to music for sleepless nights. He listened carefully to the first few bars of the Aria, then turned the volume down and settled on the sofa with a book. He tried repeatedly to read the opening paragraph, but his mind took none of it in. It was still lost in the drama that had unfolded in the park and, before that, the wait in the car with Suzie.

Somewhere between leaving Channel 5 with her and arriving home, his attitude towards burying the gold had changed from one of dread to pleasure. The sole reason for the change was Suzanne Denning. When he was around her he felt swept along in the moment. But she seemed completely unaware of the effect she was having on him and he had felt cheated when she dropped him in his driveway and sped off into the night.

He gave up on the book and turned on the television, scanning the channels for the American news programme he thought she must be watching. He eventually found the *NBC Today Show*. He tried to take an interest as the show's hosts Bryant and Jane presented a potpourri of news that segued from

American foreign policy to tips for making a better pasta sauce. Roland persisted until Willard the weatherman joined them and talked for five full minutes about everything except the weather. The whole experience brought him no closer to Suzanne. He flicked the standby switch and went to bed where he quickly fell asleep.

He woke suddenly around three, tormented by a nightmare that combined his recent experiences at Channel 5 with a story of piratical treasure hunting. He had just been on the losing side of a sword fight with a fanatical pirate queen who looked and sounded exactly like Suzanne Denning. Drenched in his own sweat, Roland lay in the dark as he recalled the ghastly details: Suzanne, the distant pirate queen, who had easily parried his own feeble swordplay and plunged her blade through his heart; Phil her evil henchman, struggling to keep a huge Dobermann on the leash while he held a lit cigarette to Suzie's lips; and, on the sidelines, Dalton cheering every stroke of Suzanne's blade, calling out, 'You're connecting with him real good there!' He imagined B.B. or one of her analysts picking their way through this fertile territory and shivered at the thought.

He fell into a more restful sleep and woke after nine when his neighbour started a lawn mower under the bedroom window. Tired and irritated, he got ready for work. He fully expected that B.B. and Dalton would want the details of the burial and looked forward to being briefly the centre of their attention. He also hoped he might bump into Suzie again, thinking that another few minutes alone with her might make it clear if there had been anything in their kiss.

When he reached Channel 5 both B.B. and Dalton were missing. Disappointed, he stayed in his office all morning working on anagrams for the competition clues. On a visit to the gents toilet, he met the newsreader, David Burton. Roland noticed that Burton's normally fair hair had been streaked even lighter and that he now had an earring stud on his left earlobe. Burton stood humming to himself at the urinal, and nodded when Roland joined him. 'It's going to be a big one, Roland. I can feel it.'

'What is?' Roland asked, almost afraid to ask.

'Today, I mean. You've heard about last night, haven't you?'

Roland was about to reply *Heard about it, I was the one who buried it!* when Burton added, 'The Environmental Justice Army.'

Admitting ignorance of the news to an anchorman was probably as low as Roland could sink at Channel 5. But Burton was in a hurry and took pity on him. 'The EJA kidnapped Lloyd Balchin's daughter last night.'

Roland knew he was supposed to have heard of Lloyd Balchin and felt sure that he had. Burton guessed this, and explained. 'Lloyd Balchin the land developer. You know, Lloydton, Balchin Downs, Virginia Waters.'

'Oh yes, of course.'

'He was in the news recently when he got approval to clear an area of swampland in Brisbane's northern outskirts. It's the last area of natural wetland of its type in South East Queensland. Every conservationist group in the State opposed the development. Somehow it got the go-ahead on a technicality.'

'What do the EJA want with his daughter?'

'They haven't said. She was reported missing last night and her car was found abandoned on the Pacific Highway early this morning. Inside was a message from the EJA saying that Virginia Balchin was a hostage.'

'No demands?'

'Nothing. The police are combing the area where the car was abandoned, but it's really a case of waiting for the next step from the EJA.' As he washed his hands, he added, 'I've got to get back to work. Dalton's waiting for me. Don't forget to keep your TV tuned to Channel 5.'

Roland returned to his office where he tried to pick up the threads of his puzzle. Dalton had asked for 20 clues, so he began by dividing his blotter into a five-by-four grid. He tried to fill each box with a vital nugget of information that, step by step, would reveal the precise location of the prize. It was slow work, and by one o'clock he was more than ready for the diversion offered by the news. David Burton read the bulletin, but had nothing new to add to the exclusive broadcast he'd made earlier in the gents toilet. The truth was that no one knew what had happened to Balchin's daughter. It was a matter of waiting for the EJA to make its next move.

Roland switched the TV off and went back to work. He had only just started when Phil arrived, beaming. 'Gidday Roly. Coming to lunch? I'm driving down to Paddington.'

Roland, who hadn't seen Phil so happy in weeks, gladly took the chance to escape the office. He put his notes and the blotter into the top drawer of the desk, locked it, and followed Phil out of the building.

'This kidnapping story is just what Channel 5 needs,' Phil said, when they were in the car. 'Dalton has decided to launch the *Newscenter5* format from tonight. It means a whole hour of news, so we can devote the best part of 30 minutes to the EJA story. It's a good decision and I've spent the whole morning telling him so.'

Roland couldn't adjust to a business that profited so nakedly from the misfortune of others. While most Queenslanders were expressing concern for the well-being of Virginia Balchin, a small group of people, mainly based on Mt Coot-tha, were rubbing their hands together and allocating resources to milk every drop of emotion from the story. Phil spoke for all of them when he said, 'What would be really great is a break in the story just before the six o'clock bulletin.'

'Have you any idea what you sound like?' Roland asked. 'David Burton was almost whistling about it earlier and now you're practically floating on air.'

'Don't get mixed up between our personal and professional feelings. Channel 5 needs big news stories and we need them now. We were lucky this one came along. For *Newscenter5*'s sake I hope it lasts a week. On the other hand, for Ginny Balchin's sake, I hope it's over today. I've met her and she seemed really nice.'

'You know Virginia Balchin?'

Phil nodded as he turned a corner. 'Our paths have crossed socially a couple of times, yes.'

'What do you think the EJA is trying to achieve by taking her?'

'The consensus in the newsroom is that they're a bunch of ratbag greenies who think they can save the planet with stunts like this.'

'Abducting Virginia Balchin will save the planet?'

'It might save the bits that Lloyd Balchin wants to flatten and turn into a brick-and-tile wilderness. Some people might think that isn't a bad achievement.' Changing the subject, he asked, 'How did you go last night?'

'Very smoothly. No thanks to you.'

'Mate, I'm sorry. I really did have important business to attend to.'

'And thanks for telling Suzie I was too shy to ask her out.'

Phil chuckled. 'I'd forgotten that. You can't deny it though, can you? I've seen the way you look at her in meetings. I didn't think it would do you any harm if I forced the pace between you a little.'

'Well, we did kiss,' Roland said, unable to keep it to himself. 'And I enjoyed every minute of it. But it doesn't mean anything.'

'Doesn't mean anything! Do you think Suzanne Denning, Ms

Living Breathing My Career In Journalism Comes First, walks up to everyone and flings her arms around them? What did you do about it?'

'Nothing. I asked her in for coffee when she dropped me home, but she had to get back home to watch the late news.'

'You could at least have told her you always watched it too and asked her in. I dunno, Roly. I think we might have to ask Beeb to organise some assertiveness training for you. What do you reckon?'

'Phil, Suzie only kissed me to make a jogger think we were a couple of lovers in the park, instead of a burial party. It was just a bit of quick thinking on her part. It means nothing.'

Phil wouldn't let it go. He ribbed Roland mercilessly about the kiss until they arrived in Paddington. Roland endured in silence, regretting he had said anything at all. He worried that Phil might try to do something to force things with Suzie, or worse tell B.B. about it.

Luckily, as soon as they found a table at a sidewalk cafe, Phil's thoughts turned to his number one passion. Food. He scanned the menu for its most tactile dish and settled eventually on a Cajun Caribbean Chicken Salad. He made Roland order the same. When the meal arrived on a banquet-sized platter, he dug his hands into the plush bed of warmed lettuce and extracted a heavily spiced chicken leg. He ate it like an extra in a medieval movie scene, tossing the stripped bone onto a side plate before plunging his hand into the lettuce for another morsel.

As Roland chewed on a chicken wing, the conversation turned to Dalton. Phil was worried Roland wasn't involved enough with events in Dalton's office. Between chicken legs, he produced a small plastic container and passed it across the table to Roland. 'That little beauty is the answer to our problems.'

Roland noted that Phil's problems were now his problems too. Already worried, he asked, 'What is it?'

'An electronic listening device – a bug.'

'Phil, you're crazy. I refuse to have anything to do with this.'

'Have I asked you to do anything yet? I'll do the dirty work this time, but I need help and you're the only person I can trust.' He picked up the box and opened it. 'I'll install it. It transmits to a voice-activated recorder. All you have to do is keep the recorder in your office and make sure the tapes are changed regularly. I told you, I'll be out of the office a lot, otherwise I'd do it all myself. Come on, mate. What do you say?'

'It's illegal, Phil.'

'I think that might be a grey area. Anyway, it would only be wrong if I used it to the detriment of Channel 5. I'm frozen out at the moment and I'm desperate to get more involved. I need to know what Dalton's up to. He won't be here forever, and I want to make sure Dad leaves me in control when Dalton goes back to America. With the tapes I'll be prepared. I can get onto the same frequency as Dalton and gain his confidence.'

Roland hesitated long enough to realise that the idea of a bug was quite attractive. It meant he would no longer be responsible for passing information on. Changing tapes on a cassette recorder seemed the lesser of two evils. 'All right, I'll do it.'

'Thanks Roly. It's times like these that you find out who your friends are.' He checked his watch. 'We should get a move on. I want to test this thing out when we get back.'

9

Roland devoted the rest of the afternoon to testing the range and quality of the listening device. Through a pair of Walkman headphones he heard Phil's voice in varying degrees of clarity saying things like: 'I've just placed the bug on the underside of my desk drawer and I'm sitting behind the desk. Can you hear me?'

'Yes, Phil,' Roland would reply wearily into the telephone.

Phil, who had his own phone cradled on his shoulder, would then move on to the next test. 'I'm standing now about three metres from the desk. Everything okay?'

'Loud and clear.'

'I'm walking across the room to the window. About four, no maybe five, metres away.'

And so it went on. Worn down by this, Roland even agreed to stay behind and help Phil test the bug after it was installed in Dalton's office. It meant a second late night at work, but he could see that Phil was obsessed and wouldn't rest until the task was complete.

Eventually, even Phil tired of playing with the new toy. He accepted Roland's plea that he needed to put in some time on the competition clues. Roland had been happily avoiding this but, exhausted by Phil's game with the bug, he gladly opened his desk drawer and spread the notes and papers across the desktop. Then he stared blankly at them, the meagre results of his work, and felt like feeding them into Beeb's new high-speed shredder. He ploughed on, but doubted that anything usable was likely to emerge.

The next distraction at six o'clock was the debut of *Newscenter5*. Roland turned on the TV hoping to be impressed. At the very least he knew that the perambulations of the news team on their bucking anchor buggies would guarantee a little light relief. It was also his first chance all day to see Suzie and he realised he would happily watch anything where she was the star attraction.

Newscenter5 opened conventionally enough with a strident news theme, all brass and percussion, urgent yet somehow reassuring. It played over a montage of charcoal helicopters, speedboats and news cars. After this, Burton and Denning slid noiselessly across the screen like two orbiting satellites and docked in front of the big *Newscenter5* screen. The only changes Roland noticed from the prototype video were the new charcoal-coloured jackets and scarlet accessories of the overexcited co-anchors.

Denning's voice faltered several times as she introduced the lead item, the Balchin Kidnapping. The story hadn't developed since lunchtime. Suzie made her way with growing confidence through a summary of the kidnapping, while the screen behind her displayed pictures of Lloyd and Virginia Balchin.

Her buggy glided abruptly to the side and Burton's moved to the centre of the set. 'We'll come back to that summary later, Suzanne. There is a development in the Balchin story and we are crossing live to Brian Marshall for an update.'

The wind-tunnel-wild hair of veteran reporter Brian Marshall appeared at the top of the screen. Then the photographs of the

Balchins faded, revealing the rest of Brian's craggy features. The two buggies manoeuvred so that the anchors were facing Marshall whose own *Newscenter5* jacket already looked as old and crumpled as its owner. 'Thanks David. We've just learned that a communique has been released by the Environmental Justice Army. Details are sketchy at this point, but we're working to clarify them now.'

LIVE FROM POLICE HEADQUARTERS appeared on the screen. 'Brian,' Suzanne asked, 'do you have anything on the content of that communique?'

Marshall's earphone popped out of his ear. He pushed it back into place and held a finger against it. 'I've just heard that a new demand has been made by the EJA. The details are not clear yet but I can confirm that a demand has been made.'

Burton asked, 'How was the communique released?'

'That is also unclear. We hope to bring you more details shortly.'

'Thank you Brian. Stick with it,' Suzanne said, as her chariot rotated to face the camera. 'That was Brian Marshall at Police Headquarters. David.'

'Thanks Suzie. We're now crossing live to Lisa Demchek who is outside Lloyd Balchin's home at Balchin Waters.'

Lisa Demchek, at first glance, might have been Suzanne's younger sister. Blonde, in her case bottled, slim, and eager, she appeared to have been manufactured from the same young female reporter mould as Denning. They were referred to in the newsroom as the Denn-chek twins, but the on-air rivalry between them was intense.

When her camera went live, Lisa was swatting a fly away from her face. She straightened quickly when she heard a smirking Suzie ask: 'Lisa, what's the latest from the Balchin home?'

'David – I mean Suzanne – we understand that Lloyd Balchin has now been made aware of the contents of the communique.

He has been here at his mansion waiting for developments. A short time ago he was joined by senior police officers connected with the investigation. We'll keep you posted if there are any developments, but for now back to you in the studio.'

'Thank you, Lisa,' Burton said, as his buggy jerked towards the front. It stalled at a 45-degree angle. Burton, ever the professional, casually rotated his head to face the live camera. 'We'll be returning to Lisa and Brian later in the programme. Suzie.'

'After the break we'll bring you a roundup of the other top stories of the day, followed by our new international segment. Stay with us for more of *Newscenter5* momentarily.'

Roland turned down the sound during the commercial break. He needed a rest. The news team had tossed each other's names around like frisbees. So much had been said, with live crosses to two outside broadcasts, but no real news had come out of it. All it had achieved was to prove that when something did happen, *Newscenter5* would be there, wherever there was.

The bulletin returned and, as promised, dealt with other news stories. In this segment the buggies were strangely still and the presentation more relaxed. About 15 minutes later, during a report from the Middle East, Burton again cut in: 'We are standing by to cross to Police Headquarters in Roma Street, where a news conference is just getting under way. Brian Marshall, are you there?'

The picture cut to a room filled with reporters, cameras and microphones, all directed towards a central podium. Brian Marshall was in a corner of the picture squeezed between two camera crews. Over the noise of background conversation he said, 'David, we are waiting for the arrival of Acting Assistant Commissioner Russell Lockhart, the senior officer in charge of the investigation. We believe he will provide us with details of the communique released by the EJA. In fact he's coming into the room now, so let's cross to him.'

Assistant Commissioner Lockhart manoeuvred his top-heavy frame through the media scrum and rested his substantial belly against the podium. He removed his cap, placed it on a side table, and adjusted his gun belt which had slipped below his waistline. He spread his papers on the lectern, looked up and nodded, signalling that he was ready to begin.

'Ladies and gentlemen. As you know, Virginia Balchin disappeared late last night as she drove home from a meeting in the centre of Brisbane. Her car was found this morning, abandoned at the side of the road on the Gold Coast Highway. Inside the car was a letter addressed to Mr Lloyd Balchin, Virginia's father. It claimed that Ms Balchin had been taken into custody by a group calling itself the Environmental Justice Army.

'The letter stated that she was safe and well and would not be harmed, but that her release depended on the actions of Mr Balchin. A team of police investigators has been working on this case all day. Shortly before 6 p.m. this evening a second communique from the EJA was received by a television studio at Mt Coot-tha. The contents of that letter are as follows.

'Point 1. The EJA alleges that Mr Balchin is guilty of crimes against the environment.

'Point 2. They demand that Mr Balchin pay substantial reparation to the environment.

'Point 3. He must also publicly denounce his past development activities and devote himself to sustainable development.

'Point 4. Mr Balchin's daughter will be held hostage until he has complied with these demands.

'Mr Balchin has no comment at this stage and neither do we. Thank you.'

Lockhart picked up his papers and his cap and left the room amid howls of protest from the assembled media.

Phil chose this moment to burst into Roland's office. 'Roly, there's a major crisis in the *Newscenter5* studio. Dalton and B.B. have both gone to the control room to sort it out. It's our chance to plant the bug.'

Roland followed without a fight, having already decided that the line of least resistance was the simplest. As they walked along the corridor, Phil explained how the crisis had arisen. 'The computer system controlling the anchor buggies has crashed. The floor crew is taking it in turns to sit behind the buggies and push them round the set. The cameras have been zoomed in tight on Suzie and David since the first commercial break so you can't see all the pushing and shoving.'

They reached the door of Dalton's office. Phil stopped and said, 'Stay here. If Dalton comes back, don't let him in.'

Roland paced nervously around for a few moments while Phil placed the bug under Dalton's desk. He breathed easy again when Phil quickly reappeared and closed the door. Encountering no one, they were back in the safety of Roland's office less than three minutes later.

'That was so easy,' Phil said through a huge grin. 'This whole industrial espionage lark is a breeze.'

Roland collapsed into his chair and glanced at the television to see what was happening. Phil saw this, leaned over and switched it off. Picking up the tape recorder, he said, 'Just check this regularly and change the tape when it runs out. I'll drop in every day to pick up the tapes. Maybe you should leave them in your top drawer, so I'll know where they are if you're not here.'

'Okay,' Roland replied, wearily.

'And keep the drawer locked. We don't want Beeb rummaging around and finding them. Give me your spare key.'

Roland separated the keys to the top drawer and handed one to Phil, who turned and crossed to the door. 'I'm off to the control room to agree with everything Dalton says. You coming?'

'No. I've just about had enough of *Newscenter5* for one night.'

He had heard enough about the Balchins too. The early planting of the bug finished the day sooner than he had expected. He dropped his competition notes back into the desk drawer next to the tape recorder, changed into his cycling gear and went home.

10

Dalton and B.B. spent most of the following morning analysing the premature birth of *Newscenter5*. Roland was excluded from this huddle and directed instead to step up the pace on the competition clues.

Right from the start, he was distracted by the thought of the recorder in his desk. He had always wondered how the Americans operated when they were alone and now he had the means to find out. Eventually his curiosity got the better of him and he reached guiltily into the drawer for the headphones.

The first few minutes were disappointing, nothing more than the sound of papers being shuffled and the clicking of keys on a computer keyboard. His heart beat a little faster when the voices of the Americans filled his ears in stereo.

> DALTON: So what are the pluses and minuses?
> BEEB: Overall, we're in a good place. A few minor concerns about Suzanne, but that's been put down to first night nerves. The technical problems with the set are an obvious negative, but the software engineer worked on it through the night. He swears we can factor that out too.

DALTON: Any changes for tonight?
BEEB: Not from my angle.
DALTON: Then we stick with the game plan. How about the publicity angle?
BEEB: We have features on both Burton and Denning in the Sunday magazines. Front cover treatment. The problem is with the follow-up. There's not much new we can write about David, so we're pushing his family man angle. The real issue is Suzanne. Our star reporter doesn't appear to have a social life.
DALTON: I thought the whole workaholic thing was an act.
BEEB: 'Fraid not, Hilary. And it's already showing as a negative in last night's audience survey. She's seen as too clinical and unfeeling.
DALTON: Your solution?
BEEB: Viewers need to know she's in a caring, sharing relationship with a man. *Toot sweet.*
DALTON: Pictures in the glossy magazines relaxing at home with the new man in her life. Hints about wedding bells, but it's too early to say. Maybe one day even babies. Tell me anyone who doesn't like that.
BEEB: The problem being, there is no man in her life right now.
DALTON: So fix her up with someone, if she can't do it herself.
BEEB: I already talked it through with her. She knows what she has to do. And she knows how urgent it is.
DALTON: Keep on top of this, Beeb. Work your magic …

Roland pulled the headphones off and locked them in his desk drawer. He was ashamed of himself for listening as long as he had. Phil was welcome to anything he could learn from the tapes. The only snippet he considered worth passing on was that Dalton's first name seemed to be Hilary.

He immersed himself in his competition and after two solid days had produced a convoluted set of cryptic clues, anagrams and cyphers. He thought of them as clever but worried they were just a little too clever. He decided to take the results to Dalton for his opinion.

'Good work, Roly,' Dalton said, as he flicked through the folder containing the clues. 'I want you to seal each night's clue inside an envelope and give them all to me for safekeeping.'

Roland was incredulous. 'Don't you want to work through them? I've been working in a vacuum on this. What if they're impossible to crack? Or worse, so ridiculously easy someone finds the gold on the first night.'

'I trust your judgement. Let's just see how the viewers react. If there's a problem, we can always make changes once it's under way.'

Crossing to the sofas, he said, 'Come over here. I want to bring you up to speed on some changes we're making to *Newscenter5*.'

Reluctantly, Roland followed him across the room. When he was seated, Dalton pressed the play button on the video player. 'This is an idea we used in the States a couple of times. We call it *Newsrap*.'

The screen showed the empty *Newscenter5* studio. A rap music beat started and a young black street rapper dressed in baseball cap and oversized clothes strutted onto the set. The camera zoomed in on his head and shoulders and he turned and seemed to notice for the first time that he was on air. He stretched out a finger directly at the centre of the screen and, to the rhythm of the music, said:

Wait a minute brother, don't touch that dial,
I'll give you some news to make you smile,
I'll give it to you straight, you won't run a mile,
When you hear the news in the Newsrap style.

He spun around and launched into an elaborately choreographed dance that ended with him spinning on his back. He sprang up, clapped to the beat and wrapped up the day's news while a video montage of the top stories played on the screen behind him:

A dude got killed, shot by his wife,
Stopped by a bullet that ended his life.
A heist went wrong, they didn't get far,
Caught in a trap, they totalled their car.
Mr Balchin Downs alone on his hill,
The EJA, they took his little girl.

We're rappin' the news in the Newsrap style,
Rap the news,
Yo! Newsrap!

Banana Republic, that's the Aussie way,
The balance of payments gets worse every day ...

Roland by now was laughing so hard that it hurt. He couldn't stop. As a pop video it was brilliant – the young rapper could move with the best of them – but how it could possibly be connected with a news broadcast escaped him. He turned to Dalton and spread his hands.

'Like it, huh?' Dalton said, slapping his thigh to the beat. 'I talked Dwayne into a holiday Down Under until we can hire some local talent. *Newsrap* will run for three minutes at the midpoint of each *Newscenter5* hour. It starts Monday, just after your first treasure hunt clue. This will knock people dead.'

'It's just amazing,' Roland managed. 'Things in the States must be so far ahead of us here.'

'I guess they are in a lot of ways,' Dalton replied, missing the sarcasm. He seemed about to expand on the topic, but changed his mind. 'So, now that your competition clues are finished, I guess it leaves you with not much to do. Any plans for the next few days?'

Roland shook his head.

'Then I want you to go talk with Suzanne Denning. She's looking for help on background research for *The Green Scene*.'

'The what?'

'Our new environmental news show. She's not getting the resources she needs from the newsroom's Chief of Staff. I want you to give Suzie whatever help you can.'

'Okay, Dalton.'

Roland was at the door when Dalton stopped him. 'One more thing. I'm counting on you for tomorrow. Check with Beeb for details.' When Roland looked blank, Dalton added, 'You don't know about the film shoot? Roland, you've got to stop being so passive. Engage, already! Make it your business to find things out. We're shooting some advertising for *Newscenter5* tomorrow.'

'But it's a Saturday.'

'So? That's not your religious day, is it? Get Beeb to give you the details. And bring a towel for the pool party after. Beeb and I have been in Queensland for exactly two weeks tomorrow and we're celebrating with a barbecue.'

Roland left Dalton's office depressed. He still had no idea if his competition clues were in any way workable. Now his weekend was violated by work. And, after being continually excluded by Dalton, he was being rebuked for not knowing what was going on. He arrived in the newsroom certain that the encounter with Suzie would also lead to trouble.

He found her at her desk with a telephone pressed to her ear. She shooed him away, pointing to the staff breakout area on the far side of the newsroom. He took a seat with a view across the landscaped gardens at the rear of the studio buildings. It was the hottest day of the summer, but a gardener was hard at work on a ride-on mower. Roland watched as he worked relentlessly up and down the parched lawn.

Suzie arrived a few minutes later. She flopped onto the sofa and rubbed her face heavily before turning to Roland. 'Has Dalton spoken to you yet?'

'About doing some work for you? Yes.'

'Good.' She showed a sudden interest in the gardener, who was now weaving around the base of a jacaranda tree. Roland could feel the tension in her, but had no idea what was causing it. He decided it must be something to do with their moment in the park. Eventually, still facing the window, she said, 'Tell me what you're good at.'

He shrugged. 'If you give me long enough I'm sure I'll come up with something.'

He had been trying to lighten the mood, but it only seemed to irritate her. She caught her breath and scowled at him. 'Phil told me you've been working for Porter Corp for ages. What exactly did you do there?'

'A bit of everything really. The last job I had was writing advertising copy for the mail order division. You know, the Porter Vault stuff we advertise in all the glossy magazines. Genuine diver's watches for $29.95, solid gold bracelets for $9.95, bar mirrors etched with portraits of the Royal Family. That sort of thing.'

'You're kidding.' She picked up a magazine from the coffee table. 'I saw one of those ads in here earlier.'

She found it and started to read: '*How I became a millionaire in the last six months ... effortlessly and working from my own front room.*'

'That's one of mine. For a new book we were trying to offload.'

'*This is not a book about mail order selling*,' Suzie read. '*Follow my techniques and I guarantee you will make more money than you could possibly need.*'

She rolled her eyes at him. 'It's all made up, isn't it? And the endorsements from contented customers, J. Smith of Coolangatta, R. Plumber of Mt Gravatt and all the others. These people don't exist, do they?'

Roland tried to look inscrutable. 'What is this? An interview for *The Investigators*?'

'Sorry, Roly. I was just curious.'

'Look, I can come back later when you've thought of something concrete I can do.'

'No, stay.' She ran her fingers through her hair and stared at the table top. He wanted to ask her what was wrong but knew she would overreact. He settled back in his seat and waited until she was ready.

After a short silence, she said, 'Tell me what you know about local green issues? A few of us wondered if you might be a bit of a greenie yourself.'

'What makes you think that?'

'Your bike, for one thing. Why else would you sweat all the way up Mt Coot-tha every day in the middle of summer?'

'I ride my bike because I never learned to drive. I don't think it's being particularly green, I just don't believe that people in cities need cars.'

'You were glad of my car the other night.'

'I'm not an idealist. I don't want to stop other people using them. And there are times when I find it pretty useful to be transported in one myself. But owning one in a city feels like a waste of resources and money.'

'Then by some standards you are a greenie.'

'I have a few friends who'd make me look a very pale shade of green in comparison.'

Suzie leaned forward, interested. 'They're involved in organised groups?'

'Well, yes. One has connections with several.'

'Could you talk to them? I'm trying to develop as many informal contacts as I can. *The Green Scene* is an opportunity to reach a large audience with a wide range of local green issues. I want to gain the trust of as many green groups as possible, so I want you to say nice things about me to them.'

She smiled at him long enough to make sure he was thinking only of nice things. 'I also want to know of any leads they might have on radical environmentalists. There must be a limited number of people in Brisbane who'd get involved with the Environmental Justice Army. Maybe your friends have met or heard about such people. It'll probably come to nothing but it's worth a try.'

'That's all you want me to do?' Roland asked, surprised.

'For now. Talk to your friends. Find out what they've heard about the EJA. Get them to ask around. Just make it low-key. But make it clear we're in a hurry. Okay?'

'Okay.'

'I've got to get back on the phone. Keep in touch with me.'

She gave him a reassuring pat on the arm, then returned to her desk and picked up the phone. As he crossed to the exit, he glanced back and caught her watching him. She looked away quickly, speaking into the phone, and he left the newsroom bewildered by her mood.

Beeb looked up from her desk when he walked into their office. Her eyes seemed to reach into his mind. 'Everything all right, Roland?' she asked, obviously hoping he would share whatever it was that was bothering him.

'Couldn't be better, Beeb.' He collected the Brisbane phone directory from its resting place under the fax machine and flicked through it.

'Roly, honey, I don't feel like we've had the time in the last week just to talk. Why don't we take a moment now and tell each other something we normally wouldn't tell a stranger. If we share just one private thought, then we're on the way to being better friends.'

'I'd love to, Beeb,' he lied. All of his private thoughts at that moment were about Suzanne Denning and they hadn't formed into a coherence he wanted to share with anyone, particularly his new best friend. 'I have to make a phone call first.'

'We'll take coffee together when you're through,' she persisted.

He dialled the switchboard at the University of Queensland and asked to be transferred to Dr Gwen Roswell's office. Her answering machine triggered on the third ring. He was about to leave his name and number, when he noticed that B.B. was still watching him. Afraid of the next step in her bonding process, he pretended that Gwen had just picked up the phone. 'Gwen, it's Roly ... Yes, it's lucky I caught you. I'd like to come and see you as soon as I can ... This afternoon. Great. I'll explain when I get there. Bye.'

He looked at B.B. and shrugged. 'I'm really sorry, Beeb. Let's have that coffee on Monday. Dalton's got me helping Suzie and I'm going out to the university to get some information for her.'

'That's cool, Roland. I'll be here.' As he hurriedly packed his bag, she added, 'And I won't forget. This is important to me.'

11

At home Roland tried Gwen's number again. He left a second message on the answering machine, then sat on the front verandah with a book while he waited for her to return the call. When six o'clock came he thought about tuning in to *Newscenter5*, but rebelled and stayed outside until it was too dark to read.

The mosquitoes were about to drive him inside when a familiar white sports car raced along the street. It turned into his driveway and announced its arrival with a final rev of the engine. Suzie emerged, still in her *Newscenter5* skirt and jacket. She crossed the overgrown lawn to the steps, straightening her wind-blown bob on the way.

At the top of the stairs, she realised there was someone sitting in the shadows. 'Roland, is that you?'

'Yes.'

She walked slowly along the verandah and leaned on the railing opposite him. 'Beeb told me you left in a hurry to meet someone. I thought it might be your contact.'

'It wasn't,' he replied, unable to admit he had lied to Beeb.

In the silence that followed, they fought off the growing fleet of mosquitoes. The tension was there again but he still couldn't understand what it meant. Eventually, he asked, 'Suzie, is everything all right?'

'It's work stuff. Something I really don't want to do. But I've sold my soul, haven't I? Willingly too.'

'Tell me about it, if it helps.'

'I can't, Roly. You'd hate me.' She paced along the verandah. 'I was actually hoping you'd come out with me for a bite to eat. Just something casual. Say you will. I feel like company tonight.'

'As long as we don't talk about Channel 5 or the EJA.'

She nodded and, with her index finger, drew a cross over her heart. 'Hope to die.'

The gesture made him laugh. They both knew the promise would be impossible to keep. But at least she had tried. 'I'll get changed, then.'

She followed him through the French doors into his bedroom. When he switched on the light, he saw the room through a stranger's eyes and blanched. A week's dirty clothes overflowed from the laundry basket in the corner. In the space between this and the wardrobe lay an over-balanced pile of library books. Worst of all, the paisley-patterned pyjamas his mother had given him for Christmas sat at the foot of the bed where he'd left them that morning.

'Perhaps you'd rather listen to some music in the lounge,' he suggested.

'I'm fine here. I'd rather not be alone.' She sat on the end of the bed beside his crumpled pyjamas. 'I know a quiet Italian restaurant just a few minutes away. I'll call them.'

She opened her bag and hefted out a mobile phone. It was surprisingly sleek, the length of her hand from the base of the palm to her fingertips, with a squat antenna that extended another few inches beyond its body. Roland had never used one, and he watched with interest as she turned it on and dialled the number.

While she made the booking, he picked out clean clothes and escaped to the bathroom to change. He hurried in case she followed him, but when he returned she was checking her make-up in the wardrobe mirror. She finished by brushing her hair with his brush, then picked up her bag and said, 'Right, let's go.'

After ten minutes in the open-topped sports car, she had to spend more time in front of the rear-view mirror, straightening her hair and fiddling with the knot in her silk *Newscenter5* scarf. Pavarotti's, a sidewalk restaurant in Milton, was neither casual nor quiet. Roland realised that he and Suzie were the centre of attention as they walked past the outdoor tables and into the air-conditioned interior. He felt a mixture of emotions, discomfort at the attention mixed with pleasure from being seen out and about with Suzanne Denning.

When they were seated and scanning their menus, he asked, 'Is it just my imagination or is everyone watching us?'

'Just pretend we're the only two people in the room,' she replied, giving him a suggestive glance.

'I'm not entirely sure, but I think you might enjoy all the attention.'

She smiled and looked around the room, catching a number of diners staring at her. 'I'm not entirely sure either, but I think you're right. If I didn't, I'd be in radio or newspapers, wouldn't I? Television news is one part journalism to three parts showbiz. And that's especially true of *Newscenter5*.'

'Have you seen Dalton's *Newsrap* video?'

'Please, I don't think I can even talk about it. There are limits to what should be done with television news and we're about to cross that line with *Newsrap*.'

'I didn't think you'd mind. After all, I distinctly remember you telling Beeb you were willing to do whatever it takes.'

He'd said it as a joke, but it seemed to cut right through her. She looked down at the menu again.

'Suzie, I'm sorry. I didn't mean anything.'

'Forget it.' She opened her handbag and dug around inside it. 'I've got to have a cigarette.'

'Go ahead, I don't mind.'

'You shouldn't tell lies, Roly. You're not very good at it.' She lit up and took a long drag. 'Beeb doesn't think so either.'

'I don't remember lying to Beeb.'

'You really are hopeless at it, aren't you? That's your second lie in under a minute. Beeb knew there was no one on the other end of the phone this afternoon.'

'I don't know how she could possibly tell. It happens to be true, but I just don't know how she could know for sure.'

'My theory is that she has a sixth sense. She knows exactly when people are at their most vulnerable. And she knows how to milk it for maximum effect.'

She stubbed out her cigarette and looked intently at him. It was her confession stare, the one she used in interviews to extract the truth from stubborn guests. He smiled and decided to share everything with her. 'For some reason I want to run away every time B.B. Olsen enters the room. That's why I lied to her this afternoon. I just had to get out of the office.'

'Keep running, Roly. It's the one thing she can't control.'

'How about you. Will you run eventually?'

'I can't. There's a clause in my shiny new contract expressly forbidding it.'

Their meals arrived. As they ate, a photographer walked into the restaurant. He spoke briefly to the manager, then approached their table. 'Do you mind if I take a few pictures?' he asked Suzie.

'Please do.'

The photographer stepped back and took a couple of shots of Suzie on her own. Then, to Roland, he said, 'Would you mind moving around so I can take one of you together?'

Suzie took his hand and tugged on it. 'Come on Roly, don't

be a spoilsport.'

She dragged him around the table until they were sitting close together. The photographer twisted the lens into focus. 'Go on. Make it look like you know each other.'

Suzie put her arm around Roland and pressed her cheek against his. This delighted the photographer, who held the shutter button down for an extra half-dozen frames. 'Great. Thank you very much.'

As he disappeared across the restaurant, Suzie disengaged herself and went back to her dinner as though nothing had happened. Roland shuffled his chair back around the table and stared at her. 'What was all that about?'

'Who knows,' she replied, concentrating on her meal. 'But the rule is you just smile and do whatever they ask.'

'Whose rule is that?'

She stopped eating and looked at him. 'It's my rule, actually, but it could have come from Beeb or Dalton. It's just something you know you have to do ...'

'... to get ahead in this business.'

She nodded. 'I'm going to climb to the top of the greasy pole. Breaks like this don't come often, so I'll cling to it like a demon. And when I say the top, I don't mean co-reading the news on Channel 5 Brisbane. Despite what people around here think, Brisbane is not number one under the sun for anything, except possibly melanoma. It's still very much a big country town as far as news is concerned, which is why I'll be heading south as soon as I can.'

The news disappointed him. He must have shown it, because she smiled, and touched his hand. 'Cheer up. I'm not leaving tonight. I just don't believe in hiding things from people.'

She was a quick eater and finished well before him. While he caught up, she tried to check her watch without him noticing. Seeing this, he asked, 'Is there somewhere else you have to be?'

'I'm sorry. We're expecting a statement from Lloyd Balchin and I don't want to miss it. I know it's rude, but do you mind if I pop out to the car for the nine o'clock radio bulletin?'

He shrugged his agreement. It was an acknowledgement that the time he had with Suzie Denning, however long that was likely to be, would always be shared with her work. 'Do we have time for dessert?'

She shook her head and signalled to a waiter for the bill. Roland took a last mouthful of pasta and put the fork on the plate. They argued briefly over splitting the bill, but Suzie insisted on using her corporate credit card. She took Roland's arm as they strolled back to the car in the cool evening air. When they reached the open-topped Mazda, she said, 'Thanks for coming out tonight, Roly. I needed company and I wanted it to be you.'

'I enjoyed every minute of it. But next time let's plan on having the full three courses.'

She put her arms round him and kissed him. 'There. I've wanted to do that again since our night in the park. I had to know if it was you or the gold that attracted me.' Seeing the query form on his lips, she added, 'And, if you dare ask me which it was, you can find your own way home.'

She sat in the car and turned the radio on, leaving him to pace along the kerb. With one ear on the radio, she said, 'B.B. asked me to remind you about being at work early tomorrow.'

'Tomorrow?'

'You know, the film shoot, as Dalton keeps calling it.'

The radio signalled the nine o'clock pips and the ABC's news theme followed. She turned the volume up just as Roland absorbed her statement about the film shoot. 'How did Beeb know you'd be seeing me?'

'Later,' she answered dismissively as the EJA story headed the bulletin.

Concern for the safety of Virginia Balchin grew tonight when her father released a statement condemning the Environmental Justice Army as a group of cowardly ecological socialists.

Speaking outside his Brisbane home, Lloyd Balchin said he was proud of the part he had played in making the Australian dream come true for many Brisbane home owners.

Mr Balchin rejected claims that he had broken the law or damaged the environment in any way. He called on the EJA to release his daughter immediately or face the full weight of the law. He said he would never give in to the demands of a group of faceless cowards.

Overseas now, and there is renewed tension in the Middle East tonight ...

Suzie turned the radio off. 'Roly, I have to get back to Channel 5. There could be some work on the story tonight. Do you want to come?'

'Are you kidding? I spend all week in the place. Why should I want to go back on a Friday night?'

'I just thought you might want to be with me.'

'Well, I thought it might be more interesting if we talked and listened to some music at my place.'

'I'd love to do that some time, really I would. But not tonight. I'll drop you home on the way to the station.'

12

Two helicopters, in tight formation, completed their sweep across the northern suburbs and turned in a wide arc towards Mt Coot-tha. The pitch of their engines rose as the pilots levelled off and selected Roland's scarlet *Newscenter5* wind jacket as their target. Sitting alone on the edge of the ridge, he watched them grow larger. Then, remembering his job, he lifted the walkie-talkie and pressed the transmit button. 'Dalton, this is Roland.'

'Go ahead, Roly.'

'They're on their way.'

'Understood. Stand by.'

Roland stood by. In his earpiece, he heard: 'Dalton to all crews. Stand by. Roll cameras. Light the fires.'

The lead chopper thundered at tree-top height over Roland's head, shaking the bushes he had been sitting in all day. He pressed the transmit button again. 'Roland again. Overhead now!'

Dalton's voice crackled through the static. 'News car. Go! Go!'

The helicopter swept over the ridge and raced across the quarry. Roland watched as it was engulfed in the thick black smoke from the fire that had been started against the cliffside.

He heard Dalton's voice come over the radio again: 'That's way too much smoke! Cut it back! Cut it back!'

A *Newscenter5* news car crested the ridge on the far side of the quarry and raced down the gravel road into the crater. The stunt driver reached a hairpin bend and slid the car around it in a carefully choreographed manoeuvre. Roland knew from the briefing that a camera concealed near the bend would have zoomed in on David Burton who was in the car's passenger seat. At the same time, the second helicopter passed over Roland's head. He saw a figure in a scarlet wind jacket lean out of the open door with a news camera on his shoulder.

The downdraught from the rotors thickened the air with a mixture of gravel, dust and black smoke. Roland edged closer to the precipice. He could just make out the dark figures moving around the quarry. As both choppers circled past again, Dalton triggered an explosion that sent a huge ball of orange flame into the air between them.

Moments later, the *Newscenter5* car arrived on the quarry floor. Roland watched mesmerised as David Burton jumped out with a camera crew and disappeared into the smoke. The lead helicopter landed near the stationary car. Suzie Denning, wearing one of the scarlet wind jackets handed out to everyone by Dalton that morning, stepped out and walked in a half-crouch away from the open door. She was followed at a predetermined distance by another camera crew.

The smoke cleared enough to reveal a small battle under way on the quarry floor. David Burton had found his way into the centre of the action. He was leaning against a boulder next to a masked man who was firing an assault rifle. Ignoring the muzzle flashes and ejected cartridge cases flying around him, Burton turned to camera and calmly began his report. Another scarlet jacket caught Roland's eye and he saw Suzanne make her way across to a command vehicle where she began to interview a senior police officer. Gradually the firing died down and the four masked men surrendered to the police. Burton followed with his camera team. A fire engine arrived and its crew laid out hoses to quench the fire which still burned in the quarry. Suzanne moved across and pressed a microphone under the nose of the fire crew's senior officer.

Roland, who was designated as Dalton's eyes and ears on the ridge, had been essential for starting the action when the first helicopter passed an agreed point on the horizon. After that he was supposed to be on standby for further instructions. In reality he had been a spectator for most of the day. He had enjoyed every minute of it. Dalton clearly knew what he was doing when it came to film-making and the edited film would be spectacular.

The earpiece for the walkie-talkie had fallen from his ear. He pushed it back into place in time to hear Dalton say, 'Cut everybody. That was fantastic. Now let's do it one more time. Start time in 30 minutes.'

On the final take, the action in the quarry looked more chaotic, but the aerial shots were prettier because of the setting sun. With daylight fading, Dalton called it a day, congratulated everybody and reminded them that they were expected to attend the barbecue at the Channel 5 studios.

Roland arranged a lift to the studios with Phil, who had played the role of Dalton's yes-man throughout the day's shoot. As they drove up Mt Coot-tha from the quarry, Phil was still infected with the enthusiasm everyone had felt during the day. 'This is a real triumph for Dalton. He should be making movies. Once this thing is edited together, it will knock the competition dead.'

'You'd better watch out, mate. You're beginning to sound just like him. I hope we're not losing you to the dark side.'

'Don't get me wrong. I'm not a total convert, but I can see things that are obviously going to pull in the viewers. On one level I appreciate what he's doing, but on another, it disturbs me. If this is where we're going with television news, I'm really not sure I want any part of it.'

Phil parked in his reserved space at Channel 5. They followed the path around to the entertainment area at the back of the studio buildings. Most of the crew had already arrived. Some were in the kidney-shaped pool, others were playing half-court tennis. A few had clustered around the sound system to argue about the next CD on the playlist. The majority were at the drinks table, washing a day's quarry dust from their throats. Phil ran straight for the pool, pulling off his clothes as he went. He arrived at the diving board with only his togs on and hit the water in an enormous belly flop that left the other swimmers protesting.

Alone, Roland was instantly uncomfortable. He looked for a quiet corner where he could wait out the painfully long time until it would be acceptable to leave. He opened a bottle of beer, collected a bowl of nuts, and started his practised art of circulating without actually speaking to anyone. Dalton saw him a few minutes later and called him over. He gave Roland a friendly punch on the arm which later developed into a bruise. 'Roly, what a day! It couldn't have worked out better. Come and have a drink with me later. We need to talk.'

Dalton opened a stubby of beer and slipped it into a Styrofoam *Newscenter5* bottle holder – part of a range of new merchandise that had appeared at Channel 5 that day. He recognised one of the helicopter pilots and crossed to shake hands with him. Together they re-enacted a series of complex aerial manoeuvres, using their free hands to simulate the Channel 5 choppers.

'Roland!' B.B. shouted from beside the pool. She was alone and he crossed to join her. He offered her a nut but she pushed the bowl away. 'I just can't eat nuts, Roly. All that salt. And you have no idea of the exploitation that's taken place in some third world country to get you the contents of that bowl!'

'They're from Kingaroy, Beeb. I saw the packet.'

'Where's that?'

'It's the nut capital of Queensland.'

'My point stands. Australia is still seen in some quarters as a developing country. Someone somewhere in that supply chain was almost certainly exploited.'

Roland gave up and turned to watch Phil who was playing water polo in the pool.

'Roly,' B.B. said, eventually, 'I think you should know there will be a picture of you and Suzanne Denning in the social section of the *Sunday Mail* tomorrow.'

'What picture?'

'I haven't seen it yet, but I think it was taken by a freelance photographer at a restaurant last night. It shows the two of you sitting cheek to cheek by candlelight and looking very happy in each other's company. They are also printing a rumour that you and Suzanne are, well, an item – you know, sleeping together. Is that true?'

When he looked at her darkly, she backed away a little. It allowed him to catch a movement behind her. Lumbering towards them like an overweight cruise missile was Mal McDarrow, his bullet head tucked low for the impact. The target might have been Beeb or Roland, but her sudden step back meant that the momentum was carrying the 15-stone payload towards Roland alone.

There was no time for evasive action. He was scooped up in Mal's outstretched arms and carried deep into the pool. He came to the surface in a flotsam of mixed nuts. Mal held him there for a menacing moment, then relaxed the arms that encased him. 'Sorry, mate,' he said. 'I must have slipped or something. Bloody dangerous, those tiles.'

McDarrow turned and climbed out of the pool. Roland stayed where he was. The shock quickly gave way to anger. It mounted when he realised that everyone was standing around the edge of the pool laughing. Laughing loudest was Dalton who knelt down and stretched out a hand to help him out of the water. Without thinking, Roland took the American's hand and yanked it hard, pulling him into the pool.

A shocked silence fell over the entire party. Dalton surfaced eventually, roaring with laughter. Roland was shocked again, this time by his own actions. In return, he allowed himself to be half-drowned by Dalton. The horseplay ended when the American gave him a final playful double slap on the face and got out to be wrapped in a large towel by Beeb.

Roland stepped out on the other side and sat in a puddle of water on the warm poolside tiles to dry off. When Dalton went to get himself another drink, Beeb came back over. 'You didn't get a chance to answer my question, Roly. About you and Suzanne. I don't want to pry into your personal life, but I have to know for purely professional reasons.'

'Beeb, there's absolutely no truth to the rumour at all.'

She looked disappointed. 'Then if anyone asks about it, we need you to tell them you have no comment to make. Sometimes it can be helpful to let rumours like this persist for a while. For publicity purposes. Would you do that for me?'

'I'm not sure Beeb. I'll have to think about it.'

'This is very important for Suzanne and for Channel 5. I know I don't have to tell you where your loyalties lie, Roland, honey.'

Dalton returned with drinks for the three of them. Roland accepted a scotch on the rocks without protest. Dalton passed B.B. her drink, then held up his own glass. 'Here's to *Newscenter5* and to our little team.'

He waited for Roland to take a mouthful before drinking himself. 'You know, Roland, you just surprised me there. I didn't think you had the guts to pull me into the water. Here's to you.'

They all took another mouthful, then Dalton added, 'I've been wanting to talk to you all day. I've tied up another sponsorship deal for your little competition. As well as the gold, we are now giving away a top-of-the-line Mercedes. I want you to dig up the treasure chest and put the car keys in it.' He felt in his pockets, but couldn't find what he was looking for. 'Beeb, will you go get the car keys from my office.'

'Sure Hilary.'

When Beeb was gone, Roland said, 'Hilary?'

'Now you know my little secret,' Dalton replied, laughing. 'But using it is a private thing between Beeb and me. Okay?'

Roland nodded. 'Look, about the car keys. I think it's too risky going back to the treasure site. Eventually, someone will see me.'

'The sponsor insisted the keys are found with the gold. Just make sure you put them in the ground before Monday.'

Dalton took Roland by the arm and steered him over to the drinks table. He held the whisky bottle out, but Roland held up a hand to stop him.

'Go on,' the American insisted. 'Enjoy yourself. Everyone else has let go.' He waved his arm at the rest of the party. 'No one gets to leave tonight unless they can prove they've enjoyed themselves to the max. And they're all going home in taxis on my orders. That includes you. So drink up.'

Why not, Roland thought. He took his hand away and allowed Dalton to pour a generous measure.

'There's something else I want you to do for me,' Dalton continued. He looked around and checked that no one was listening. 'You're Phil's friend. And I think you know what he's trying to do to me.'

Roland sipped nervously at his drink. 'I'm not sure I follow you.'

'Come on, Roly. Phil is trying to disrupt my work and I need it to stop. Take a look at him now.'

On the far side of the pool Phil was in earnest conversation with Malcolm McDarrow and Lauren D'Aussey. They looked deeply conspiratorial. As if aware they were being watched, Lauren glanced over at Dalton and gave him an icy stare.

'I want you to make Phil see that we should be working together. That it's in his interests if he wants to remain in control when I move on. Talk to him, will you?'

Roland wondered what he was getting into, but agreed. 'Okay. I'll do what I can.'

'Good. I also want you to keep an eye on him for me. You know, talk with him regularly, find out what he's thinking and doing. And keep me informed. I know he's up to something. I can feel it, but I don't know what.'

'You mean spy on him?'

'Sure, if that's what you want to call it.'

Roland began to see the symmetry of this. It occurred to him that spying on Dalton for Phil might actually be made easier if he was also spying on Phil for Dalton. He tried to decide if this was a logical thought, but the whisky was beginning to cloud his judgement. He decided to give up. 'You're the boss, Dalton. I'll do anything you want.'

'I'm glad to hear that, Roly.'

13

A beer followed closely by two double whiskies was enough to make Roland light-headed and a little uncoordinated. It also had the pleasing effect of giving him the confidence to be around others. He loaded a plate with food and attached himself to the largest group, the one that happened to contain Suzie.

When his chance came, he told her about burying the car keys and she immediately offered to help. He wanted to ask her about the photograph Beeb had just mentioned, but McDarrow arrived carrying a large bowl of punch. Any chance of a quiet conversation was gone. McDarrow freely admitted that the punch was spiked to his own formula, and the story worked its way around the group. When it reached Roland, it gave him the idea for revenge.

While everyone was distracted by Dwayne, who had started to give an impromptu lesson in rapping to David Burton, Roland crossed to the drinks table. He opened a stubby of beer, tipped half the contents over the railing, and topped it up with vodka. He opened a second beer and sought out McDarrow.

'Here you go, Arrow,' he said, being careful to give McDarrow the spiked drink. 'Let's have a drink and make up.'

The big man grinned and tapped his bottle against Roland's.

Tilting his head back at a well-practised angle he drained the stubby in a few seconds. He finished by wiping his mouth on the back of his hand and directing an enormous beery burp into Roland's face.

'Jeez, mate,' he said, in the friendliest tone he had used on Roland yet, 'I'm glad it's not your shout. You're too fuckin' slow, you piker!' The vodka seemed to have no immediate effect on him, although shortly after he wandered over to the pool and insisted on dancing with Beeb.

Thanks to the punch he had mixed earlier, McDarrow had a pervasive effect on the evening. Everyone who tried his special brew found themselves letting go. This included Suzie, who joined Burton and Dwayne in a breakdancing display on the tiles around the pool. Even Dalton became expansive, telling tales about the goings-on at a string of stations across the US. He was ecstatic about the way the day's shoot had gone and told this to anyone who stood still long enough to listen.

Phil was one of the few who retreated into himself. When Roland saw him later in the evening, he was sitting morosely by the pool, snacking on cold sausages and charred onion rings. Roland thought it strange. Phil was usually upbeat after a few drinks, the centre of attention at any party he attended. He decided to investigate.

'You look as though you feel a bit left out, mate,' he said, trailing his feet next to Phil's in the tepid water.

'We can't all make the sort of splash you made tonight.'

Roland produced a mock smile. 'The funny thing is, Dalton thinks more of me for giving him a ducking. He thinks I've got hidden depths.'

'Hidden depths! Is that something we should all be worried about?'

'It's probably a false diagnosis.'

Phil offered Roland a sausage from the stack on his plate and they nibbled in silence for a while. 'I'm sorry,' Phil said eventually. 'I'm not much company tonight. I've got a lot on my plate at the moment.'

Roland was conscious that he now had the power to bring Phil and Dalton together. He decided to try a little team building. 'I think I can help you there.'

'Roly, there's nothing you can do. It's already out of control.'

'Don't forget you're part of a team,' Roland continued, conscious that he was slipping into Beeb-speak. 'If you try to work a little more closely with them, things wouldn't seem so desperate.'

'What are you talking about?'

'You and Dalton, of course. He genuinely wants you both to work together.'

'Oh, that. I wasn't talking about him.'

'What then?'

Phil breathed in deeply, then exhaled slowly until his shoulders sagged forward. 'I can't talk about it, yet. And if I could, you probably wouldn't understand.'

Roland gave up in frustration. He wanted to help, but knew better than to press Phil when he wasn't ready to be pressed. He decided to wait it out, hoping his friend might open up.

Phil finished his sausage and began to suck the fat and flavour from his fingertips. He let out a burp and this seemed to lift his mood. 'Maybe you're right. Maybe I shouldn't worry so much. If I can control the things it's in my power to control, it might still turn out all right.'

'Everyone else has already lost it, but it's not too late for us to keep a grip on things,' Roland said, surveying the revellers. 'Anyway, I'm going home. Do you want to share a taxi?'

'No thanks. I'm hoping that if I hang around this lot long enough, it might make me feel better.'

The music had switched down a gear. It was more mellow

now, and the party seemed to be slowing down. Roland decided it was acceptable to leave. He slipped away and rang for a taxi from the foyer.

While he waited outside, he heard the huge V8 engine on McDarrow's Commodore throb to life. He watched in horror as it squealed out of the car park and raced away down the mountain towards the city. There was no telling how much McDarrow had drunk that evening. All Roland could think of was the half-stubby of vodka he was personally responsible for. He closed his eyes and prayed that Mal made it home safely.

As Roland's taxi arrived, Dwayne and Suzie swayed out of the foyer. They were only just holding each other upright. Suzie had been drinking steadily all evening and looked as if she had been, or was about to be, sick.

'Yo, Rollo,' Dwayne said. 'Dalton wants Suzanne to go home right now. Can we share your cab?'

Roland nodded and helped push her limp body into the back seat. Dwayne got into the front, leaving Roland to climb in after Suzie. The driver looked warily at his back seat passengers, then turned to Dwayne. 'Where to, mate?'

Dwayne gave the address of his own apartment, which was not far away, and they started down the mountain. As the taxi twisted through the corners, Suzie leaned against Roland. He squeezed her arm to make her focus. 'Suzie, I don't know your address. We need to tell the driver where we're going next?'

She shook her head. 'Let's go to your place, Roly. I want to talk and listen to music.'

'I don't think that's such a good idea tonight. Where do you live?'

'I have to go to sleep now.'

'Suzie.' He shook her arm, but there was no reply.

Their taxi was caught in a snarl of traffic as they neared the Toowong Cemetery. It crawled slowly forward until they were stopped by a police random breath testing unit. The cabby tested negative and pulled away. As he did so, Roland recognised a white Commodore sitting at the kerbside. Being led away from it by a police officer was McDarrow. A stab of guilt struck Roland and he watched through the rear window until the taxi turned the corner. Facing forward, he closed his eyes and tried not to think about what he had done.

The taxi arrived at Dwayne's unit. The American turned and said, 'Thanks for the ride, Rollo. Stay cool!'

'Wait a minute, Dwayne. Have you any idea where she lives?'

'How should I know? I only just met her. You deal with it, man.'

He slammed the front door and walked up the driveway, leaving Roland with a dozing Denning on his shoulder. The cabby turned and said, 'Come on, mate. Give sleeping beauty a shake. Then we can all go home.'

Roland shook her, but it only produced a groan. With her eyes closed, she raised her head a little. 'Fuck you, Roland Kendall. Why can't you leave me alone!' She groaned again and smiled weakly. 'Roly, I didn't mean it. I love you, you know. I really do.'

He gave up and let the cabby have his own address. Ten minutes later, when the taxi pulled into his driveway, Suzie was still resting on his shoulder. He tried one more time. 'Suzie, wake up.'

'I think I'm going to be sick,' she said. She opened the door and leaned out, but was held in place by the seat belt.

Roland paid the taxi driver. He helped Suzie up the verandah steps and along the hallway. In the lounge he guided her to the sofa. 'Don't go to sleep, Suzie. I'll make coffee.'

He put the TV on and turned it up, then went into the kitchen and switched on the kettle. When he returned a few moments later, she was sound asleep, snoring lightly with her mouth slightly open. He turned the TV off and sat watching her as he drank a mug of strong black coffee. It was, he realised, another nail in the coffin for his vision of the perfect Suzanne Denning. She was all too human, more so than she would ever admit to. Somehow it made him want her even more.

He found a blanket and pillow and put them on the floor beside her. Then he switched off the lights and went to bed. It was a humid night and after the alcohol and coffee he knew he wouldn't sleep. Having Suzanne Denning snoozing on the sofa did nothing to help. After an hour of listening to a mosquito lurk around him, he got up and checked on her. She was sleeping peacefully, and he decided not to disturb her. Instead he went through the French doors onto the front verandah. He sat on the battered sofa, disturbing the neighbour's cat which had been nestled against a cushion. It climbed onto the back of the sofa, washed its face then jumped onto his lap and made itself comfortable.

Roland stroked the cat and sat wondering about the changes that were happening in his life. He knew that late at night after drinking too much at a party was hardly the best time for reflection, but he couldn't switch his brain off.

His life was in need of a shake-up and he had been waiting for one to come along. But he hadn't expected it to include an attraction to a work colleague. He wasn't even sure what, if anything, they had in common. There only seemed to be opposites: she was talkative, he was quiet; she was the life of the party, he was the first to leave; she had a successful career, his was a complete failure. He went on, listing pluses for her and minuses for him and double minuses for the chances that she could be more than a little interested in him.

Resigned to the fact that he would have to wait until morning to see how things turned out, he went back to bed and listened to her snoring until he too fell asleep.

14

Roland woke to the sound of voices outside. He struggled out of bed and stumbled onto the verandah, finding it hard to believe it was morning already.

Suzie, wearing a pair of very dark glasses, was standing on the footpath. She was talking to his elderly neighbour, Mrs Campbell. Roland ran back into the bedroom for a T-shirt. When he returned, Suzie was getting into the front seat of a taxi. He called out to her as he ran down the steps but the car reversed onto the road and drove away.

Mrs Campbell was hosing the nature strip in front of her house. She heard Roland and turned to wave, sending a jet of water onto a passing power walker. 'Roland!' she cooeed.

He realised he would have to go and speak to her.

'Who's a dark horse then, Roland Kendall?'

'I'm sorry?'

'You and that lovely Suzanne Denning. I just introduced myself and we had a nice little chat. She seemed pleased about this.' She held out the newspaper, folded open at the social pages. Prominent among the pictures of the usual social set at the week's functions was one of Suzie and Roland, pressed cheek to cheek. The caption read:

Love is on the air for Channel 5 anchor Suzanne Denning, pictured celebrating the success of her Newscenter5 debut with new man in her life Roland Kendall, mastermind of the Channel 5 viewers' treasure hunt competition.

'You both look so happy,' Mrs Campbell said as Roland read the caption, and he had to admit this was what the picture appeared to be showing.

'It's not the way it looks, Mrs C. We just had dinner together. I hardly know her.'

'And I suppose she didn't sleep here last night. I saw you both arrive in the same taxi.'

'That's not the way it looks either.'

'She's such a nice girl, but she should take off those dark glasses when she's talking to people. It's rude, and it's not as if she's a film star. You will tell her that, won't you?'

'I have to get dressed, Mrs C.' He turned to leave then glanced at the picture again. 'Do you mind if I keep that page of the paper?'

'Of course not.' As she pulled out the page, she added, 'If you ask me, settling down with a nice girl like that is just the sort of tonic you need.'

Roland had heard enough. He started up the driveway but Mrs Campbell called after him, 'She's on the front cover of the TV guide too, but I need that till the end of the week!'

He went back to bed where he found a note sitting on the spare pillow.

Roly,
I hope you don't think I'm too rude, but I have to run off early and I don't want to disturb you. Fraser, my stepfather, is coming to stay for a few days. He arrives

on an early flight this morning and I have to go out to the airport to pick him up. He can't stand it if people are late.

To tell the truth I'm glad you're still asleep, because I'm really embarrassed about getting so completely drunk last night. I don't think I could have faced you this morning in case I did something shameful last night.

I'll come back around 10.30 tonight and we can bury the car keys. Ring me if that doesn't suit.

Thanks again for looking after me.

Suzie. xxx

P.S. I took $20 for the taxi from your wallet. I think I must have left my purse at work.

Roland pulled the pillow over his head and tried to get back to sleep, but it was already too hot. He showered and ate breakfast, then sat on the verandah with a book on medieval Europe, hoping that the complexities of Charlemagne's civil administration would distract him from the machinations at Channel 5 and from his own confused feelings about Suzanne Denning.

He ignored the phone which rang twice during the morning and was a hundred pages further into the book when a shabby orange Toyota turned into the driveway. He watched as Gwen Roswell shifted across to the car's passenger seat, catching her skirt on the gear lever on the way. She opened the only door that worked and struggled out. On the footpath, she straightened her skirt, flattened her wild dark hair, then slammed the car door and walked across the long grass to the front steps.

'You're slipping, Roland,' she said as she climbed the front steps. 'Letting your guard down. You can hardly pretend you're not in and then sit brazenly on the verandah like that.'

'Was that you on the phone earlier?' he asked as she sat beside him on the sofa.

She nodded. 'I knew you'd be in, so I rang Mrs Campbell to make sure. She thinks you should answer your phone when it rings, and I agree.' Gwen had once shared the house with Roland and Phil, and of the three, she was Mrs Campbell's favourite.

'I'm so lucky to have the two of you keeping an eye on me,' he said, using the photograph from the social pages as a bookmark.

'She also told me you were engaged to some TV star, but I assumed she's been hitting the cooking sherry a bit early this morning.'

'Have you seen this morning's paper?'

'I've got better things to do with my Sunday mornings than read the *Sunday Mail*.'

Roland was relieved. He decided to change the subject. 'Did you get my phone message on Friday?'

'Why else would I be here?'

He began to explain his new job, but Gwen's contempt for the electronic media was enormous and she refused to listen. 'So, you're finally doing something important with your life. You're in television.'

'Well, it was either that or starvation. Phil talked me into it, really.'

'Phil? Well, if he asked you, then it must be all right!'

'Don't start, please!'

Phil and Gwen had once been close friends, and Roland thought there might for a while have been something between them. If this was true, neither was willing to talk about it now. In fact, neither talked at all about the other any more, except in negatives. 'Roly, it's about time you let go of him. He's only using you. Move out of here. Make the break.'

'I will, I will. But not yet. I'm caught up in a number of things at Channel 5 and I want to find out how they turn out.'

Gwen threw her hands up to her chest and simulated a coronary. 'Are you feeling well? This is Roland Kendall talking. You just said you were interested in your work.'

'I didn't say that. I just feel committed to staying there a little longer.' He tried to steer the conversation away from himself again. 'I rang on Friday to ask for your help. I'm doing some background research for a new environmental programme called *The Green Scene*. The presenter is Suzanne Denning and she's asked me to help her establish links with active environmentalists.'

'Suzanne Denning! That's the name of the TV star Mrs C. said you were in love with. Come on, Roly, spill it.'

Gwen exerted a power over Roland that no one else did. He caved in and showed her the picture from the social pages section. When she read the caption, she started to laugh. 'So you're the mastermind behind a viewer competition and the new man in someone's life. Famous at last, Roland Kendall.'

'To be honest, I'm completely out of my depth. The last couple of weeks have been like a rollercoaster ride. I don't know what's coming from one moment to the next. I've been attacked, I've sacked people, I eavesdrop and I've buried $50,000 in gold. It's so different from the dull safety I normally live in that I feel almost anything can happen.' He glanced at her and saw that she was listening open-mouthed. He decided to go for broke. 'And then there's Suzie Denning. I know it sounds ridiculous but I think I've fallen for her.'

'What's she like?' Gwen asked, no longer laughing.

'Well, she's blonde, with the most amazing blue eyes ...'

'I can turn the TV on and see that, dummy. I mean what's she interested in, what does she think about things?'

'I'm really not very sure. We've mostly talked about work. She's very serious, and I think she's genuinely interested in environmental issues. She's been pushing hard to get *The Green Scene* off the ground.'

'Well, she can't be all bad if she's a little bit green, can she? What does she think of you?'

'I have absolutely no idea.'

'Why don't you ask her then?'

'I don't think I want to know just yet. It might be bad. It's more likely she just doesn't think about me at all.'

'Suit yourself. But if I were you, I'd sit down with her and tell her straight out how I felt. It can't hurt and you'll know then if you're wasting your time. You should do it before this new man in her life bit gets taken seriously.'

'It wouldn't hurt my cause if I could tell her you were helping to get some information together.'

Gwen smiled wickedly. 'I was going to tell you to get lost, but in the interests of your love life, I'll see what I can do.'

'She wants to know particularly about the EJA.'

'Who doesn't. It's the only thing my friends are talking about. We're all deeply suspicious of their green credentials. No one had ever heard of them before and some people think they could be phoney. Using environmental issues as a cover for extortion. We can't believe environmental activists would get into kidnapping and blackmail. It could set the cause back years.'

'You don't know of anyone who could be involved in this sort of thing?'

'No way. There are plenty of people who'd willingly chain themselves to trees or lie in front of Lloyd Balchin's earth movers, but that's essentially a non-violent act. Passive resistance at most.'

'Would you ask around for me, Gwen?'

'Yes, and I'm only doing this for you. If Denning had asked me directly, I'd have told her to piss off.'

15

Roland decided he would try following Gwen's advice about Suzie. During the afternoon, he rehearsed his way through a number of theoretical conversations but, when Suzie arrived just before midnight, the theory of being assertive around her immediately gave way to reality.

'You can't go dressed like that,' she insisted, when they met on the verandah. She rolled her eyes at his fluorescent pink T-shirt. 'You're glowing like a beacon.'

As a committed cyclist, he habitually dressed in clothes that made him more visible on the road. Suzie, on the other hand, was wearing dark jeans and a black, long-sleeved blouse.

'I'll get changed,' he said, retreating into the house.

She followed him into the bedroom and sat on the bed while he rifled through his drawers for something dark. She had a black beret in her hand. While she waited for him, she tried it on. Roland thought she was being ludicrously overdramatic but reminded himself that he needed to work on curbing negative thoughts.

'I like the beret,' he said, just to see how being positive sounded. Pleasantly surprised by her smile, he truthfully added,

'It suits you.'

'I know it's over the top, but I thought it looked suitably clandestine.' She got off the bed and checked herself in the wardrobe mirror, adjusting the angle of the beret. 'I don't suppose you've got one. It would look very *covert operations*.'

'The best I can do is an old Greg Chappell cricket hat.'

He assumed from the look on her face that this was a bad idea. The search for an item of dark clothing continued and eventually he found a navy T-shirt in the dirty linen basket. He thought about asking her to leave the room while he changed, but she was still at the mirror. The beret was off and she was shaking her stunted bob vigorously. 'My hair is a total disaster.'

Turning to him as he pulled the blue shirt on, she said, 'Don't tell anyone I said that. I don't mind everyone else thinking it was a massive mistake, but I don't want them to know I agree with them.'

He saw his chance to be assertive and took it. 'I think you're perfect just as you are.'

She glanced at him in the mirror, then stuck out her tongue at her own reflection. 'Thanks for last night, Roly. The pressure of the last two weeks must have got to me.'

'That, and Mal McDarrow's secret punch recipe.'

'I've never been comatose before. So could you not mention to anyone that I spent the night on your sofa.'

'That's the least of our worries. Have you seen the picture in the paper this morning?'

She nodded. 'I thought it was rather sweet.'

'The caption didn't bother you?'

'Why should it? That sort of thing happens all the time. People will have forgotten about it by tomorrow. Come on, let's get going.'

They hardly spoke during the short drive to the park. Roland was preoccupied by their different reactions to the photograph.

He wondered why the caption bothered him so much. And why she had been so dismissing of his concerns. Was she one of the many who would have forgotten about it by tomorrow?

He was still chewing this over when Suzie pulled the car into the same parking space they had used on their first visit to the park. They carried the tools across the deserted park to the monument, then retraced the pattern of moves recorded in Roland's notebook to the burial spot.

'We did a pretty good job,' he said, shining the torch over the ground in front of him. 'There's no trace of the previous dig.'

She passed him the slender steel rod he had found under the house. He used it to probe below the surface. It took a few minutes of prodding to locate the strongbox. He lifted the turf and dug down until he had uncovered the lid of the box.

Suzie aimed the torch at the lid and they saw the Channel 5 logo stamped across it. Roland cleared the earth from the sides of the box and hefted it out of the ground beside Suzie. She undid the catch and opened the lid.

'You're not going to believe this,' she said. 'It's gone!'

'Stop messing around. We're in too much of a hurry.'

'I'm not kidding. Look.'

He took the torch from her and aimed it into the box. She wasn't joking. The gold had disappeared. 'I don't understand. We're the only two people who knew it was here.'

'Well, I didn't tell anyone,' she said defensively.

'I didn't mean it that way.'

He lifted out the cloth liner and a small envelope fell out. It was unaddressed, but sealed. He ripped it open and unfolded the paper. A message, printed in large text, read:

> *The contents of this box have been confiscated by the Environmental Justice Army. The gold will be used in the struggle against environmental crimes.*

Also in the envelope was a driver's licence. In the torchlight, they could read Virginia Balchin's name on it and recognise her picture.

'Shit,' Roland said, 'what do we do now?'

Suzie shrugged. 'Put the box back in the ground, fill in the hole and hope nobody finds the prize until we've figured out what to do.'

'But the competition starts tomorrow. At the very least, we've got to find a new location. I don't think I can reconfigure the clues in time.'

'Just dig another hole near the monument.' She pointed towards a gum tree about 20 metres away. 'Over that way.'

While Roland dug the new hole, Suzie tore a page out of his notebook. She wrote:

> *Congratulations. You have located the burial place of the Channel 5 treasure. For security reasons the gold is held at the Studios of Channel 5. Contact Channel 5 to claim your prize.*

She signed it and passed it to Roland when he finished digging the hole.

'Good idea,' he said. Even as he said it, he knew they were clutching at straws. 'If we get lucky, the winner might just think we planned it this way.'

He folded the note and placed it in the strongbox. Suzie added the car keys and closed the lid. Together they replaced the strongbox in the hole.

'This is absolutely the last time I bury this bloody box,' he said as he tipped soil into the hole.

In the car, they tried to decide how to handle the situation.

'I think we should call Dalton right away,' Roland said.

Suzie shook her head. 'We don't know who we can trust on this.' Turning to face him, she added, 'I think we can trust each other, right?'

He stared back at her and, for a moment, wasn't sure. 'Yes, of course.'

'But can we be sure about Dalton?'

'Of course we can.'

'I mean, who else knew?'

Roland replayed the events of that day. 'I carried the package around with me in an airlines bag Dalton gave me. I met David Burton in the morning and took the bag to the canteen at lunchtime. I didn't tell anyone what was in it. Dalton might have, but I didn't. The only person I spoke to was Phil, who talked to you. The way he is at the moment he might have mentioned it to a dozen people before he came across you.'

'But he didn't tell me what you wanted me for. Remember, he said you wanted to take me out.'

Roland smiled at the memory. 'I did actually. I didn't want you to know, of course, and I was annoyed at Phil for saying it, but I wanted to get to know you better.'

'Phil wasn't the only one who could see that, Roly.'

'And I'd like us to go out again.'

She smiled briefly. Then her mind went back to the missing prize. 'But, what did you tell Phil about the gold?'

'I told him I had the gold bars with me and I needed help to bury them. He said he was busy that night and sent you to see me. He knew I had the gold, but not where I was going to put it.'

'What about Dalton. Did he know where you buried it?'

'He wasn't interested in the details.'

'So, there are four main suspects. You, me, Dalton and Phil.'

'There's B.B. too. Dalton shares everything with her. And I'd feel better if she was on the list.'

'Plus anyone else they might have talked to. And then there's the sponsors. Anyone could have followed us to the park.'

'But it looked deserted.'

'How hard did you look?' Suzie asked. 'It was pretty dark and I was looking at the hole most of the time.'

'We must have been alone.'

'What about the jogger? The one who ran past us?'

'I don't know. I don't think so. He just went straight past us and kept going.'

They ran out of ideas and lapsed into silence. Suzie lit a cigarette. 'You did mean that, didn't you? About going out again.'

'I thought we might try it on a night when you're not distracted by a breaking story.'

'Or when you're not burying gold in a park.'

The mention of the gold killed the conversation again. 'We really have to tell Dalton,' Roland said after a while. 'There's no real reason to suspect him or anyone else at Channel 5.'

'I agree. But not tonight. It can wait till the morning.' She looked at her watch. 'I have to spend an hour or so with my stepfather before he goes to bed. He isn't the sort of man you can afford to ignore.'

As she drove Roland home she told him more about Fraser. 'He arrived last night instead of this morning. When I wasn't there he let himself into my flat. Actually, he broke in. He writes adventure and spy stories and he's beginning to think he's one of his own characters. He picked the lock on my front door and got in.'

'He sounds a little unorthodox.'

'That's putting it mildly. I think he's relatively harmless, though. He got worried when I didn't get back last night, and rang the station to find out if I was working. They told him I'd left with you and Dwayne, so he gave me the third degree when

I got back this morning. I cracked and told him the truth.

'The thing that worries me most is that he'll tell my mother. And he'll give her the photograph from the paper. I know I sound like a teenager, but she has permanent wedding bells inside her head. She's getting worried about me, still single at 28, when some of her friends' daughters are dutifully producing grandchildren.'

At Roland's house, Suzie turned into the driveway. She left the engine running and leaned over to kiss him goodnight. Roland was too tense to enjoy it properly. The outline of Mrs Campbell leaning out of her darkened bedroom window did nothing for his mood.

'I won't let you take me out, you know,' Suzie said after the kiss. 'Not if it means getting a double on your bike to a restaurant. You'd better let me do the organising again.'

'That's fine by me,' he replied as he got out of the Mazda. 'As long as you can also organise what the hell we're going to tell Dalton about the gold.'

'Don't worry about it, Roly. We've done nothing wrong. I'll pick you up in the morning and I'll hold your hand while you tell him. We're all adults. He won't sack us or anything.'

'He can't sack you. Me, I'm not so sure about.'

As the car started to reverse up the driveway, she called out, 'Goodnight, Roly.' Then she turned to the house next door, where a dark shape was silhouetted against the lace curtains. 'And goodnight, Mrs Campbell!'

16

A fringe environmental group, the Environmental Justice Army, has claimed responsibility for last night's firebomb attack on earthmoving equipment at the Virginia's Green land development site.

In a statement released to the media, the EJA said its attack had been provoked by the refusal of developer Lloyd Balchin to halt land clearing on the site.

The EJA said it would continue to act against Mr Balchin until he announced he was ceasing development of the area, which is a natural habitat for a number of endangered species of flora and fauna.

Mr Balchin has so far made no comment on last night's attack. His daughter Virginia Balchin was kidnapped by the EJA last week.

Our reporter Lisa Demchek is on the scene ...

Dalton muted the sound and turned to Suzanne who was on a sofa beside Roland. 'Anything interesting at the site?'

'Nothing. The earthmoving equipment is a write-off and the site office is too. Balchin spent a lot of money this morning getting replacement equipment out to Virginia's Green. He's holding a press conference at two o'clock where he will personally clear the first plot with a dozer.'

'Jesus! He's taking a risk with his daughter's life, isn't he?'

'He likes to remind people that he got where he is today by taking risks.'

Beeb came into the room and sat next to Dalton. 'How did it go?' he asked her, as he poured coffee for her.

'He got a fine, a disqualification and 200 hours of community service.'

Dalton whistled. 'Can we keep the lid on this, Beeb?'

'Too late, H. It's going to be in tomorrow's newspapers. They got pictures of Malcolm coming out of the court.'

'Are we talking about Mal McDarrow?' Suzie asked. 'What's he done?'

'Drink-driving,' Dalton replied. 'They stopped him on Saturday night after the party.'

Roland felt a spasm of guilt. 'Oh God!'

'I know,' Dalton agreed. 'He was under strict orders not to drive home after the party. We're still trying to figure out why he did it. But Beeb thinks we can turn it to our advantage.'

'I know we can,' B.B. said confidently. 'Malcolm will have to work very hard with me on this, but I think we can use it to remake his image. You know, a big man realises the dangers of drugs, has a change of heart, and takes his message to the young people of Queensland. There's a wonderful opportunity in this.'

'It's in your hands, Beeb,' Dalton said. Turning to Roland, he continued, 'Now we're all here, let's talk about your little problem with the gold.'

Earlier, Dalton had barely reacted to the news that the gold was missing, insisting that they wait for B.B. before discussing it. The only significant change Roland noticed now was that the missing gold was officially his problem. He worried about what he might have to do to make good the loss.

'We have to assume that the four of us are innocent,' Dalton said. 'That's a bit of a risk, right? But I don't see a motive for any of us taking the stuff.'

'We can't rule out everyone at Channel 5,' Suzie interrupted. 'We'll need a list of all staff who knew we were burying the gold.'

'It's not that simple, Suzanne. There's something I haven't told you or Roland yet. Beeb, will you get the box?'

B.B. opened his desk drawer and retrieved a plastic container. She put it on the coffee table in front of Roland and Suzanne. Through the clear lid, they could see two small plastic objects. Both were the size of a fingernail with a short black wire tail. Roland recognised one of them immediately. He tried to maintain an exterior calm but, on the inside, he was one stage below panic.

'They look like little plastic sperm,' Suzie said, laughing.

'They have a similar purpose,' Dalton replied. 'Penetration. They are electronic listening devices. I had a security expert sweep the office early this morning. It's a routine procedure I used to do in the States but I foolishly let it lapse when I started here.'

'But who would put them there?'

'The most obvious answer is industrial espionage, probably our competitors at one of the commercial channels.'

Roland realised he was still holding his breath. He forced himself to exhale.

'The thing is,' Dalton continued, 'Roland and I were here in this room on the morning I gave him the gold. Anyone listening would have heard me tell him to bury it that night. They only had to follow him and watch the two of you bury the box.'

'So anyone could have known about the gold?'

'Add to that the sponsor and people who supplied him with the gold and the chain gets even longer. Eventually someone connected with this Environmental Justice Army found out about it. The only advantage we have is that only the four of us know you went back to the box and discovered that the gold is missing.'

'How do we use that to our advantage?' Suzie asked.

'I don't know yet. Roland, you're looking pretty quiet. You got any ideas?'

Roland was still wondering about the second bug. He thought it unlikely Phil would have planted another one without telling him, so it must have been put there by an outsider. He cautiously replied, 'Call in the police?'

'Hell, no. Then we lose control. The police would have nothing to go on anyway. They'll be told at the right time.'

They sat in silence for a while, until Dalton said, 'Beeb, help us to get some ideas flowing here.'

'We could brainstorm it.'

'Sure. Tell them the rules.'

Turning to Roland and Suzie, she said, 'Say anything that comes into your head, however fantastic, and don't make any negative comments. I'll record what we come up with and we'll prioritise the results. Now, task number one is to agree the desired outcome.'

Suzie, a veteran of Beeb's team-building sessions over the past two weeks, was happy to play along. 'We want the gold back.'

'In the box, in the ground,' added Roland, getting the hang of it. 'I'm tired of digging holes in that bloody park.'

B.B. looked at him darkly. 'Don't forget the rules, Roly. You've got to suppress anything negative.'

'I'd also like to know who took it and why,' he replied as cheerfully as he could.

'You mean, who actually followed you?' Dalton asked. 'And how did they find out about the gold? I'm already ahead of you on that. The driver's licence proves it was the EJA, but we'll probably never find out who actually planted the bugs.'

'The alternative is to make the competition so hard that no one wins it. That way, no one discovers the gold is gone.'

'Or we could just cancel the promotion,' Suzie added.

'We can't cancel,' Dalton said. 'The sponsors are locked in. We'd look like a bunch of amateurs if we had to admit we cancelled because Roland lost the prize.'

Roland wanted to deny he had lost the prize. He decided this was probably the kind of negative he should learn to suppress.

'Getting back to the desired outcomes,' Suzie went on, 'I think we should find some way of using this information to our advantage over our competitors on the EJA thing.'

'You mean use it in a story?' Roland asked.

'Not exactly. Let's assume the EJA did it. They obviously don't intend us to discover for some time that they've taken the gold.'

'Makes sense,' Dalton said, catching on. 'Otherwise, they would have announced it in one of their communiques, or just kept the gold and we'd never have known who did it. Maybe they need the money, but the one thing they want even more is air time. They are anticipating the media reaction when the winner of our competition digs the box up and the gold's gone and there's a note inside saying the EJA took it. That's a big story.'

'Every news outlet would carry it,' Suzie confirmed.

'So how do we use this, Suzanne?' Dalton asked.

'You tell me. I just know it's a lead and an exclusive one.'

Here, the conversation stalled.

'Okay Beeb,' Dalton said after a pause. 'Tie this together for us.'

'Sure. Point 1. We need the treasure hunt to go ahead, and we'd like the gold back.' Glancing at Roland, she added, 'In the ground, and without anyone knowing it was gone.

'Point 2. We'd like to know who did it, but that's not critical.

The Balchin driver's licence points to a legitimate EJA act.

'Point 3. The way forward involves a choice. The passive approach is to call in the cops. The alternative is to take our own action.'

'And your preferred option?' Dalton asked her.

She pulled off her glasses, which today were red-framed again, and swung them slowly in the air as she considered this. 'The key issue here is that we lose control if we go with option one. I'd never vote for losing control of anything.'

'I'm with you on that. Here's what I want us to do. We're going to get the gold back.'

'How exactly do we do that?' Suzie broke in, echoing Roland's thoughts.

'Easy. Roland is going to find the EJA for us.'

'I am?' Roland rolled his eyes and ran his hands through his hair.

'My bet is the EJA will be monitoring the progress of the competition. They need to know how close our viewers are to digging up the prize. So, tonight you are going to change the first clue to include a cryptic message the EJA will understand.'

'Rewrite the clue! I can't. It's too late.'

'Roland, you need to get the gold back, and you've got to make contact with the EJA to do it. If you don't have a better idea, then I say we all commit to my plan.'

Roland took this as a veiled threat. He remained silent while Dalton finished. 'Give Beeb and me half an hour to think this through, then you can rework your clue. I don't care if it makes no sense so long as the person who took the gold understands it. Everyone else will just think it's a wacky competition that needs time to get their heads around. I'm going to offer the EJA a deal. We give them all the publicity they want, but only if they give back the gold.'

'Why should they want to do that?'

'Because we'll persuade them it's in their best interests. You can't just walk into a bank and deposit gold, especially when the bars are imprinted with the *Newscenter5* logo. My deal is better to them than money. They get access to the media instead.'

Turning to Suzie, he said, 'Roland will set up a meeting using the coded message. If it works then the story is yours.'

Suzie began to salivate at the prospect. When she left the room with Roland she gripped his arm and tugged at it violently.

'It's madness,' he said to her in the corridor. 'We should go to the police. Dalton has Virginia Balchin's driver's licence in there.'

She stopped and stared at him. 'Roly, I'm counting on you. If there's a chance of making contact, we should try it. Promise me you'll do what Dalton wants.'

A moment's eye contact was enough to pacify him. 'Okay, I promise.'

She squeezed his arm a final time and smiled. Then she left him and walked down the corridor to the newsroom.

'But only within reasonable limits,' he called after her.

If she heard him, she chose not to respond.

17

Roland had thought he was finished with puzzles and word games for good. He found it harder than ever to mould an EJA message into a clue in just one afternoon. The result, which Dalton collected just before news time, was barely acceptable and he watched with some embarrassment as it was broadcast.

Suzie introduced the competition at 6.30.

'Welcome to the first night of our *Newscenter5* Viewers' Treasure Hunt competition. You can win $50,000 in gold and a new Mercedes simply by staying tuned to *Newscenter5*. Each weeknight we'll broadcast a clue at the midpoint of the news hour. All you have to do is solve each clue and piece the information together until you know the exact spot where the treasure chest is buried. The clues will take a number of different forms – it's up to you to work them out – so good luck. David.'

'Thanks Suzanne. Here's the first clue.'

Their anchor buggies glided apart and the clue appeared on the giant screen between them.

Clue No. 1
POOR GUESSES FAIL CATCH FUTURE DEFECTS ON THE HILL BE WARNED R

'That looks too hard for my tired old brain, Suzanne.'

'No problem David. It's the first night of the competition, so I'll go easy on you and give you a hint. That clue could be an anagram. Let me give you an example of how it might work.'

The clue disappeared and the example flashed onto the screen.

Sample Clue
LICENCE FOUND DO A DEAL RETURN SITE OF GOLD ELEVEN PM MEET RK

'David, if you worked on rearranging the letters – during the commercial breaks, of course – you'd eventually come up with this.'

The words on the screen bent into a circle and began to spin until the letters were a blur. One by one, they fell from the circle to form the message:

Sample Clue Solution
FEEL LEVEE LEDGE AT EAST CORNER OF DUCK POND IN EMU RD MILTON

'So the gold might be somewhere on that ledge in Emu Road?'

'That's right, David. But only if this was a real clue. It's only an example of the information you can expect from us each night. I'll say that again. This is just an example. There is no Emu Road in Milton. And there is definitely no duck pond.'

'I hear you, Suzanne. Now let's take a look at the real clue once more, just in case it already makes sense to anyone.'

The message to the EJA was replaced by the real clue. After a pause, Burton added, 'I can't wait for tomorrow night. Now let's recap the main news stories of the day. We'll be doing that every night around now with our new *Newsrap* format. Take it, Dwayne.'

Burton and Denning's consoles trundled apart to allow space on the studio floor for Dwayne to spin on his neck, leap to his feet and say:

Wait a minute brother, don't touch that dial,
I'll give you some news to make you smile,
I'll give it to you straight, you won't run a mile,
When you hear the news in the Newsrap style ...

The *Newsrap* chorus was surprisingly catchy. It played endlessly through Roland's head throughout the rest of the evening. As he sat near the monument in the park waiting for a meeting he was certain wouldn't happen, he composed endless verses to the *Newsrap* beat. His best effort was:

Dalton's a fool, that's plain to see,
Out of his head, and so's B.B.,
Only one thing's worse, and this is the key,
I'm sittin' here! What's that make me?

He stopped when the rhymes became worse than he could bear. He leaned uncomfortably against the trunk of a tree, watching the clouds pass overhead in the moonlight and listening to the leaves rustling in the gentle breeze. Around midnight he decided he was wasting his time. He collected his bike, which was leaning against the base of the monument, and went home to bed.

After his late night out, Roland allowed himself a leisurely start the next morning. He timed his arrival at Channel 5 to coincide with morning tea. With a mug in his hand, he read a note from

Dalton which he'd found on his desk:

> *Roly,*
> *Congratulations on last night. Brilliant reaction. Call me when you get in.*
> *Dalton.*

The message made him curious enough to call straight away, but the line was engaged. As soon as he put the phone down, Phil called him. 'Roly, how are you? Where did you get to last night?'

'Last night?' Roland replied, curious.

'I tried to get you all night.'

'Sorry. I was out. Was it something urgent?'

'Well, yes and no. It's about the tapes.'

Roland had forgotten about them. Phil obviously hadn't. 'I checked your desk yesterday and there was no tape. You're not deserting me are you?'

'It's not a matter of deserting you, Phil. It's Dalton. He's found the bug.'

'Shit! Does he know you did it?'

'What do you mean, I did it?'

'Well, you are doing the taping.'

Roland decided to let this go. 'Dalton found a second bug. You didn't plant that too, did you?'

'Of course not. Now that's interesting.'

'Dalton thinks it's industrial espionage. One of our competitors.'

'He's probably right. Look Roly, I'd better come over and collect the recorder and the spare tapes. It won't do any harm to destroy the evidence. You have been keeping your desk drawer locked the whole time, haven't you?'

'With Beeb in the same room, I'd be crazy not to.'

'Okay, I'll be over in a minute to collect the gear.'

Phil collected the tapes, but left immediately, insisting that he was still flat out with his special project. Roland suspected this had something to do with watching television alone in his office. Phil's parting words were that Roland should stay in touch as they would now have to rely again on verbal reports of Dalton's plans. Roland nodded, but was left with the impression that Phil was slowly becoming unhinged by the presence of the Americans.

He tried calling Dalton again, and this time got through.

'Roly, how are you? I'm glad you're in. I've been on the phone all morning taking complaints about your puzzle. Come on over to my office. We need to talk.'

Dalton was on the phone again when Roland arrived. 'Yes, Lord Mayor. I appreciate your position. You will understand I can't confirm or deny that the prize is buried in any of your parks ... If viewers choose to go digging holes in the ground on the basis of one clue, then they must be plain crazy, don't you agree? ... Look, why don't we get together on this in a couple of days. There's an opportunity in this for the city of Brisbane ... Good. I'll get my people to talk to your people and set up a meeting ... Thank you for calling, Lord Mayor. Goodbye.'

Dalton put down the phone and beamed at Roland. 'City Hall is apoplectic about us burying the prize in one of their parks. Did we do that?'

'Actually, we did. But viewers don't have enough information yet to know that for sure. Last night's clue was an anagram for *Follow their clues and disturb the surface of the green space.*'

'Green space. That could just get us off the hook. The Lord Mayor says that burying anything in parkland would contravene a number of council by-laws.'

'Does it?' Roland was well aware of this, but didn't want Dalton to know that he knew. 'I suppose I should have thought of that.'

'She's putting out a press release complaining about our actions.'

'There can't be much damage from one hole in the ground.'

'Haven't you heard? Dozens of people were out this morning in parks all over Brisbane. Most of them with metal detectors. No one's found anything yet, but they've made one hell of a mess. It's a fantastic response. The publicity is just great. We'll get even more when the Lord Mayor issues her press release. Beeb is working right now on a way of ramping this up into a war of words.'

'But we can't let people dig up parks all over the city.'

'You must have known this would happen.'

Roland hadn't even considered the possibility. He shook his head. 'Honestly, my mind was focused on burying it.'

'You can't put a pot of gold in the ground and not expect people to try digging it up.'

'I didn't even know if anyone would work out the clue. Shouldn't we do something about this?'

Dalton shook his head. 'Nope. Not yet, anyway. In a couple of days the publicity should have peaked. Then I'll meet the Lord Mayor and offer the city an incentive for playing along with us. We'll pay for any damage or we'll donate money for greening the city.'

'So we keep going with the competition?'

'Hell, yes.' He rubbed his hands together happily. 'But have a think about whether we can tailor the rest of the clues to minimise the damage. Now about your other project. How did it go last night?'

'Nothing happened. I stayed till midnight then went home.'

'Stay with it Roly. It was too much to expect them to respond in one day. You can keep Suzanne involved in this too. This sits neatly within the scope of *The Green Scene* and I've given her control over the whole story. She'll be on standby every night near you. She'll have her mobile phone, and you can borrow mine for the next couple of nights.'

He opened his desk drawer and produced his mobile phone. Roland took it and stared helplessly at the buttons. 'Don't worry,' Dalton said, 'Suzanne will show you how it works. If you make contact try to involve her, but don't crowd them. And keep in touch with me.'

18

On his third night alone in the park Roland was starting to doubt his sanity. Left to himself he would have been at home in bed with a good book, but Suzie had insisted on driving him to the park and was waiting in the car nearby. She was as convinced as Dalton that the EJA would make contact. Their need to believe this, Roland thought, was clouding their sense of reality. As he sat once again against the familiar tree trunk near the monument, he told himself that this was the last time. After tonight they were on their own.

It was a warm evening and eventually the exhaustion from three consecutive late nights overcame the discomfort. He closed his eyes and dozed off. A freight train rumbling past at the far end of the park woke him an hour later. He stood and stretched his stiff limbs, then paced around to loosen his muscles.

When he was a few metres from the monument he saw a sheet of paper taped to the plinth at the base of the column. In the moonlight, he had no trouble reading the printed message: *Kendall – be at the shelter on the bikeway opposite the Regatta Hotel 11.30 p.m. sharp.*

He had five minutes to cover the 400 metres to the river. He half-ran, half-jogged down the hill to the corner of the park, turned left under the railway bridge and crossed the road to the Regatta Hotel. He dodged a few cars on the four lanes of Coronation Drive, and ran down the slope to the riverside cycle path.

The shelter was a few metres away. He slowed to a walk and caught his breath as he neared its steps. He sat down to wait. After 15 minutes he was beginning to think nothing would happen when a shadowy figure came out of the bushes along the bike path and walked towards him. He – the build and posture were clearly male – was dressed in an army surplus uniform. On his head he wore a ski-mask with holes cut for the eyes and mouth. It was either the EJA contact or a mugger.

Roland backed away a little when the contact climbed the steps. The man put up a hand to stop him. 'Sit down, Kendall. We don't have much time. We expected you last night.'

'Last night?' Roland replied. 'The note wasn't there last night.'

'It was. You just didn't see it.'

The contact was edgy. He stayed on the move as he talked, scanning the cycle track for signs of trouble. Satisfied they were alone, he turned to Roland and asked, 'So why are we meeting?'

'How do I know you're from the EJA?'

'What do you want, a letter of introduction?' He fished a credit card from his pocket. 'You do take Visa Card, don't you?'

Roland took the card and saw Virginia Balchin's name and signature.

'Keep it,' the contact man said. 'She can't use it at the moment.'

Dalton had given clear instructions on how the deal should be worded. Roland now delivered this verbatim. 'We want to film an interview with your spokesperson and we want to talk with Virginia Balchin. We guarantee to give it prime time airing. In return you give us back our gold.'

'I think we can come to an arrangement. But we need to protect our safety. We will control how the interview takes place. You supply a reporter, but no camera crew. We say when and where it will occur. If anything looks wrong then we cut contact. You get one chance and one only.'

Roland thought for a moment. It sounded sensible, but Dalton had given him certain non-negotiables. 'We can accept most of that but there's one condition. We need to take a camera crew. We need good-quality video or there's no point.'

'Don't waste my time. We're risking a lot to do this. You've got to take a risk on the quality.'

'I can't give a final say on this. It sounds workable to me but I don't make the decisions.'

'Take it back to the decision maker. We'll set up the interview. If you don't like the deal, then just don't show. Okay?'

Roland nodded. 'How do I arrange for our news team to contact you?'

'We deal through you alone. You accompany one reporter when we meet, and we meet here on this bike path. Both of you should cycle along the bike path for the next three nights. Start at the city end under the Victoria Bridge at midnight and ride towards Toowong. Just the two of you. If everything looks okay, we'll make contact.'

'I'm not supposed to come along. My job is to arrange the contact.'

'And now you're the go-between. If you don't show, the deal is off.'

'Okay, okay. I'll be there.'

'I need the name of the reporter.'

'Suzanne Denning.'

'Okay. Now leave me and head back the way you came. Don't look back.'

Roland did as he was told. He climbed the slope to

Coronation Drive, crossed the road and walked back towards the park. After a hundred metres he remembered the mobile phone in his backpack. He turned it on and pressed the speed-dial button Suzie had programmed for him.

She answered immediately. 'Had enough for tonight?'

'I'm in Sylvan Road, Suzie. Come and collect me. I've made contact.'

'I'll be right there.'

She stopped across the road a few minutes later, did a U-turn, and leaned over to open the door for him. He could smell smoke as soon as he got in and saw from the overflowing ashtray that she had spent the evening chain-smoking.

'What happened, Roly? Why didn't you call me earlier?'

'There wasn't time.' He had actually forgotten about the phone during the jog to the river.

She continued the interrogation on the journey home. In the driveway, she insisted on calling Dalton on her mobile phone, but his answering machine was set and Beeb's voice delivered a message that Dalton had gone to bed.

'Beeb seems to look after his home life too,' Suzie said as she hung up.

'That woman is everywhere. Another couple of months and she'll be tucking us all in at bedtime. Do you feel like coming in?'

She hesitated for a moment, then shook her head. 'I'd like to, but I don't think I should. Fraser thinks I'm ignoring him. I've been out every night since he arrived and he's beginning to wonder what I'm up to.'

For once, Roland was relieved she had turned the invitation down. He needed to digest the exchange with the EJA contact and could only do it alone. As her car roared along the street, he climbed the verandah steps and opened the front door.

A light was on at the back of the house. On edge, he walked

down the hallway to the kitchen and was startled to find a stranger sitting at the kitchen table reading a book. 'Who the hell are you?' Roland asked. Seeing his book on Frankish kings in the man's hands, he stupidly added, 'And that's my book you're reading!'

The intruder was around seventy. He had close-cropped grey hair and a hard, weathered face. He looked down at the book, appeared to finish reading a sentence, and replaced the newspaper photograph Roland was still using as a bookmark.

'Don't worry,' he said. 'I haven't lost the place.' His voice carried the traces of an English accent. 'I'm tempted to stay and finish the chapter. It's unusual to find someone else with similar tastes in non-fiction.'

'Who are you?' Roland repeated.

'My name is Urquhart, Fraser Urquhart. And I'm here to have a quiet word with you, Roland Kendall.'

'Fraser? You're Suzie's ...'

'Stepfather. She's mentioned me?'

'She also mentioned your habit of breaking into people's houses.'

'How can you be sure you didn't leave a door unlocked? Besides, you wouldn't have wanted me to sit on the front steps for hours when the two of you are off God knows where, doing who knows what.'

'The door was locked,' Roland replied, sure of himself. 'How did you get in?'

'It's not so hard. Particularly with these old Queenslander houses. Don't worry, I haven't broken anything. I'm very careful.'

'Suzie also said you write books.'

'Not in my own name of course. I'm Brian Caffrey for the spy stories and Jack Torrance for the adventure-thrillers. I didn't see any in your bookcases. You should try one. They really are quite good.'

Roland was amazed he was talking with an intruder about books. 'You said you wanted to have a word with me.'

'Just a friendly little chat. You see, I've decided to stay on in Brisbane for a little while longer. Doing a little research for a book and a little consultancy work.' He smiled and asked, 'That was Suzie's car in the driveway just now?'

'Yes.'

'I have an ear for things like that. She makes it too easy, though, the way she keeps revving the engine. I love that girl but she's almost all show.'

'She was hurrying home because she was worried about leaving you alone for too long.' Roland understood now how right she had been.

'You've been seeing a lot of her lately.'

'We're working together on the research for her new programme.'

'Research? What sort of research would keep her out every night of the week with you?'

'You'd better ask her about that.'

'The thing is, Roland, I'm watching you. I just wanted you to know that I know you're up to something. I haven't figured out what it is yet, but I will. I dropped in on Suzie at work the other day and met Dalton. When he heard about the work I used to do, he asked me to sweep his office for bugs. I swept yours too and found your tape recorder.'

'You went through my desk?' Roland felt his face flush with a mixture of anger and guilt.

'Well, I had to take a quick peek, didn't I? It's all part of the service I provide.'

'Some service. The desk was locked.'

'Was it?' Fraser looked up at the ceiling, apparently trying to remember. 'The real issue is the recorder. It had a blank tape in it, so I couldn't prove anything. Maybe there's a perfectly innocent explanation for it being in your drawer. But I've got a feeling about you.'

Roland had heard enough. 'I think you should leave.'

'My theory is that you stole the gold. Anything to say to that?' When Roland refused to answer, Fraser continued, 'So, a little warning to you. I'm watching you. Eventually I'll find out what you're up to. And when I do, I'll do everything I can to protect Suzie. I know she's sleeping with you, and I want it to stop. For her sake, and for her mother's.'

Roland stared back at Fraser. It was too much.

Having achieved the purpose of his visit, Fraser stood. 'If you don't mind I'll leave through the front door. It's so much simpler. Don't forget. Every step you take, I'll be right behind you. And I'll catch you in the end.'

19

Roland was still awake an hour later when a car pulled quietly into his driveway. Worried that Fraser might have returned, he crossed the bedroom to the French doors to see who it was. A familiar white Mazda was sitting in front of the house and he was relieved to see Suzie crossing the lawn.

'I know it's late,' she said when he opened the French doors for her, 'but I have to talk to you.'

'Is your entire family nocturnal?'

'It's Fraser I want to talk about. Can I come in?'

He stepped back into the bedroom and she followed him in. She sat on the end of the bed. He settled into the cane chair in the corner of the room.

'I've just had a massive fight with him,' she said. She picked at a chewed nail and tucked her hair behind one ear. 'He told me he'd had a quiet word with you, and that you won't be making a nuisance of yourself to me any more. What the hell happened between you?'

'Oh, nothing much. He was waiting for me in the kitchen when you dropped me off.'

She didn't seem surprised. 'He just walks into places. You should be more careful to lock up when you go out.'

'I'm pretty sure I did. I always do. He must have picked one of the locks.'

'Look, I'm sorry this happened. Fraser is a little unhinged. He sometimes thinks he's one of his own characters. If he's done any damage I'll get him to pay for it.'

'He's not one, is he?'

'One what?'

'A spy, or a government agent or something.'

From the way she laughed he could tell that she wasn't entirely sure. 'As far as I know he only writes books. If he ever was one, it must have been a long time ago. But I don't think I could separate fact from fiction where he's concerned. I'm not sure he knows the difference either. What exactly did he want?'

'He just wanted to let me know that he knew what I was up to. Which makes him a whole lot better informed than me, because I haven't a clue what's going on around here any more.'

He laughed nervously, but Suzie was curious now. 'Roland, what exactly are you up to that he would be interested in?'

'Well, a couple of things. First, he said we've been seeing a lot of each other lately.'

'That's true. So?'

'He thinks that because we're out together every night there's something going on between us.'

'Typical of him to get ahead of the game. What else?'

'I think he suspects me of being in the EJA.'

'You?' She shrieked with laughter. 'How did he come up with that one?'

'He knows about the bugs in Dalton's office. He said Dalton hired him to do a sweep. He also knows about the missing gold, and only Dalton could have told him about that.'

'But why would Dalton hire him in the first place? I wouldn't trust him to sweep the back steps, let alone sweep an office for bugs.'

'That's why I asked you if he was an ex-spy or something. Anyway, after he found the bugs, he searched my office and found a mini-recorder in my desk.'

'And from that he concluded you planted the bugs? There are a dozen of those things in the newsroom alone. It doesn't make sense.'

Even to Roland it sounded thin. He still had no idea why Fraser rightly suspected him and it worried him. Suzie seemed to sense this too. 'Roly, you didn't plant the bugs, did you?'

'I swear I didn't plant either of them.' This was technically accurate. But he was lying by omission, and he felt his face flush as he said it.

Despite this, she chose to believe him. 'I'm sorry. I shouldn't have asked. I'm glad it's only the bugs he suspects you of. I was worried it was something worse.'

'What could be worse than industrial espionage?'

She stood and crossed to the verandah door. Leaning against the door frame, she lit a cigarette and drew deeply on it. When she was ready, she said, 'I was afraid he thought you were my stalker.'

'Stalker?' To Roland this was the limit, the craziest thing he had heard in a bizarre week. He wanted to throw his head back and laugh. But the look on her face told him to hold back. 'You have a stalker?'

'For a while now. Mostly he's been quite harmless. Random gifts, flowers, chocolates. Occasional notes, the odd poem – and when I say odd I'm not talking about their frequency or the rhyme scheme. Everyone in this business has fans who are a little extreme. David Burton is considered a sex symbol by women of a certain age. Lisa Demchek got a half-dozen offers of marriage in her first few months at Channel 5. I was quite jealous of that tally until my admirer showed up.

'About a month ago it all turned a little weird. That's when the phone calls began. Things started disappearing from my flat and from my car. The police are investigating. But I don't hold out much hope for a resolution.'

'Suzie, I'm so sorry.'

She shrugged. 'Mostly, it's something I just live with. But I mentioned it to my mother last week and bingo – Fraser is now on the case.'

'But how can he possibly help?'

'Well, for a start, he's doing something called a full risk assessment. Which would be laughable if it was happening to someone else. He's got me changing all the locks at my place, my phone number too. The car is the next thing. An MX5 is too visible, apparently – well, you can imagine what I told him to do with that advice.'

'Maybe he has a point about the car.'

'Don't you start. I'm not changing the way I live because of some weirdo. This will blow over.'

She finished her cigarette and stubbed it out on the verandah. When she came back into the room, her mood had lifted. 'Roland, don't worry about Fraser. He likes to play games with people to see how they react. You'll probably turn up as a minor character in his next book.'

'I'd settle for that, so long as he just stops bothering me.'

'I hope he hasn't ruined our friendship too.'

'If you mean, will he put me off spending countless nights near that park with you, then the answer is no. But I was getting a little tired of that game anyway.'

'I told Fraser I like you and that if I want to keep seeing you I will.' Peering at him in the half-light, she added, 'I do like you. I like how different we are, that you're grounded and measured and calm. I don't know how long you could stand to be around someone like me, but I think it's worth finding out. I also told him I was coming here to spend the night with you.'

'You did?'

She interpreted his raised voice as a note of alarm and backed off. 'Maybe I got a bit carried away in the heat of the moment.' She paused, hoping he would give her some hope. When he said nothing, she added, 'Now I'm here I can't really go home until the morning. I was wondering if I could, um, spend the night on your sofa again.'

He knew what she really meant. On any other night, he would have welcomed it. But his head was still spinning from the clandestine meeting on the riverbank and the weird encounter with Fraser that came after it. It even seemed possible that the old man might pop up again at some time during the night. That thought alone put any notion of romance firmly on ice. 'I'd really like you to stay, and it doesn't have to be the sofa. I've got a spare bedroom, you know.'

'Oh,' she replied, and he thought she sounded a little surprised. Suzanne Denning was obviously used to getting her own way. 'Okay. I'll just get my bag then.'

While she went out to the car, he rifled the linen cupboard for some spare sheets and a towel. And he thought about what he should have said. He knew a moment like this might not come again, and that he should have taken it without hesitation. Glumly, he wondered whether there might still be a chance of some assertiveness training from Beeb.

He found Suzie on the verandah, where she was smoking a final cigarette. She stubbed it out and reached out for Roland's hand, pulling him onto the sofa beside her. She put her arms around him and kissed him.

'Roly,' she said, 'I can see that you think I'm pushy. But it's only because I'm sure we want the same thing. I'm prepared to take a risk right now, but I'm also willing to wait until you're ready. At least I think I am.'

She kissed him again, and smiled at him. 'We'd better get to bed before we do something we might regret. What would Mrs Campbell think if she saw us?'

'Nothing more than she already does,' Roland replied. He was still searching for the release button on the mental handbrake that was keeping him out of life's fast lane.

Suzie squeezed his hand and got up. 'I'm down the hallway, I suppose.'

He was barely able to look at her. 'Second door on the right.'

'Goodnight, Roly.'

'Goodnight, Suzie.'

He turned off the lights and went to bed. Lying there in his paisley pyjamas, he felt distinctly middle-aged. He slipped the jacket off and lay on top of the sheets, wondering if she was asleep and thinking how little rest he would get that night. He listened for a sound but, for once, the house was strangely quiet. Even outside, the night seemed uncommonly still and he was left entirely alone with his thoughts.

There was, he realised, no perfect time in life for anything. Instead, a string of opportunities presented themselves and you either took them or you didn't. He closed his eyes and tried to imagine how things would develop if he just went down the hallway to her room. As he did this, his own door crept open and Suzie slipped quietly into the bed beside him.

'Your time's up, Roland Kendall,' she whispered. 'What are you going to do about us?'

20

Around midnight the following evening, Roland and Suzanne wheeled their bikes down the access road to the jetties at North Quay. They cycled to the end of the street and joined the bike path that ran below the concrete underbelly of the riverside expressway.

There was plenty of time and they cycled slowly, allowing Suzie to experiment with the gears on her new bike. She had last ridden a bicycle in high school and the childhood skill took longer than expected to relearn. After a few minutes the freeway above them merged onto Coronation Drive and the cycle path rose away from the river. Suzie accidentally selected her highest gear and had to labour breathlessly up the slight incline.

Roland stopped and waited for her to catch up. Laughing, he said, 'You should get more exercise. A tiny hill like this shouldn't faze you.'

'Shut up, Roland,' she replied between breaths. 'I get plenty of exercise on the job.'

'Smoking doesn't help either.'

'If I didn't think I'd fall off, I'd lean over and thump you. You're risking any future we might have together, with just a few careless words. Let's do a deal: I won't stop you reading tediously long history books or listening to mind-numbing classical records. In return, you accept me as the chain-smoking, news-loving couch potato that I am.'

He was enjoying having the upper hand for once. As he pulled ahead again, he said, 'If you talked less and pedalled more, you'd find it a lot easier.'

The path dropped again to river level and they coasted past the floating restaurant on the Milton Reach of the river. Roland tensed when a cyclist approached from the Toowong end of the bike path, but the figure swept past with his body low over the handlebars and his legs pumping hard. He soon disappeared round the corner.

Ahead of them on the river, a paddlewheeler restaurant was making its way slowly downstream. Beyond it, the navigation lights of a small powerboat were just visible. As it rounded the paddlewheeler's stern, it changed course and raced for the riverbank. Two figures, dressed in ski-masks and camouflage gear, were just visible in the powerboat. One was at the wheel, the other crouched low on the bow.

Roland and Suzie stopped and watched as it drifted towards the bank. The bowman jumped onto the rocks and held the craft steady. 'Kendall,' he whispered. 'Ditch the bikes in the bushes.'

Roland recognised the voice of the contact man from the night before. They pushed their bikes behind a bush and Roland shackled them to a post.

'Hurry up!' the bowman whispered.

They stepped down the rocks to the water's edge and climbed aboard. The bowman pushed off. A few metres out, the helmsman opened the throttle and the vessel jumped forward, lifting its bow in the direction of the opposite bank.

In midstream, they turned in a loose circle while the two EJA men scanned both banks for signs of trouble. 'We're good,' the bowman said. 'Let's go.'

The helmsman nodded and opened the throttle again. The powerboat raced upriver toward the distant lights of a Toowong apartment block. A few minutes later on the St Lucia Reach, the boat turned for the southern bank. They floated the last few metres into the Dutton Park ferry jetty, where the bowman jumped ashore.

'Come on!' he said to Roland and Suzie. They stepped ashore after him and watched as he pushed the boat clear.

'Follow me.' He jogged along the jetty and into the car park. Suzie, breathing hard, followed and Roland brought up the rear. He glanced over his shoulder and saw the boat in midstream again heading upriver. The landing had taken seconds.

A white delivery van was waiting in the shadows at the far end of the car park. The bowman slid open the side door of the cargo bay. 'Get in.'

Roland and Suzie sat on the empty floor of the van. The door slid shut and they were pitched into total darkness. 'Well let's hope we've made contact with the right people,' Suzie said from the gloom opposite him. Roland wished he felt like laughing.

The engine started and the van picked up speed as it moved out of the car park. It was a struggle at first to stay upright. Roland braced himself as the van twisted and turned to the top of what he guessed was Gladstone Road. He felt a right turn at the top of the incline, but soon had to admit that he was lost.

In the silence and the enforced confinement with Suzie, his thoughts returned to the previous evening. Would it always be like this with her, he wondered? Would they always be coming from, or heading towards, some strange nocturnal encounter? He hardly knew what was coming next, and realised that was part of the attraction. He found himself staring at her outline on the other side of the van.

She somehow sensed this. 'Am I getting paranoid, or is someone staring at me?'

'I was thinking about last night. I've been thinking about it all day.'

'I was afraid I pushed you into something you weren't ready for.'

'Well, you did give me a bit of a nudge. But I needed it and I'm glad you did. And, in case you can't see it, I'm smiling right now.'

'Me too. But it sort of changes things, doesn't it?'

'For one thing, it makes it hard to concentrate on anything else.'

'Try reading autocues or having stage directions delivered in your earpiece when your head is elsewhere. Even now, I should be concentrating on the interview.'

He tried not to talk, but couldn't help himself. 'Just one more thing and then I'll shut up. I just want you to know that, Fraser or not, I'm expecting you to be a regular visitor at my place from now on.'

'That's the most tempting offer I've had all day.' She crawled across to his side of the van and tried to kiss him. In the dark, her lips found the tip of his nose. 'Let's make it later, Roly. There's a lot riding on this interview.'

'I won't say another word if you'll just stay on your side of the van.'

'It's a deal.'

Eventually, the vehicle picked up speed and made fewer turns. Roland guessed they were on a highway. 'We must be outside the city,' he said after a while.

He checked his $29.95 Porter Vault genuine diver's watch. The marketing copy he'd written for it claimed that the dial was luminous, and he had to concede that from a few centimetres away he could just make out the time. 'It's maybe 30 minutes since we left the car park.'

'32, to be exact. And you're supposed to be quiet.'

'Sorry.'

They continued for almost the same time again, before the van slowed and turned onto an unmade road. After ten more minutes of slow, uncomfortable travel, the van came to a standstill. A heavy metal door banged nearby. The van crawled forward a few metres and came to a halt.

The cargo door slid open and they were greeted by the contact man.

'We're here,' he said.

21

The interview took place in an empty storeroom behind the garage the van had arrived in. The sole furnishings were an ancient laminated kitchen table and a half-dozen plastic chairs. They were arranged in front of a breeze-block wall that had recently been painted in an off-white. A video camera on a tripod pointed towards the table.

Three EJA people, dressed identically in camouflage gear and ski-masks, were already in the room when Roland and Suzanne arrived. The smallest in the group was clearly a woman. The other two were of average height and build, with one slightly taller than the other.

The contact man guided Roland and Suzanne across to the camera. He pointed to the tallest of the trio at the table. 'This is our spokesperson. The others will assist him and I will operate the camera.'

'Do we start now?' Suzie asked.

'As soon as you are ready.'

The three EJA people seated themselves behind the table. Suzie sat facing them so that the camera was above her left shoulder. Roland stood behind the contact man and watched as he adjusted the sound levels and focus. When he was happy, the contact man said to Suzie, 'Ready when you are.'

'Okay.' She composed herself, and began. 'Can you identify yourself, please.'

'We are an active service unit of the Environmental Justice Army. I am its spokesperson.'

'What is the Environmental Justice Army and what are its aims?'

'The EJA is dedicated to direct action against those who commit crimes against the environment. Our mission is to expose and punish wrongdoers and provide a direct incentive to change their behaviour.'

'Why haven't we heard of your group before?'

'We have existed in secret for some time. We concentrated initially on intelligence gathering operations, but have now concluded that direct action is necessary.'

'Why do you say that?'

'This is a crisis point. As custodians of the environment for future generations, we have to make sure there is something left to protect.'

'Why have you targeted Lloyd Balchin?'

'Lloyd Balchin is the biggest land developer in the state. The expansion of residential land in the south-east corner of Queensland is the greatest single threat to the environment this state faces.'

'In your communiques you claim he is guilty of crimes against the environment. If that is true, why punish his daughter?'

'Virginia Balchin is being well looked after. She was taken for three reasons. First, as a lever to make Lloyd Balchin see his errors and give him an opportunity to express regret and to offer compensation – he has failed to do this. The second reason applies to Virginia herself – she has lived comfortably on the proceeds of his crimes and done nothing to stop him – guilt by association. Third, we chose her because we wanted to make a clear statement that anyone who is not with us is against us – there are no undecideds in an issue like this.'

'When will you let her go?'

'When Lloyd Balchin acknowledges the damage he has done to the environment. He must renounce his development activities. He must also donate $1 million to established Australian environmental organisations. Finally, he must commit himself to working with conservationists and scientists to produce model green housing developments that are both non-intrusive and energy neutral.'

'$1 million is a lot of money.'

'It's a fraction of his net worth, and he made it all by exploitation of the environment.'

'If he refuses to pay, what will you do?'

'He won't refuse. His daughter's life is at stake.'

'But if he won't pay.'

'Her life is in his hands.'

'How long has he got to find the money?'

'The deadline is set for seven days, but he could find the money tomorrow if he wants. We know that.'

'So far you have only taken action against Lloyd Balchin. Why have you singled him out?'

'He is simply the first of many. In fact we have prepared a statement about our next target and will read it now.'

He removed a sheet of paper from his pocket, unfolded it and began to read. 'The Environmental Justice Army has gathered conclusive evidence from tests on effluent discharged by the Coverdale Chemicals plant at Lytton, and from examination of official company documents, that dangerous levels of toxins are being knowingly released into the Brisbane River and Moreton Bay. The company is guilty of crimes against the environment and so are the directors of the company. They must immediately admit their guilt and offer compensation or face the consequences. They have 48 hours to respond to this statement.'

He finished reading the statement. 'You have further questions?'

'What consequences do they face?'

'These people have knowingly caused damage to the environment. Now they are being called to account. We see nothing wrong with that, and if you examine your conscience, neither should you.'

'Why do you think you have the right to sit in judgement on anyone? Surely the legal system exists to deal with anyone who breaks the law.'

'The courts have failed us, just as the legislators have. The wealthy and the powerful can and do escape justice. All it takes is money.'

'If Lloyd Balchin is watching, what message do you have for him?'

'You can free your daughter. Only you can do this. And we have told you how.'

'Is Virginia here?'

'Yes.'

'Can we talk to her?'

'She has a prepared statement which she will read at the end of this interview. No questions are allowed. If you break that condition, the videotape will be destroyed.'

'It won't do any harm to ask her a few questions,' Suzie complained. 'You still control the camera.'

'No. If you want to stay in the room, keep quiet. Now stand over there behind the cameraman, both of you.'

Suzie reluctantly joined Roland in the corner behind the camera.

'Is the camera ready?' the spokesperson asked.

The cameraman nodded and the EJA woman sitting next to the spokesperson left the room. She returned a few minutes later leading a blindfolded woman. She guided her to the table and helped her to sit in the middle chair. An EJA person sat on either side of her. When one of them removed the blindfold, Roland recognised Virginia Balchin. She looked drawn and tired as she shielded her eyes from the glare of a spotlight.

One of the EJA people spoke to her and she took a folded piece of paper from her pocket. Roland could see the handwriting from where he stood. At a signal from the cameraman, she began to read:

> *I have been allowed to prepare a statement to read to you tonight. The EJA have reviewed it but have not edited it in any way. These are my own words. My purpose in speaking is to ask anyone with influence over my father to convince him that he must cooperate with the EJA.*
>
> *I have not been treated badly although I am watched 24 hours a day. I have spoken with several of my captors and I believe they are reasonable people. I am not in any doubt, however, about their motivation and their determination to see their cause through. Therefore, I do fear for my future.*
>
> *They told me, and I believe them, that they are willing to take a life to save many lives in future generations. I believe I am safe for now, but maybe not forever. I ask all of you listening to call or write to my father asking him to change in a small way the way he does business. It is possible for him to still make a profit while ensuring that future generations can enjoy a healthy environment.*
>
> *Please do what you can to make him see this, for my sake and for the sake of the future.*

She stopped reading and stared intently at the camera. In her eyes there was a flash of defiance, but it gave way quickly and was replaced by fear and uncertainty. Roland could hardly bear to watch. The whole pantomime sickened him. He wanted to speak, to say something that would give her hope, but knew there was nothing he could do.

After several seconds, the cameraman signalled the cut and the spell was broken. The woman beside Virginia leaned across and spoke to her, then the blindfold was placed over her eyes again. She submitted to this mechanically as though used to it and her guard helped her from the room.

Roland turned to Suzie. He could tell that she too had been moved by Virginia Balchin's demeanour. But her face hardened again when the cameraman handed the videotape to her. She said, 'Won't you let me speak briefly with her?'

'Absolutely not.'

'Then at least let me check the quality of the tape. We didn't come all this way to get back and only have the memories of it.'

'The tape is good. Just trust us.'

Cocooned alone together on the return journey, they reacted to the interview in opposite ways. Suzie's mood skyrocketed. She talked endlessly about the interview and what a coup it was for Channel 5.

Initially, Roland let her rattle on, but after a while it began to irritate him. When he couldn't stand it any longer, he cut her off abruptly. 'Please will you just shut up.'

It stunned her into silence. Pleased with the effect of his words, he ploughed on. 'You enjoyed every minute of that charade, didn't you?'

'Yes. I feel great.'

'What about Virginia Balchin. You saw how she looked. How

can you feel anything but frustration that we weren't able to bring her back with us?'

'Roland, I'm in the business of gathering news. I have to put my own emotions aside when I'm on the job. Of course I feel sorry for her. I'd be a monster if I didn't. But I was there to get the story and that's what I did. Job done. There was no way that asking them to let her go would have done any good.'

'Well, it just isn't right,' he replied.

They lapsed into a silence that made the journey home seem interminable. Roland soon tired of bracing himself every time the van turned. And eventually he admitted to himself he had been wrong to vent his frustrations on her.

It was a relief when the van finally stopped, and the contact man slid the cargo door open. 'Everybody out,' he said. 'This is the end of the line.'

Roland and Suzanne climbed out of the van and stretched.

'Where are we?' she asked, as she massaged her back.

'Close to home,' the contact man replied.

'I know where we are,' Roland said, recognising the street.

'Here is our part of the deal,' the contact added. He held up a leather overnight bag.

Roland felt the weight of the gold as he put the strap over his shoulder. The van drove off and they were left on the footpath of a suburban street. They stared at each other until a dog barked at them from behind a fence.

'My place is just around the corner,' he said, as they started along the footpath.

'Truce, Roly,' Suzie replied. 'I admit I was on a high after the interview, but I don't feel I've done anything wrong.'

'Okay, truce. It's just that looking at Virginia Balchin made me see that this is for real. I've been doing so many crazy things for the past few weeks that it took me a while to realise it isn't just another game.'

22

For the second night in a row, Roland and Suzanne lay naked together on his bed. This time, the gold bars and the videotape sat at their feet on the rumpled sheets.

'If Mrs Campbell walked in on us right now,' Suzie asked, 'do you think she'd still see me as a good influence on you?'

Roland pretended to consider this carefully. Recalling the first conversation he'd had with his neighbour about Suzie, he replied, 'So long as you always take your sunglasses off when you get undressed, Mrs C. will think you're a lovely girl.'

Suzie laughed so hard that she began to cry. The infection quickly spread and he was soon clutching his stomach in pain. When they were exhausted, they lay in silence for a while, happy in each other's company. Eventually, he said, 'This is the first time in days that I don't feel completely controlled by Dalton or Beeb.'

He rolled towards her and stroked her hair, leaving his fingers at the nape of her neck. With his other hand he traced patterns down her body until she pulled him closer. She kissed him and they began to make love again.

Afterwards they dozed until the light of another summer's day crept into the room and the hum of suburban life grew more noticeable. Suzie walked out onto the verandah to smoke a cigarette. Roland lay in bed, content that she wasn't rushing off somewhere.

Breakfast was leisurely but subdued. Ahead lay an important day for Channel 5, possibly the biggest its news team would ever have. Neither of them wanted to discuss it. Instead they went through the motions of learning to be around each other at the beginning of a day.

They hardly spoke during the taxi ride up the mountain. In the empty corridor outside Roland's office, they kissed briefly. With the worst possible timing, B.B. opened the office door and caught them. All three were taken by surprise. Roland was embarrassed but Suzie seemed unconcerned. She laughed and walked along the corridor to the newsroom waving the tape in the air.

Beeb smiled conspiratorially at Roland. She retreated into the office, leaving the door open for him. He followed reluctantly and settled behind his desk while he waited for the inevitable discussion.

She didn't keep him in suspense for long. 'You know, Roly, I feel real mixed about what I just saw out there.'

He thought at first she was taking a moral tone, but she went on to say, 'I always feel uncomfortable when there are mixed messages showing in the data.'

'I'm sorry, Beeb. I have absolutely no idea what you're talking about.'

'I'm talking about you and Suzanne. And the pluses and minuses of it. When the rumours started about the two of you – when that picture came out in the *Sunday Mail* – I inserted some questions into the audience surveys about you as a couple. You should be happy about this because the results are very positive.'

'You've been gauging public opinion about me and Suzie?'

'I'd be crazy not to, wouldn't I? It's part of my job description, after all.'

'Maybe I'm being a bit slow this morning. Can you explain to me why anything private that goes on between me and Suzie has anything to do with your job?'

'Dalton put me in charge of all things Suzanne, remember? You were sitting on the sofa with us when he did it. The pleasing thing is that our viewers see you as a big plus for her.'

'I couldn't be happier to hear that.'

The sarcasm was entirely lost on her. 'I can print out the results if you're interested. We knew that changes in Suzie's personal life would boost her scores. It rounds out her character, softens her image. This is the sort of thing that makes people love her instead of just liking her.'

'So why should it worry you?'

'The problem, Roland, is this. I'm utterly convinced that the relationship can't last. I'm only sharing this with you because I'm concerned as a colleague and a friend.'

Roland wished the whole conversation hadn't started. 'That's extremely good of you, Beeb.'

'I knew you'd be upset. But this is something you have to hear. I've compiled personality profiles for all of the key personnel at Channel 5. The correlation between yours and Suzanne's really is troubling.'

'You mean our handwriting slopes in different directions?'

'You're a sceptic about things like this – I'm okay with that – but data doesn't lie. My analysis is extremely reliable for team-building purposes, even for a team of two. I don't get any pleasure from telling you this, but you're in a doomed relationship.'

The news had a dramatic effect on him. He felt energised, determined to prove her wrong. 'I'm beginning to see your problem. The viewer surveys tell you we should go for it, but the personality correlation says we're toast.'

She nodded. 'I only wish I'd completed the analysis before Suzanne okayed the whole thing with me.'

'She what?'

'Your relationship. You do know that, don't you?'

'No, I didn't know that.'

'Then I can't go any deeper into this. You two should take some time out together on this. Real soon.'

Roland tried several times during the morning to return to the subject, but Beeb had said all that she intended. She had successfully planted a seed of doubt, and it quickly began to germinate. He remembered the bugged conversation where Dalton had told Beeb to fix Suzie up with a man. It played on his mind and he was desperate for Suzie to call and clear it up.

When she did ring, he realised how hard it would be to talk about. 'We're both hot property this morning,' she gushed. 'Everyone has seen the edited tape and thinks it makes great television. We're running it during a special edition of *The Green Scene* tonight at 6.30.'

'That's great news, Suzie.'

'Dalton is thrilled with it too. He wants to talk to us right now. I'll meet you in his office.' She hung up before there was a chance to ask about the discussion with Beeb.

Roland walked next door and found Suzie and Dalton talking animatedly on the sofa. Dalton pointed to the coffee maker. 'Help yourself, Roly.'

Roland was light-headed from the lack of sleep. He was delighted to learn that the filter machine for once contained a fully caffeinated blend. As he poured himself a mug, he tuned in to the conversation on the sofa. Dalton said, 'I'm thrilled with how this has turned out. You both did great work. This will turn the corner for Channel 5.'

Roland sat beside Suzie. He stirred the milk into his coffee, and half-listened to the rest of the discussion. Dalton noticed after a while and said, 'Roland, you look kind of stressed. Are you okay?'

'I'm fine. Just tired. I haven't been getting much sleep lately.'

'I guess not. I know we've made major demands on you and we really appreciate it. So, after tonight, I want you to go home and forget about Channel 5 for a couple of days. Switch off, do your own thing, and come back refreshed and refocused. Okay?'

Roland was surprised and pleased by the offer. Then he realised that it was Friday and Dalton was only offering him a weekend off. Three weeks ago he would have known this instinctively. Now every day seemed taken up with Channel 5 and the people connected to it. 'What do you mean *after tonight*?'

'I hope neither of you have any plans for this evening. If so, cancel them. I've arranged for the police in charge of the Balchin kidnapping to talk with you after the interview airs.'

'Police?'

'You had to know they'd want to talk to you.'

'It could be more of a grilling than a talk,' Suzie added with relish.

Roland had been avoiding eye contact with her since coming into the room. He made himself face her now and she rewarded him with a smile so warm that he wanted to forget everything B.B. had told him. 'What do you mean?' he asked.

'We've done a number of things they're not going to like.'

Dalton agreed. 'Your first problem is that you failed to report the theft of the gold. Then we – or rather, you, Roland – had contact twice with the EJA. Finally, we have information about their next target and we're sitting on it until news time. That should be enough for starters.'

'Why do you sound so pleased about this?'

'I don't think there's too much to worry about. You've got all day to get your story straight. They're coming here at 7 p.m. and have no idea why we want to see them. The Channel 5 lawyers will be on hand all afternoon to prepare you. I don't want you to hold anything back, but I don't want you to give them anything that might be useful to our competitors.'

'Surely those two things conflict?'

'Roly, why do you always see things in such a complicated way? You'll be intensively coached all day. Relax, you'll give a terrific performance.'

23

Beeb was on the phone when Roland returned to his office. He gathered from her side of the conversation that she was talking to Malcolm McDarrow. The warm, intimate tone suggested that they had somehow become firm friends.

When the call ended, Roland couldn't help wanting to know more. 'What's the latest with Malcolm?'

'A major development, something Dalton and I are extremely excited about. I've talked Malcolm into going cold turkey. I'm taking him down to a private clinic in Sydney next week and we're going to shoot a documentary on the whole thing. He'll come back from Sydney a totally new man.'

Roland was amazed. 'What does Arrow think about this?'

'He was reluctant at first, but now he's fully on board. He sees the benefits of it, both personally and financially.'

'Financially?'

'Well, for starters, there was a possible termination of contract if he didn't go along with it. I guess that's more of a negative incentive than a benefit. But we also just negotiated a major deal with a non-alcoholic beer maker. And Malcolm's court-ordered community service will be exchanged for commercials and appearances aimed at lowering youth alcohol abuse. Malcolm

McDarrow is about to become a temperance god.'

Roland couldn't keep his guilt to himself any longer. He told Beeb about the vodka he'd added to Mal's drink. She listened in a stunned silence. 'Thank you for trusting me with this, Roly. I understand better now where Malcolm has been coming from this week. He insisted all along that he only had a couple of drinks on Saturday night. I just wasn't prepared to believe him.'

'I think I should tell him this before he goes down to Sydney. I'm not looking forward to it, but I feel he has to know.'

'Don't even think about doing that. For some reason he's taken against you already. Wrongly handled, it could throw out the whole programme.'

'Beeb, I have to get this off my chest.'

'By telling me, you just did. Now let me handle it. I have excellent relations with him at the moment. When the time is right, I'll pass it on.'

'Well, if you don't mind.'

'Of course not, Roly. That's what friends are for.'

'Thanks Beeb. Now, about Suzie and me.'

She held up her hand. 'I can't talk about that. It would be wrong of me. Anyway, we have a lot of work to do on your story for the police.'

Roland watched the *Newscenter5* broadcast from the control room with Dalton. As the seconds ticked down to 6 p.m., there was a palpable excitement and a growing sense that nothing could possibly go wrong that night. The EJA interview led the bulletin, with a few tantalising excerpts from the videotape. Then came the revelation that the next EJA threat was to Coverdale Chemicals.

At 6.30, Suzie hosted an extended edition of *The Green Scene*. She led with the tapes. Viewing the edited interview for the first time, Roland was both impressed and disturbed. The gloomy lighting and the grainy recording gave the whole event a more sinister and desperate air than he had remembered. The masked EJA figures were more shadowy and menacing on the small screen. Virginia Balchin seemed more drawn and isolated when she read her statement appealing for help.

As the interview ended, Beeb arrived in the control room. She drew Dalton aside and whispered, 'The police are here. They wanted to speak to Suzanne but I convinced them to take Roland first.'

'Good idea,' Dalton replied. 'Thanks, Beeb.'

'Yes,' Roland added, 'thanks a lot, Beeb.'

She ignored the remark and beckoned him to follow.

Two crumpled, overweight detectives were waiting in the conference room. One, dressed in a short-sleeved shirt with an unfashionably wide tie, was lurking near the window. The other, wearing a brown suit, was seated at the huge oval table. He stood as Roland and B.B. walked in.

'Roland,' Beeb said as the detective approached, 'this is Inspector Derek Murphy.'

Murphy was in his forties, with thinning, shaggy fair hair and a broad, weathered face. He wrapped a fierce hand around Roland's and tweaked it sharply. 'Thanks, Miss Olsen,' he said to Beeb. 'I'll call you when we're done with him.'

'Sure, Inspector. And that's Ms, you know.'

Murphy ignored her and smirked at Roland. His lips parted to reveal two rows of glistening teeth. Roland felt like a lone swimmer in the sights of a white pointer.

Murphy nodded to a chair at the end of the conference table. 'Sit down, Mr Kendall. Please.'

Roland was perspiring freely – one armpit, his left, had gone into panic mode – and his pulse was racing. Murphy sat uncomfortably close to him on the edge of the table. He jerked a thumb at his colleague. 'That's D.C. Cleary over there. And we're both desperate to know just what the hell is going on between you and the EJA.'

Roland smiled innocently. His instructions from the lawyers, and from Beeb, were clear: be pleasant, be placid and answer only specific questions. In the growing silence, Cleary walked around the table and began to circle behind him. It added to the impression of a feeding frenzy.

After a lengthy pause, Murphy said, 'You're in a bit of trouble, Kendall. Did you know that?'

Roland had already suspected it. Now he believed it totally. 'I don't feel I've actually done anything wrong, Inspector.'

'Then let me help you to a better understanding of it. Number one, you set out to communicate with a terrorist organisation, knowing that it had committed a serious crime. Two, you succeeded, according to Mr Hinsley's account, in meeting a member of that terrorist organisation, after which you did nothing to inform us. Three, you then arranged another meeting in order to record an interview. And four, having done this with your accomplice, Miss Denning, you took no action to inform us for nearly 18 hours.'

Murphy leaned close enough for Roland to smell the garlic on his breath. 'I think you'd better start from the beginning and tell us everything.'

Roland felt queasy, but decided it would be unwise to look away. 'Do you think I could have a glass of water first?'

Murphy snapped his fingers and Cleary filled a glass from the jug on the table. 'Come on Kendall. Tell me all about it. Tell me why you were able to find the EJA when we weren't.'

Roland accepted the glass and drank slowly from it. 'I'm not sure I understand the question. You want me to tell you why you haven't been able to locate the EJA?'

'Don't be a smart-arse. Let's just start with how you managed it.'

'I didn't have to do anything. The EJA made the first move.' He felt the drops of sweat rolling down his armpit. He was a hopeless liar and wondered why Dalton was making him do this. 'It all started because of the treasure hunt. Have you heard about the competition?'

'Yeah, we know all about that. We've had some nasty incidents in parks over the last few days. And a couple of private garden ponds have been damaged.' Murphy straightened and walked behind Roland. 'You were telling me how the contact happened.'

Roland tensed again. This was the part of his story that was closest to a lie. He hoped to get through it without stumbling. 'I got a note asking me to a meeting on the riverside bike path. Just a time and location. When I got there, he turned out to be from the EJA.'

'Tell me about the meeting.'

He recounted the riverside meeting with the EJA contact. He went on to describe the second meeting, the journeys by boat and van, and finally the interview. Murphy sat opposite him and listened intently without interrupting. Cleary took notes as Roland spoke.

Murphy made him describe the building he had been in during the interview, and the EJA people he had met. This took some time but, by the end of it, Roland sensed that the animosity towards him was fading. Murphy ran out of questions and glanced at his colleague. They both shrugged their shoulders. 'Well, Kendall, I think we're going to let you go for now. I'm not sure what we'll do about the charges.'

'Charges? What exactly have I done wrong?'

'Let's just say it will depend on how things turn out. If you cooperate with us, things will be all right. If there is any more contact between the EJA and you, we want to know about it immediately. Understand?'

Roland nodded.

Murphy smiled. 'And take a good look at Cleary here. Ugly mug, isn't he? But all that facial hair makes him pretty much unforgettable.' He grinned at Cleary, who smirked and stroked his thick, drooping moustache. 'You'll be seeing him around a fair bit from now on, because until this is sorted out we'll be keeping a close eye on you.'

Roland made his escape and returned to his office. He found a note from Dalton on his desk, asking him to stay back for a meeting after the police had gone. Thinking this might be some time away, and anxious for a chance to recover, he went outside for a walk in the night air.

More than an hour later Beeb called from Dalton's office and asked him to join them. When he arrived, Suzanne was already in full flow. 'It was straight out of a B-grade cop show. They really tried to put the frighteners on me. I presume they did the same with Roly.'

He nodded as he sat down opposite her. Before he could say that Murphy's tactics had been one hundred per cent successful, she continued, 'They threatened charges, unspecified of course, and demanded cooperation in future. A lot of hot air, really.'

'It sure sounds that way,' Dalton replied. 'The important thing I want you both to realise is, we've done nothing wrong, despite what Murphy might say. We were doing our jobs. If you have any further contact with the police, let me know immediately. Don't be concerned about any pressure they put on you. Just come straight to me. Understood?'

Suzie and Roland nodded, Suzie more enthusiastically. She even looked like someone who would welcome a further confrontation with Murphy.

Changing the subject, Dalton said, 'Roland, you'll be pleased to know that your competition is still causing people to dig holes in parks all over Brisbane. So far without success.'

Roland felt mixed about this news. On the one hand, he was concerned about the damage. On the other, he was quietly pleased with the competition's success. Lamely, he said, 'I hope it's not making too much of a mess.'

'The way I see it, there's no such thing as too much of a mess. The Lord Mayor has been putting out damning news releases all week. I've agreed to buy her off with a very generous sponsorship deal for the City's Parks and Gardens division. It will cost us mega-dollars, but the publicity will just last and last. There's a front-page story on it in tomorrow's *Courier Mail*.'

'It's early days yet,' Roland said as he rose to go. 'I don't think there will be enough clues to logically locate the prize for at least another ten days. Barring an outrageous guess, that is.'

Turning to Suzie, he said, 'I really need to talk with you.'

'Not now, Roly. Dalton and Beeb are taking me out to dinner.'

'Make it a foursome,' Dalton said. 'It's kind of a celebration and you deserve to be part of it too.'

'Thanks, but no thanks,' Roland replied. 'It's Friday night. And, as you promised me earlier, my weekend starts now.'

24

Early the next morning Roland crept into Mrs Campbell's front garden to borrow her *Courier Mail.* He picked it off the lawn, worked at the plastic wrapper until it came away, and unrolled it as he walked back to his own garden.

The treasure hunt article was above the fold on the front page. It was accompanied by a huge picture of a middle-aged couple standing waist-deep in a hole in the ground. The man, who was heavily bearded and wearing a navy singlet, held a pick in both hands. His wife, dressed in overalls and an Akubra hat, was pointing a metal detector into the hole at her husband's feet. The article gave an account of their efforts and those of scores of other treasure hunters searching in different parts of the city. Roland noted with pleasure that no one was anywhere near the correct location.

Inside, an interview with a still angry Lord Mayor was positioned beside a conciliatory response from Dalton. There was even a small picture of Roland at the bottom of page two. It was a cropped version of the photograph taken in the restaurant, minus Suzanne and the wine glasses. The caption read: *Roland Kendall – only he knows where the treasure is buried.*

If they only knew, he thought, that the secret was shared with the EJA. He rolled up the paper, shrouded it in its plastic wrapper, and tossed it back over the fence. Minutes later he saw Mrs Campbell retrieve it from under the bush where it had landed. She waved to him on her way indoors. He waved back and hurried inside in case she saw his picture and wanted to make a fuss.

His work-free weekend got off to a bad start after breakfast when Gwen rang and he discovered that even his friends were now calling to talk business. 'I need to talk to you about Virginia Balchin.'

'Did you see *Newscenter5* last night?'

'I did, and I was impressed. Channel 5 have reached a new high – or should that be low – in sensationalism.'

'You're probably right,' he conceded. 'But I only started paying attention to their style recently. I can't say whether it's any worse than before. Have you got anything new on Virginia?'

'I came across something you might find interesting. In her first year at university she quickly developed a reputation as an environmental radical.'

'So do lots of people, Gwen. You did.'

'Yes, and I stayed one too. Unlike some people.'

He knew who she meant and braced himself for the usual vitriol. 'Are you thinking of Phil by any chance?'

'Yes, Phil. I thought he and I would continue to share the same beliefs.'

'People change.'

'It must have had something to do with the smell of his father's money. Or maybe he was just stringing me along in the first place. I'd rather have someone like you, with no discernible beliefs at all, than someone who abandons their principles as soon as they get access to a trust fund.'

Roland thought Gwen would actually prefer strong but changing opinions to the bland fence-sitting he excelled at.

Rather than pursue this, he steered her back to the purpose of her call. 'What about Virginia Balchin. Did she do a Phil?'

'It looks that way. She had always been the first to chain herself to trees or go diving to block effluent pipes, that sort of stuff. Then at the end of her second year she gave it all up. She told everyone she wasn't at uni just to have fun.'

'I thought university was supposed to be all about having fun.'

'You would think that, wouldn't you.'

'And Virginia just walked away from the cause?'

'She was a meeting attender and a motion seconder for a while. Over time she faded from the scene altogether. Her friends from that period said she just seemed to get serious about her studies. When I saw the interview last night I thought it a little strange they had chosen to abduct a woman who was once so active in the same cause.'

'It does seem odd. But I suppose her value to the EJA is solely as Lloyd Balchin's daughter. Or maybe they think, like you, that it's worse to have been a believer and then dropped it for material gain.'

'Anyway, that's all I have. I expect you'll pass it on to your reporter friend.'

This was Roland's cue to end the call. The last thing he wanted to discuss with Gwen was his reporter friend. 'That's exactly what I'm about to do. Thanks Gwen, talk to you later.'

He hung up and called Suzie, but had to leave a message on her answering machine. This was a relief as he was still unsure of the best way to tackle the subject of Beeb's intervention in their relationship. Worried she would ring back or come over before he was ready to talk, he decided to go out.

It took him half an hour to walk to the cycle path and reach the point where the EJA boat had collected them on the night of the interview. He was beginning to feel like a regular visitor, having gone there the night before to collect his own bicycle.

Suzie's bike was still shackled to the lamp post, and remarkably still in one piece despite two nights in a public place. Roland adjusted the saddle, mounted and started towards the city. Going nowhere, just riding to clear and concentrate his mind, he quickly resolved to confront Suzie directly about Beeb.

He turned for home and had covered less than a hundred metres when he encountered the drooping bulk of Detective Constable Cleary. The policeman was dressed in shorts and T-shirt, with a baseball cap and sunglasses completing the disguise. The moustache and the sag of his rounded shoulders gave him away. Roland considered stopping to say hello, but changed his mind and merely nodded as he sped past, keeping up the pace until Cleary was out of sight.

At the end of the bikeway he joined the two lanes of Saturday morning traffic winding along Coronation Drive to Toowong. Competing constantly with cars for road space had developed in him a kind of sixth-sense survival instinct. It was probably this that saved him from serious injury shortly after passing through Toowong. He turned along a side road he often used as a shortcut and sensed rather than heard a car follow him.

When it closed on him, he half-turned and saw a grey Commodore come level to overtake. Without warning, it swerved into him, catching his rear wheel with its bumper. He let himself fall with the bike, clenching his hands tight on the handlebars and tucking his elbows into his body. When his shoulder hit the road, he lost contact with the bike and rolled into the gutter, cracking his helmet on the kerb.

Seconds later, the pain started in his left shoulder. It also came into his wrist and then his hip. He tried not to look at his legs, which were bleeding at the knees. Instead he scanned along the street for a sight of the car or the driver who had deliberately hit him. It must have turned up the next side street. He was left alone with a broken bike and a mounting anger.

As he walked slowly home, he tried to make sense of the incident. He replayed it in his mind and was certain it couldn't have been an accident. Reaching that conclusion was the easy part – deciding who had been at the wheel of the car was an entirely different problem. A few weeks earlier, he would have been hard-pressed to think of anyone who might try to hurt him. Now, the walk back to his house was barely long enough to consider the list of contenders.

At home he had just showered and was dabbing himself gently dry when Suzie returned his call. He told her about the accident and then about Virginia Balchin. He deliberately downplayed the incident with the car, and it hardly surprised him that she was more interested in the latest update from Gwen. 'It's another piece in the puzzle, Roly, but who knows where it fits. It might be useful background. Can you follow this up with Gwen. Find out who we can use as sources on this. Just names and phone numbers. I'll call them and ask if they'll talk to me on air.'

'Okay.' With the discussion on Virginia Balchin at an end, he decided to ask the question that had been nagging at him for 24 hours. 'Suzie, there's something we really have to talk about. It's difficult for me to say on the phone, so please hear me out.'

'Oh God, you're not pregnant, are you? I thought you were supposed to be taking precautions.'

'Please, this is serious.'

'Okay. You have my full attention. I promise not to interrupt.'

'Beeb talked to me yesterday after she caught us in the corridor. She seems to think you manufactured a relationship with me as a publicity stunt.'

'She told you that?'

'She also said you got her approval in advance.'

He waited for a denial. When it didn't come, he pressed again. 'I need you to tell me it isn't true.'

'Of course it isn't. Well, not exactly, anyway.'

'What does that mean?'

'Calm down, Roland. I'll be honest with you, if you give me a chance to explain.'

His concerns were mounting now. Somehow, he managed to remain silent while she spoke. 'Beeb thinks she started this when she identified the areas where we needed to modify my image. It was quite a list, from minor things about my appearance through to softening the impression that I'm too focused on news. But the biggest issue for her was this thing about me not being in a relationship. I thought I could handle her, but she's incredibly persistent. She kept coming back to it, even though I told her what to do with her analysis.

'It was around this time that I helped you bury the gold. I found myself attracted to you, I really honestly did. Anyway, next time she talked to me about it, I got desperate. I told her that, as a matter of fact, I had just met someone I liked a lot.

'That only made it worse. She demanded details, and when she found out it was you, she went full-on Beeb crazy. She arranged for the photographer to appear that night in the restaurant. Roly, that's the one thing I'm totally ashamed of. I knew it was a set-up and I went along with it. I just didn't think you'd mind very much and I thought it would keep B.B. off my back. It was just a picture and a few lines of gossip.'

'Well I do mind,' Roland said. 'Quite a lot, actually. I don't see why my private life should be splashed deliberately across the social pages. And I don't see why Beeb should be going around thinking I'm some sort of factor she can tweak on her spreadsheets. You know how it makes me feel? Like I can't be sure of your motives any more.'

'That's ridiculous! Are you suggesting I deliberately trapped you?'

'I don't know what to think.'

'I wouldn't do that. I just wouldn't.'

He wanted to believe her and tried hard to make himself say it. But it was undeniable that she had deceived him. He wondered what else she might be holding back. 'I want to believe you, Suzie, I really do. I need some time to think this over.'

'No, Roly. You don't need time on a thing like this. It's a fundamental issue of trust. When I finish talking, I'll count to three. If you don't say anything, I'm going to hang up and it's over between us. The end. *FINIS*. You can just fuck off.'

She must have counted well beyond three. He was still searching for an answer when she slammed the phone down.

He wished the conversation had been different, that he had been more measured and conciliatory. He even considered ringing her back to apologise. But there was still the nagging doubt about what had come first in her mind: the need for a relationship to satisfy B.B.'s publicity machine, or her feelings for him. He wondered if the two could even be separated.

He decided that she would have to make the next move. When it came 24 hours later, it didn't look good. It arrived in the form of Mrs Campbell who came over to show him the *Sunday Mail*. Suzie was on the front cover of the magazine section. Under the picture was the headline: *Newscenter5's co-anchor talks about the media, the environment and the new man in her life.*

The article hailed Suzie as the hot new property in Brisbane television. Roland skimmed the first page, which was so complimentary that he suspected Beeb had drafted it. About two-thirds of the way into the article, he found the first reference to himself:

> *Not content with the major changes to her working life, Suzanne has also found time in the last month for a deepening romantic attachment to a Channel 5*

colleague. She confirmed that the rumours circulating on Mt Coot-tha about her and Channel 5 newcomer Roland Kendall are true.

'Roland and I met less than a month ago, but it was something that felt perfect from the very beginning. We've been working together closely the whole time and it's been a case of falling more and more for each other from the moment we met.

'I'm just so happy when we're together, and I want everyone to know it …'

He read and reread her glowing words about their relationship. Furious, he decided to have it out with her and called her home number.

When Fraser answered, Roland almost hung up. He stopped himself, and asked, 'Is Suzie there?'

'No, she's not. Who's calling? Is that you, Kendall?'

'Tell her I'll call back later.'

'I heard you had a bit of an accident yesterday. You should be more careful on the roads. You could get hurt. You're playing a serious game now, you know.'

'I'm okay,' Roland replied, wondering if he was deliberately reading malice into the old man's voice. 'I'll feel even better if you pass on my message to Suzie. I really need her to call me back.'

'I'm sure you do. But I told you, I don't think the two of you are a good idea. Goodbye.'

25

On Monday morning, when there was still no word from Suzanne, Roland decided he needed a break from Channel 5 and everyone associated with it. He spent the entire day at home reading on the front verandah. It was a nostalgic return to his old life, a simpler era when television was nothing more than an occasional diversion. He enjoyed every minute of it.

At six o'clock he couldn't resist tuning in to watch Suzie. He switched the television on in time for the beginning of *Newscenter5*. After the opening visuals with their familiar brassy fanfare, David Burton appeared alone on screen in his anchor buggy:

> *Good evening Brisbane. I'm David Burton and this is Newscenter5.*
>
> *As you can see my co-anchor Suzanne Denning is not with me tonight. Suzie is on location and we'll be crossing live to her in a moment.*
>
> *But first tonight's main story. The Environmental Justice Army claims it has placed a bomb in the home of Christopher Summers, the chairman and CEO of Coverdale Chemicals.*

In a communique released through a Brisbane radio station earlier today, the EJA announced it planned to detonate the bomb this evening.

Suzanne Denning is with our live eye unit outside the chairman's home. Suzie, can you tell us what's happening?

Suzie appeared on the screen. 'David, I'm standing outside the Summers' home in Pullenvale. The area immediately around the house has been sealed off by police. The EJA communique states that the bomb will be detonated at 6.30 tonight.'

'Suzie, have the family and neighbours been moved to safety?'

'Yes, David. This is a large property – the grounds cover more than five hectares – so the house is completely isolated from the neighbouring homes. But police are taking no chances with the safety of residents and the whole neighbourhood has been evacuated.'

As she spoke, shaky overhead pictures appeared on the screen with the subtitle *Newscenter5 Chopper Cam.* In the fading light it was just possible to make out the sprawling low-set brick homestead and its surrounding outbuildings. Suzie continued: 'As you can see the house has a large floor area. There is no clear indication of where the bomb has been placed. Police have been concentrating on securing the perimeter and are now waiting on the arrival of army bomb disposal experts.'

'Suzie, do you expect any work on locating the bomb to begin before the 6.30 deadline?'

'I can't say at this stage David. I would think it unlikely.'

'Was anyone in the house when the bomb was allegedly planted?'

'I spoke to the housekeeper earlier and she told me the house was empty from noon onwards. This is apparently her afternoon off and she was unaware of the situation until she returned home at 5.30. The other members of the household were out all day. Mr Summers was in a board meeting discussing the EJA threat when he was informed. His wife and two children are interstate on holiday.'

'Okay Suzie. We'll stay in touch.'

'Thanks David.'

'We'll cross back to Suzanne as soon as there are any further developments, and we'll have our chopper cam in the sky above the property during the entire bulletin.'

Revelling in his exclusive use of the *Newscenter5* studio, Burton gave a buoyant performance as he introduced the other top stories of the day. Roland, who had tuned in for a precious glimpse of Suzanne Denning, felt cheated. He realised now how much he had missed her over the weekend.

His thoughts were interrupted during the first commercial break when Phil arrived carrying his briefcase and an armful of takeaway containers. 'I hope you haven't eaten yet, Roly. I stopped on the way over and picked up some Thai.'

Roland crossed to the television to turn it off, but Phil stopped him. 'Keep it on. If there's going to be a bang then I hope Channel 5 doesn't miss it.'

'You sound like the rest of them.'

'What's wrong with that? We're in the news business. If we miss it we'll look like a bunch of amateurs. Anyway, you were watching when I came in and still would be if I hadn't arrived. So don't get all morally superior with me.'

Roland couldn't explain that he had been watching Suzanne Denning and not *Newscenter5*. He shrugged. 'Sorry. I think all this is beginning to affect me. I'm about as close as I want to be to the whole business. Too close.'

He collected plates and glasses from the kitchen, and they helped themselves to the selection of dishes and the beer Phil had brought. All the time, they kept an eye on *Newscenter5* which was still working through the day's other news.

When his plate was piled high, Phil sat back on the sofa. He said, 'I was looking for you today but nobody had any idea where you were. You didn't even ring in.'

'I couldn't stand the thought of being around Beeb. I couldn't even face her on the phone.'

'You needn't have worried, mate. She flew down to Sydney this morning with Arrow McDarrow. We won't see either of them for days. Not until she's rebuilt him from the ground up.'

'In which case I'll happily be back in the office tomorrow. Back on duty as the cuckoo in Dalton's nest. It's not just B.B. who kept me away. It's this thing with Suzie too.'

'The romance of the century.' Phil fluttered his eyelids. In a small high voice, he said, 'I'm just so happy when we're together, and I want everyone to know it.'

There was no need to ask if he'd read the article. 'Do you think she's using me?'

'Who can say. She knows how the publicity machine works and how to use it to her advantage. She's a journalist after all, and they spend most of their time trying to break down other people's facades. She's also very ambitious and she's been looking for a break like the one she just got. It's really up to you to decide if you feel used. And if you do, does it matter, as long as you like her and she likes you?'

It was a fair point, Roland decided. As he digested it, Phil looked at his watch. 'Hell, I forgot the time.'

It was 6.25 and *Newscenter5* was just coming back from another commercial break. David Burton in his anchor buggy glided in front of the giant screen which now carried an overhead shot of the Summers property. There was a stillness about the abandoned house that even the fuzzy helicopter camera managed to convey.

The picture cut again to Suzanne who was standing next to a

Newscenter5 car. 'Hello David?' she said, looking off-camera for a moment.

'Suzie, have you any further information for us at this stage?'

'We are now minutes away from the deadline set by the EJA. The police cordon around the building has been completely sealed. We have just been moved further back from the property for reasons of safety. Police have also blocked the roads into the area and are turning back sightseers.'

'Suzie, what's the feeling where you are?'

'There is a growing tension as the deadline approaches. An air of expectancy amongst the onlookers, and I think also a hope that nothing will happen.'

Her voice trailed off and she struggled for more to say. Outdoor lights were coming on around the property as the shadows lengthened. Suddenly, as a timer clock somewhere in the building ticked around to 6.30, spotlights flickered to life around the swimming pool and tennis court.

'Suzie, we're going to stay with you a little while longer,' Burton said.

'Yes, David. Obviously we are unable to talk to any of the police in charge at this stage, but we are trying to arrange for them to speak to us shortly.'

As they listened to her prattling on, Phil bent over and picked up his briefcase. He opened the lid of the case and rummaged around inside.

Roland asked, 'Do you think anything will happen?'

'The EJA knows how to use the media for maximum effect. They set this thing up so that half of Queensland will be tuned in live. If I was one of them, I wouldn't let that opportunity go by. It's just good television sense.' When the picture changed again to a dim overhead shot from the chopper cam, he said, 'If it was up to me I'd do it now.'

As he finished speaking, the centre of the screen erupted in a ball of orange flame. Roland was convinced he had heard the click of a detonator switch. The sound of the explosion came a fraction later and the chopper shook, causing a temporary loss of focus.

The picture cut to a ground camera which showed the fireball rising from the house. Suzie was a dark shadow at the side of the screen. She said nothing as the flames spread, wisely allowing the picture to do its work. Then, calmly, she began, 'The explosion came at 6.34 p.m., four minutes after the deadline set by the EJA. The bomb appears to have been located in the main building in the centre of the house. Flames are now visible at most of the windows.'

The chopper cam picture returned, showing flames spreading across the roof. Suzie continued: 'The fire brigade is standing by but I understand they won't move in until police are satisfied that no other detonations are likely.'

'They're hardly likely to need any more are they,' Phil said as he closed the lid of his briefcase. He picked up his plate and continued to eat his way through a mound of fried rice. With his eyes fixed on the screen, he failed to notice that a ball of rice fell into his lap and lodged in the buckle of his belt.

'Do you mind if I turn it off?' Roland asked.

'Sure. I've seen all I need to.'

Roland crossed to the set and switched it off. 'You've got an incredible sense of timing. How did you know it would happen then?'

Phil shrugged. 'It just seemed like the perfect moment.'

'Why did they do it? I just don't understand.'

'They're cranking up the pressure. Everyone in Australia will see that tonight. Every channel is showing it now, and they'll be replaying it every hour tonight and all day tomorrow.'

'Where's this all going to end? Someone is bound to get hurt.'

'I hope not. So far, all they've done is destroy property. If they wanted to hurt anyone, they wouldn't have blown up an empty house.'

'So, you're telling me they are decent people?'

'From where I sit, they just look like frustrated idealists. And I've got some sympathy for them. Don't you, just a bit?'

'Not with their methods, no. But if they have the evidence they say they have, and the government hasn't taken action against that company, then I suppose I can see their point.'

'The EJA have had an effect already. If you and I are discussing the issue, and agree that someone should take action, they're on the way to achieving their goal.'

Phil scraped his plate and put it down on the table. 'It's time I was going. I just dropped in to let you know I've almost cleared up the other projects I've got on at the moment. I have a few things to finish off tonight, then I should be able to spend more time on things at Channel 5. I thought you'd like to know that. It takes the pressure off you. I'm going to be working on Dalton myself from now on.'

He picked up his briefcase again and stood up. 'That should leave you free to sort things out with the incomparable Ms Denning.'

26

With B.B. away in Sydney, Roland hoped his absence from Channel 5 would pass without comment. But when he arrived at the office next morning a handwritten note was waiting on his desk. He recognised Dalton's flamboyant, fountain-penned script and spent half an hour avoiding it.

He skimmed first through the newspaper headlines and worked through the easy clues in the crossword, before returning to the note. It read:

> *Roland,*
> *Where the hell were you yesterday! I pay you to be here when I need you. Check in with me when you arrive.*
> *Dalton*

He decided this was serious enough to go next door right away. He found Dalton sitting in front of the window in the lotus position. His eyes were open and, when he noticed Roland, he smiled a greeting.

'Sit down, Roly, mate,' he said in a passable Australian accent. He spoiled the effect by adding, 'I'll be with you momentarily.'

Roland sat on the sofa and watched the Channel 5 live feed.

Lauren D'Aussey was hosting a telemarketing segment of *Morning Lite.* The volume was turned down but Dalton's measured breathing, the only other sound in the room, was low enough that it didn't interfere with the discussion on screen. Lauren was standing at a display counter in conversation with a middle-aged man in a plaid sports coat. He was demonstrating a stainless-steel pocket-sized digitally-calibrated electric orange peeler.

'Lauren, this marvellous device actually senses the thickness of the skin and adjusts the stainless-steel cutting blade so that the peel alone is removed. You can use it on grapefruits and other citrus fruits too.'

'That looks really useful, Brian.' She was doing a very competent job of looking interested in what he had to offer. 'What else do you have for us today?'

'I think we've seen enough of that, Roland,' Dalton said as he stood and stretched his body. 'Hit the kill switch.'

Roland picked up the remote and aimed it at the monitor. The image of Brian extracting something called the *Portable Coffee Pal* from his jacket pocket faded to black.

'Lauren is a natural in that job,' Dalton said. He ambled over to the coffee machine and poured coffee for Roland and himself. 'She made the right career move at the right time. Sir Adrian has decided to expand into telemarketing. We're going to scale up *Morning Lite* to a whole morning programme selling Porter Vault products on air. This is a win for everyone.'

Roland gave a neutral nod. He wondered how there could possibly be a market for the huge inventory of Charles-and-Di bar mirrors and fake diver's watches he happened to know were sitting in the Porter Vault warehouses.

Dalton sipped his coffee and gave a satisfied sigh. 'I'm glad you came by. Beeb's out of town on the McDarrow Project and I've just launched a nuclear strike at the news staff. I'm low on friends today.'

Roland was flattered that he qualified as a friend, even if it was one from the reserve benches. 'I thought the news team did a pretty good job last night.'

'Last night was great. I've reviewed the coverage from the other channels and we were way out in front. But in television you're only as good as your next broadcast and we missed the boat on Lloyd Balchin.'

'What's happened with Balchin?'

'He just agreed to an exclusive interview tonight with the ABC's *7.30 Report*. He says the content will have an impact on his daughter's release. We don't know what it's about and he isn't talking to anyone else.' Dalton paused for another sip of his coffee. 'Which means we're losing whatever lead we had. We need something big to get the momentum going again. Any ideas?'

Roland shrugged. Today, he couldn't care less about the Balchin story.

Unfazed, Dalton launched straight into his next idea. 'Phil came by this morning with a dynamite plan. He thinks we should offer the EJA $50,000 in return for exclusive first use of Channel 5 over the next year.'

Roland almost spilled his coffee. 'He thinks we should give $50,000 to a terrorist organisation?'

'When you put it like that it does sound a little unorthodox. But I've been working it through all morning and I can't see any negatives.'

'How about this for a negative. It's crazy.'

'Just listen to the details first. We don't actually give the money to the EJA. Instead we make a string of donations to legitimate environmental causes. Up front. We can do it as a publicity stunt for Suzanne and *The Green Scene*. That legitimises us in the eyes of the green public and with our viewers. And the beauty is we get the EJA to come to us. I really like Phil's thinking on this. And I love that he's comfortable sharing his ideas with me at last. What's your reading on it?'

Roland thought that Dalton should be instantly suspicious of anything Phil thought was a good idea. He decided to stay neutral. 'I suppose it's possible it might work, but isn't it risking a lot of money to find out?'

'This is television, Roly. There are two things you need to get used to. One is taking risks, and the other is spending money.'

'Some people might think it a little unethical,' Roland added gently.

'Unethical? How many different ways do I have to say this to you. We are talking about television news – ethics has nothing to do with it. We're in the business of being first to a story and getting it exclusive if we can. Everyone engages in a little chequebook journalism when they have to. We're just pushing the boundaries of that.'

Roland disagreed, but said nothing. Dalton read his thoughts immediately. 'Relax, Roly. I like that you're so refreshingly negative around me. It makes me work harder to think my ideas through. Stick around where I can get to you when I need you.'

Dalton crossed to his desk and began to search in the drawers. Thinking the discussion was over, Roland got up to go. Dalton noticed and stopped him. 'Roly, are you interested in classical music?'

'Yes, very.'

'I have a ticket here for the concert at the Cultural Centre tonight. Can you use it?'

'Definitely.'

'Good. It's a free one. Beeb cooked this up as another way of rehabilitating McDarrow's image. Then she decided to take him down to Sydney instead. I shouldn't tell you, but she's secretly impressed with your work on Malcolm.'

'My work?'

'The vodka in his drink. It was a risky step, but it paid off for us spectacularly. So, well done.'

Roland's mouth fell open. 'You think I deliberately set out to get him arrested?'

'Come on. This is me you're talking to and we're behind a closed door. It was common knowledge the police would have a booze bus at the roundabout that night. That's why we arranged taxis for everyone.'

They stared at each other while Roland decided how to respond. A further denial would have no effect. But a full-on confession might just make Dalton see how ridiculous his thinking was. He spread his hands and smiled. 'You have me cold, I guess. It was all part of my master plan. Get just the right amount of booze in him and point him at the police. It was surprisingly easy in the end.'

'I knew it. I knew it. That's what I like about you, Roly. You're so easy to underestimate. But underneath that passive exterior, you're just as calculating as the rest of us. You might be interested to know that Malcolm will be working with the Brisbane City Council on a tree planting scheme when he gets back. It's part of the deal I cut with City Hall. The Lord Mayor also agreed to a tree planting ceremony in the same hole you buried the gold in. I hope you put it somewhere where that can be done.'

'I did, actually.'

'I've got a second ticket for tonight if you'd like it. We really should fill the seat if we can.'

'I don't think I can use the other ticket.'

Dalton raised his eyebrows. 'From what I read and hear, you're supposed to have someone to give that other ticket to.'

'Dalton, I thought you would know better than to believe what you read in print. If you'd rather give both tickets away together, I don't mind standing aside.'

'No, take yours. I'll find someone else from the station to take the other one. Lisa Demchek, maybe. We need to start building her image with the public a little. Just one thing, though. Take my mobile phone again tonight. I might need to contact you during the evening.'

As he took the phone, Roland noticed a collection of toys in a plastic crate behind Dalton's desk. Dalton followed his gaze and smiled. 'Maybe there is someone you can take to the concert, after all.' He reached down and picked a doll out of the box. It had a blonde bob and was dressed in a miniature copy of a charcoal *Newscenter5* uniform. The doll's features vaguely resembled Suzie's.

'It's the new Suzanne Denning Doll,' he said as he passed it to Roland. He reached into the box again and spread the rest of the toys on top of his desk. 'This is the David Burton Doll. There's a Malcolm McDarrow somewhere in there too. And a radio-controlled anchor buggy.' Chuckling, he added, 'It actually works better than the real thing. We'll have news cars and Channel 5 choppers too when the range is complete. It's all part of our commitment to young viewers. They own the dial in the run-up to 6 p.m. We're going to make sure they keep their whole family tuned to *Newscenter5*.'

'I'm impressed,' Roland said genuinely. 'Is there anything you leave to chance?'

'No one can think of everything, Roland. The trick is in knowing when to try to control a situation and when to just go with the flow. It's a tough call, but that's why Beeb and I cost a lot of money.'

As he watched Roland inspect the miniature Suzie, Dalton said, 'Every joint can be manipulated. You can make her do anything you like. Keep it, Roly. I've got plenty more samples in the box.'

Roland happily accepted the gift. From the doorway, he made

her wave goodbye. Dalton waved back with a grin. 'One more thing. Make sure you're here by 8.30 tomorrow morning. And don't take any more days off without my say-so. I'm paying you to do a full day's work, not goof off at home. When Beeb gets back from Sydney, the three of us need to take some time out and talk about our future together.'

Back in his own office, Roland sat the Suzanne Denning doll on his desk. They finished reading the paper together, while he kept himself on standby in case Dalton needed him to be refreshingly negative again. Afterwards, the Suzie doll showed a keen interest in the administration of the court of Charlemagne and suggested they read a chapter on it together.

The real Suzie rang at lunchtime and an embarrassed Roland dropped the doll, which had been doing a headstand on the edge of the desk, into his daypack.

'Roly, I've rung to apologise. I really shouldn't have told you to fuck off.'

It was such a qualified statement that he decided she would have to go a lot further. He said nothing, and eventually she was forced to fill the silence. 'I've been thinking a lot since Saturday. And I think I owe you another apology. I can see how you might feel you were used, but I didn't set out to do it deliberately. Not consciously, anyway. I really want you to believe that.'

'Suzie, straight after we talked, you went ahead and gave another interview to the *Sunday Mail*.'

'You're wrong. The interview happened last Friday, the morning after the EJA interview. I was on a high and got completely carried away. You know what it was like the next day.'

'Oh, I see.' He realised he had misjudged her. And that he had wanted her to be in the wrong. 'I suppose I look a little paranoid to you.'

'Frankly, yes. Look, do you think you can forgive me just enough so that we're back on talking terms again? I promise never ever to mention your name in any future interviews. I'm crossing my heart as we speak.'

'All right. We start again, but only if there's no more publicity.'

'That sounds fair.'

'Can we meet after work? I haven't seen you since Friday, if you don't count watching you on television, or making you do handstands on the edge of my desk.'

'Handstands?'

'I think that's something I'll have to show you when we meet.'

'Tonight is out. I have to be here at 7.30 when Lloyd Balchin gives his interview to the ABC.'

He had been hoping he could still get Dalton's other ticket to the concert. He realised that given the choice between the two events, he would always pick one and she would always pick the other. 'Don't you want to switch off from all this, sometimes?'

'This is my job, Roly. I love it. Even the parts I hate, I love to hate. News gathering is part disease and part addiction.'

'So what do you do to relax?'

'I haven't really had a lot of time for that lately, have I?'

'Don't you play any sport, belong to any clubs or have any hobbies?'

'What are you, my GP or something? I thought we had a deal about not trying to change each other.'

'I don't mean to sound critical. I just wondered what you do after a hard day at the office.'

'It depends. I'm a bit of a couch potato. I might watch a movie or a documentary or try to clear something from my videotape library. Then late at night, I might watch CNN. This is turning you off, I suppose.'

'No,' he replied, unconvincingly. 'It's just not something I can share with you.'

'I don't expect you to. Does that mean you won't be staying

on to watch the Balchin interview with me?'

'I'm going out tonight and I was hoping you'd come with me.'

'Sorry, Roly. We can make it tomorrow if you like. I'll call you later.'

27

Late in the afternoon, Roland cycled along the riverside bikeway into the city and crossed the Victoria Bridge to the South Bank. On one of the many backward glances he had taken to making in recent days, he thought he recognised Cleary again. The detective was on a bicycle this time and struggling to keep up.

With plenty of time to fill before the concert, Roland cycled over to the State Library. He left his daypack and mobile phone in a basement locker and browsed through the periodicals display. He was joined at the racks by the moustached detective, and they enjoyed a game of pretending not to recognise each other.

At six o'clock he left the library and crossed the road to the Performing Arts Complex. He bought a meal from the cafe and ate outdoors near the fountain. Upstairs at one of the bars, he drank a beer and watched the crowd gather for the evening performance. When the concert hall's doors opened, he entered the auditorium and found his seat, which was only five rows from the stage. It was a football field closer than the B reserve he usually sat in.

The doors closed at 7.30 and the orchestra assembled on stage. The seat next to Roland was still empty and he concluded that Dalton had been unable to find a volunteer for the other ticket. The lights dimmed and the conductor, a lanky German with a shock of white hair, ambled across the stage. He acknowledged the applause, then led the orchestra through a pacy rendition of Mendelssohn's Hebrides Overture.

After the ritual cycle of applause that followed, latecomers were allowed into the auditorium. Roland turned as someone excused their way along his row and was surprised to see Suzie coming his way. She smiled as she took her seat and said, 'So this is what you do for fun.'

'One of the many things. I didn't expect to be sharing it with you.'

'Dalton ordered me to come. I don't suppose you had anything to do with that.'

'Nothing, I promise. But I'm glad you're here.'

'Buried deep in the fine print of my contract, it says I have to attend events like this as and when required. I really should have read all the way to the end of the document before signing it.'

The conductor reappeared on the stage to more applause. As he took his place in front of the orchestra, Suzie added, 'Apparently we sponsor this lot.'

'Shshsh,' two people behind her hissed.

Roland prayed that she would. He was relieved when the evening's star attraction, a young Chinese violinist, made it all the way to centre stage without comment. Suzie's constant fidgeting through the Beethoven Violin Concerto couldn't sour his mood. He loved having the real Suzanne Denning, warts and all, beside him again.

Over a glass of wine at the interval she apologised. 'Sorry, but these things make me really restless. I find it hard to sit still for long periods unless there's a camera pointing at me.'

They were in the foyer and he had to share her with a stream of concertgoers who wanted to say hello and tell her how much they liked her work. She seemed to enjoy it, and was just modest enough to make herself even more popular. One elderly fan, who reminded Roland of Mrs Campbell, grasped Suzie by the forearm and said, 'I just wanted to tell you how much I like the way you read the news. Much better than that other one, what's her name? A cool customer, that one. You're a perfect match for the handsome Mr Burton. And I like what you've done to your hair. It was always hanging in your face before.'

'At least she got the compliments in the right order,' Suzie said as the satisfied fan returned to her companion. 'I read the news well, and I'm decorative too.'

Roland began to find the attention wearing. He was relieved when Suzie spent the remainder of the interval in the queue for the Ladies. As they returned to the concert hall, he said, 'I keep expecting you to get a pocket television out to see what Lloyd Balchin is saying.'

Suzie laughed. 'I have been known to go several hours at a time without catching a bulletin, provided I can get myself in front of a television set soon after. Anyway, the video player at home is set to record.'

As they returned to their seats, an irate concertgoer in a neighbouring seat scowled at Roland. He said, 'I think you should know there was a ringing sound coming from your bag while you were gone. This is very annoying. Very. I hope it won't happen during the performance.'

Roland apologised and reached inside his bag for the phone. He switched it off and dropped it back into the bag. It seemed to mollify his neighbour who turned to the woman beside him and whispered something derogatory about yuppies. Embarrassed, Roland wanted to deny that he was or ever had been a yuppy, but the lights dimmed and he had to let the opportunity go.

The Radetzky March after the break was lively enough to

keep anyone awake, but afterwards came a Mahler symphony and Suzie began to struggle. Her head swayed as she fought to stay awake. Finally she settled on Roland's shoulder and closed her eyes. She revived temporarily in the middle of the performance but soon settled back on his shoulder again and stayed there to the end.

In the final minutes of the performance, a photographer crept down the aisle looking for the best angle to capture the conductor's final bow. He spotted Suzie in the audience and took a few shots of her asleep on Roland's shoulder. Satisfied, he turned his lens on the conductor who was now shaking hands with the leader of the orchestra.

The applause woke Suzie. She jumped out of her seat before properly tuning in to her surroundings and unintentionally led a standing ovation. When she realised what she had done, she turned to Roland and laughed. He put his arm around her and they strolled out of the concert hall. In the foyer, a member of staff approached and told Suzie she was expected to meet the orchestra at a post-performance supper. They followed the woman to a reception room where the same photographer inserted Suzie into a group shot of the conductor and principal players.

Before she could intervene, he had also coaxed Roland into the group. An hour later, when they were able to leave, Suzie said, 'It looks like I've broken my promise to you already. I had no idea that was going to happen.'

'It wasn't your fault. Besides, I enjoyed every minute of it. I haven't met an orchestra before let alone had my picture taken with an eminent conductor.'

'Come on. I'll give you a lift home.'

With the wheels off, his bike just managed to fit into the back of the Mazda. They screamed out of the underground car park and jumped the queue to the exit.

As they crossed the bridge into the city, Suzie said, 'I've just got to make one call.'

With one hand on the wheel, she speed-dialled the newsroom and asked for a rundown on the Balchin interview. She listened in silence, then said, 'Yes. He's with me now.' She turned to Roland. 'Kevin Hardy has a message for you from Dalton. He's been trying to get in touch with you since you left work.'

Apprehensive, Roland took the phone. 'Hello?'

The voice of the newsroom's Chief of Staff boomed in Roland's ear. 'Kendall, Kev Hardy here. I've been instructed to tell you that you're in Deep DooDoo with Dalton, whatever that is. He said something about kicking ass, so it definitely can't be good. He's been trying to call you since late afternoon. Don't you have the phone with you?'

'It's been in my bag the whole time,' Roland replied, an answer that was technically correct. Warming to the white lie, he added, 'I haven't heard it ring.'

'Must be a problem with reception. Anyway, the message is to call him immediately. He said it's crucial that you talk to him before you go home. Make any sense to you?'

'None whatsoever. But I'm getting used to that.'

'We all are, believe me. By the way, my children phoned me earlier about tonight's clue for the treasure hunt. They said it's nothing like your previous ones. Can you tell me what it means? They're family, so they can't enter the contest anyway.'

'I'll come over to your office in the morning and explain the whole thing.' He put the phone back into Suzie's bag and used his own to call Dalton.

'Where the hell were you, Roland?' Dalton asked. 'In the fucking can all night?'

'Sorry, Dalton. There must have been a reception problem.'

'Where are you now?'

'In Suzie's car. She's driving me home.'

'Well, turn around and come over to my apartment first. There's something you need to know.'

Suzie made an illegal U-turn on Coronation Drive and headed back to the city. On the way, she gave Roland a summary of the Balchin interview. 'Balchin just agreed to make the donations to green charities. He will also redesign his current residential land holdings to provide a greener environment and employ a team of advisers on an experimental housing development. He stopped short of renouncing his previous views on development, but he's turned a corner.'

'He's come a long way for a man who called them socialists a few days ago.'

'Last night's events at Pullenvale must have done the trick. He did call them criminals again, but his line was much softer than before.'

'Is it enough to free Virginia?'

'I wish I knew. I suppose it depends on how much we can trust the EJA.'

'They can't hold her forever. What else could they want that he hasn't just offered?'

'Good question.'

Dalton's apartment was on the twelfth floor of a South Bank apartment block. He buzzed them through the security door and was waiting when they stepped out of the lift. He took them into the lounge, which looked downriver towards the floodlit cliffs of Kangaroo Point. When they had all admired the view, Dalton insisted on making a fresh pot of green tea for them.

'Have you heard about Lloyd Balchin's offer?' he asked as he returned with the tea.

'Yes,' Suzie replied. 'I called the station after the concert and spoke to Kev.'

'Enjoy the show by the way?'

'The performance was excellent,' Roland said. 'And the seats were the best in the house.'

'I can't corroborate that entirely,' Suzie added a little sheepishly. 'I slept through most of the Mahler.'

'I've got to say, he does that to me too. The important thing is you were there flying the flag for Channel 5. I made sure you'll be in the paper tomorrow with the conductor. Now back to the EJA. I decided to go with Phil's concept for an exclusive offer to them. Which means we try for another meeting.'

Roland had a feeling about what was coming next. He wasn't surprised when Dalton said, 'You'll be the link-man again, Roland. They've dealt with you and they trust you.'

'Wait a minute. I don't want any more to do with this. For one thing, I don't like what they're doing. And I don't agree with us paying money for the story.'

'We're not paying them. We're sponsoring recognised environmental groups. You can't have a problem with that. Channel 5 is doing a legitimate community service here. Everybody wins from a thing like this.'

Roland turned to Suzie. 'What do you think?'

'The more I think about it, the more I agree with Dalton. The EJA gain nothing themselves. Channel 5 gives money to green groups. And Channel 5 wins on two fronts: we get the stories before the others, and *The Green Scene* gets the credit for making the donations.'

'How much money have you decided to offer?' Roland asked Dalton.

'$50,000 for an agreement over one year. Come on Roland – what do you say? All you have to do is meet them one more time, give them the details and then cut out. All other contact can go through someone else. You can't let us down.'

Roland nodded reluctantly. Dalton had worn him down. 'Okay, but this is absolutely my last contact with them. After this

I go back to looking after the treasure hunt and doing a bit of background research for *The Green Scene*. Agreed?'

'Absolutely. Now you'd better get back home. I don't want you to be out too late.'

'I never knew you cared so much.'

'Oh, you don't get it. I've set up the contact for your house at midnight tonight.'

'Tonight?'

'When I couldn't get in touch with you earlier, I changed your clue for today and replaced it with a coded message to the EJA. It's quite similar to the one you used to contact them before, so I'm hoping it will work. If they don't respond tonight, then we do the same thing tomorrow and so on until they do. Any questions?'

'What if they want to bargain?'

'They can have whatever they like so long as it doesn't cost us any more and there is no proof of a connection between us. Anything you're worried about, get back to me on it. I'll be waiting by the phone. Okay?'

'Let's get going then, Roly,' Suzie said, rising off the sofa. She put her teacup down next to a picture of Dalton and B.B. cutting their wedding cake.

28

The house seemed peaceful when Suzie turned the Mazda into the driveway. But, after the recent experience with Fraser, Roland knew that appearances could sometimes be deceptive. Cautiously, he climbed the steps onto the verandah and opened the front door. He flicked on the light and scanned along the hall. Everything looked normal, but he wasn't prepared to relax until they had split up and checked every room.

'There's no guarantee anything will happen tonight,' he said as they sat down to wait. 'It took days before they contacted me in the park.'

'I don't mind,' Suzie replied with a smile. 'I've had my sleep already tonight, remember?'

'Dalton didn't say anything about you staying.'

'He didn't tell me not to either. He knew I would.'

'To be honest, I'm glad of the company. This clandestine stuff is getting on my nerves. I half-expected Fraser to jump out of the hall cupboard when we came in.'

'Forget about him. He'll be tucked up in bed at my place rereading his favourite Ian Fleming.'

The mention of her stepfather brought Roland back to the question that had been haunting him for days. 'Suzie, what kind of car does Fraser drive?'

'His hire car? I don't know. He parks it in the street. Never get trapped in a garage, he keeps saying. A Ford, I think.'

Roland relaxed. It wasn't the car that had knocked him down.

'He's funny about cars,' she continued. 'Last Christmas, when he picked me up at the airport in Sydney, I had to put my case in the back seat, because there was a concrete slab in the boot. I mean a solid lump of concrete. He said it was an old KGB trick for fast getaways. The extra weight at the back increases the traction on the rear wheels. Can you see why I'm telling you not to worry about him?'

Roland laughed and finally accepted that Fraser could be removed from the list of suspects. To pass the time, Suzie entertained him with more Fraser stories. 'The other strange thing he does is change his hire car every few days. I've known him to go through three or four in just one visit. God knows what Hertz think of him.'

'You mean, he's changed cars on this visit?'

'Last week it was a Commodore.'

'What colour?'

She shrugged. 'I only remember him saying he'd taken the Commodore back. Why do you want to know?'

'I was knocked down by a current model Commodore.'

'Roland, don't be ridiculous.' She stood and walked across the room. In the doorway she turned and said, 'Apart from anything else, there are thousands of new Commodores in Brisbane. He might have a screw loose but he doesn't go around knocking people off their bikes.'

'I know I should agree with you. But I just can't get the thought out of my head. It takes time to get over something like that, and I know it was deliberate. If you'd seen the way it swerved towards me.'

'I really don't think blaming Fraser is the answer.'

He nodded, and told himself to let it go. Midnight came and went with no visitors arriving. About 12.30, he decided they were wasting their time. 'Let's call this off for tonight.'

'You're right. I'll ring Dalton.'

She was standing over the phone about to dial Dalton's number when they heard footsteps on the back stairs. A few seconds later a camouflage-geared figure slipped into the house and walked along the hall to the lounge. He held a finger up to the mouth hole in his ski-mask, then lifted a walkie-talkie. He pressed the transmit button and said, 'Okay, I'm in. Squawk me in three minutes.'

Roland recognised him as the contact man from previous meetings. He watched him walk through the house, checking all the rooms. When he returned to the lounge, he sat on a chair where he could look along the hall to both the front and back verandahs. To Roland, he said, 'What's she doing here?'

Suzie objected to being spoken about in the third person. She coldly replied, 'I'm part of the deal we're offering.'

'What deal?'

'Channel 5 wants to be used exclusively for communiques you release. We want you to deal with us first. We'll guarantee to broadcast the material and then make it available to other media outlets.'

The contact man leaned back in the chair and thought for a moment. 'You've got about one minute left before I walk out the door. Give me the details.'

Suzie hesitated and Roland guessed she was reluctant to talk about the money. He took over. 'Channel 5 is prepared to donate up to $50,000 to any green organisations you nominate. In return, you deal exclusively with us for a period of one year.'

As the contact man considered this, his walkie-talkie crackled. He lifted it to his lips and said, 'What's the problem?'

A woman's voice replied, 'We've got movement at the

window of the house next door. One person. Could be nothing.'

'I'm on my way out.'

'It's only Mrs Campbell,' Roland said. 'She doesn't sleep much and probably heard our voices.'

The EJA man got out of his chair. 'You'll get your answer in the next few hours. If we agree, you must donate tomorrow. No delays. Your first communique will be our answer on Balchin's offer of payment. I've got to go.'

'Wait a minute,' Suzie said. 'I want to do another interview soon. Is that possible?'

'Yes, but I can't confirm that yet. I have to go.'

Roland watched him disappear down the stairs, then followed Suzie as she hurried down the hallway. On the back verandah, he caught her hand. 'Let him go, Suzie.'

They peered across the back yard and saw the dark figure disappear over the fence into the garden beyond. Then, at Mrs Campbell's house, they heard a flyscreen door bang and the sound of feet pounding down the front stairs.

'Mrs C. hasn't run like that for decades,' Roland said, turning along the hall again.

From the front verandah, they saw a figure getting into a car about 50 metres down the road. The engine started and the tyres squealed as it sped away and disappeared around the corner.

Roland posed the obvious question. 'So who was that?'

'I'm not sure.' She returned to the lounge where she picked up the phone and dialled a number. After a few seconds, she hung up.

'Who were you calling?' he asked.

She chewed on a fingernail before answering. 'I was just checking in at home.'

'Afraid Fraser would object to you being out late again?'

'I was hoping he would pick up the phone. But I just got the answering machine. Maybe he's asleep already.'

Roland realised what was worrying her. 'You think it was him next door, don't you?'

'I can't be sure. But he was the same build, and the way he ran reminded me of him a little. Now you've got me paranoid about him too.'

'If it was him, what was he doing there?'

'It probably wasn't him,' she replied, unconvincingly. 'And if it was, he's just playing one of his little games. He does things like this all the time, as though he's acting out some scene in his latest book. There's no point in asking him why. He denies all of it.'

A toilet flushed next door, and Roland's thoughts turned to Mrs Campbell. He leaned over the side railing of the verandah and scanned along the house next door. He saw her silhouette at the kitchen window and heard the sound of a kettle being filled.

'Mrs C.,' he called, gently. 'It's Roland. Are you all right?'

'I'm fine,' she answered unsteadily. 'I think someone was in my house. It would happen in one of the few moments when I had my eyes shut.'

'Should I come over?'

'Goodness me, no. I've called the police and they'll be here soon. I expect they'd like a cup of tea, being on the go all night. You go back to sleep, Roland. I'm fine.'

When he returned to the lounge, Suzie was on the phone. 'Yes. They were just here ... We don't know yet. They're calling us back ... Okay. Bye.' She hung up and turned to Roland. 'That was Dalton. He wanted to know what was going on. We're to call him when we hear from them.'

Roland sat down in a chair near the telephone. He was determined to be first to it next time. He remained on the edge of his seat for another half-hour, and sprang up when it rang again. 'Kendall here.'

Suzie put her arm round his shoulder and pressed her ear close to his. He could barely hear the EJA man say, 'You've got a deal. You choose your own organisations but make the donations today. Our next contact is through you alone. Get an answering machine installed at home. If you need to contact us, broadcast a quiz question during *The Green Scene*. The question should be: Is the hole in the ozone layer over the Arctic or the Antarctic? Give the answer the Arctic, then correct it a minute later. Channel 5 will receive a video communique today containing our response to Balchin's offer. It'll be positive.'

The EJA contact hung up and Roland replaced the receiver. 'Did you hear all that?' he asked, thinking she had probably heard it better than him.

She nodded and picked up the phone. 'I'll give Dalton the good news.'

While she did this, Roland walked out onto the front verandah. When she joined him a few minutes later, he asked, 'Suzie, what do you think about this whole thing? Ethically, I mean.'

She looked doubtful for the first time. 'I think it's borderline okay. Just on the right side of the line.'

'You don't think we're going too far?'

'Roly, in the news business, you spend a surprising amount of your time dealing with pretty shady people. It comes with the job. Maybe we should stop worrying and enjoy the scoop.' She checked her watch. 'I'd better go. It's pretty late.'

He walked to the car with her to collect his bike. As he reattached the wheels, a police car stopped at the kerb next door. Two officers got out and walked up the path to Mrs Campbell's house. Roland and Suzie looked at them and then at each other and decided to wait for an update.

After a few minutes, one of the officers returned to the car. Roland called out, 'Is Mrs Campbell all right?'

'She's good,' the officer said, 'but she's convinced that

someone was in her house earlier. Did you hear anything outside maybe 30 minutes ago?'

Roland turned to Suzie. She stared back at him, then turned to the policeman and said, 'Well, we did hear the flyscreen door open, and someone go down the front steps. You mean that wasn't Mrs C.?'

'She doesn't sleep very much at all,' Roland added, committed by Suzie to the deception. 'She's up and about at all hours, making cups of tea, going to the bathroom, one after the other usually. Is she all right? Should I go in and sit with her for a while?'

'If you ask me, she seems to be enjoying the fuss,' the officer replied. 'She's got this huge old cricket bat beside her in the kitchen. I think she hopes whoever it was will come back. My partner's staying with her for a while, till I've had a look around the back garden. Mrs Campbell says she heard something out there too. Maybe you could pop in and see her in the morning, though. Just to make sure she's okay.'

The policeman disappeared behind the house and Suzie went home, leaving Roland alone with his bike. He took it upstairs and left it in the spare room. Then he locked the doors and windows and went to bed, hoping against the odds that he might get a few hours' rest.

29

An open briefcase on Beeb's desk announced her return from Sydney. Three telephone messages for Roland in her handwriting confirmed it. The first was from Phil. Roland had just picked up the phone to return the call when he walked into the room.

'Gidday Roly.' He was buoyant, more upbeat than Roland had seen him in weeks. 'I'd like your take on what Dalton's up to with this EJA thing.'

'You should know. He's doing exactly what you suggested.'

'But what's he really up to? What's his game?'

'He's doing the same thing as always – trying to get better ratings for Channel 5.'

'Suzie told me about last night. The meeting, I mean. She said there was someone outside who scared the EJA contact away. Any idea who it was?'

Roland shook his head. 'We saw someone get into a car down the road, but couldn't identify them at that distance.'

Phil seemed to have what he was looking for. 'I've got to go. Dad wants a report on all of this. I think the $50,000 bribe to the EJA could be Dalton's undoing.'

'Aren't you getting a little carried away? You were the one

who suggested it in the first place.'

'But I don't make the decisions any more. Dalton does. And Dad doesn't like this particular one.' At the door, he added, 'Have you seen today's *Courier Mail*?'

'Not yet.'

He chuckled. 'You should take a look.'

This left Roland curious enough to search one out. He knew he would find one in the newsroom, and hoped he would also see Suzie, who had left the second phone message. She was standing at her desk, sharing a joke with Lisa Demchek. In front of them was a copy of the *Courier Mail* open at its Diary section.

'Roly,' Suzie said, as Lisa returned to her own desk, 'you should take a look at this.'

At the top of the page was a photograph of Roland and Suzanne. They were seated in the concert hall, with Suzie asleep on his shoulder. The headline over the picture was: *Newscenter5's live eye unit catches 40 winks at concert.* The caption under the photo read:

> *After a long day in the field, newshound Suzanne Denning gets some shut-eye on the shoulder of Channel 5 co-worker Roland Knedall. Rumours on the media mountain link the two romantically, and he certainly played a very supportive role during last night's performance by the Queensland Symphony Orchestra (review page 26).*

Further down the page was a picture of Suzie, champagne glass in hand, standing with the conductor and the leader of the orchestra. It was captioned:

> *After recharging her batteries during the performance, Suzanne Denning slips effortlessly into party mode with the orchestra.*

Roland couldn't help laughing. When it went on a little too long, Suzie demanded half-seriously, 'What's so funny? That sort of thing could ruin my credibility.'

'At least they got your name right. This is my one chance for fame and people think I'm a Knedall.'

Lowering her voice, she said, 'You do know I had nothing to do with the photographer, don't you?'

'Honestly, I don't have a problem with it. After all, I'm not the one who was asleep.'

She ignored this and picked up an unmarked videotape. 'A present from the EJA. It was inside an envelope sitting at the entrance to the studio driveway.'

'When did it arrive?'

'We don't know exactly. No one noticed it until 8.30 this morning.'

'Have you watched it?'

She nodded. 'There are two interesting things. Number one is that they've accepted Balchin's offer. His daughter will be released within 24 hours of Balchin donating the money to major environmental organisations. The other thing is that they say they've chosen Channel 5 as their media release conduit. They say they're doing it because *The Green Scene* demonstrates our commitment to the environment.'

'When will this be released?'

'In a special edition at 11 a.m. I have to go, Roly. There's a lot to do before the bulletin.'

Roland's third phone message was from Dalton. When he arrived at the American's office, the door was, for once, closed. He knocked and waited outside until Dalton called, 'Yo! I'm in. Come on through.'

Dalton was against the wall behind the door, hanging by the ankles from a tubular steel frame. 'Gidday Roland,' he said. 'I just had this installed. What do you think?'

Roland had thought there was nothing Dalton could do to surprise him any more. But this was the limit. He collapsed onto the nearest sofa and buried his face in his hands.

Dalton seemed not to notice. 'It's just so relaxing. I had one in the States and used it every day.' He looked at his watch and added, 'I'll be down in a moment. Want to try it?'

'I don't think so.'

'Come on, you'll love it.'

'No, really.'

Dalton reached up to grip the bar. 'Roly, I thought you were finally loosening up a little. But you're going all cautious again.'

'Believe me, watching you enjoy it is more than enough fun for me.'

Dalton unhooked his ankles from the frame and lowered himself gently to the floor. 'I feel like a new man. Beeb found it for me in Sydney.'

He crossed to his desk, picked up a scarlet tie, which was a close match for the colour of his face, and slipped the loop over his head. 'One of the little surprises she was working on down there.'

'I thought she'd be gone all week,' Roland said, curious about her sudden return.

'Something came up and we had to change the plan. Do you know the secret of our success?'

Once, Roland might have just shrugged his shoulders. Now he felt he had seen enough to hazard a guess. 'Keeping everyone else completely in the dark, and stunning them with off-the-wall surprises.'

'That's not a bad effort. And it's partly true. The real answer is ideas and motion. Beeb and I are full of amazing ideas and we know how to make them happen. We also know how to pace ourselves so that the next challenge is under way before the last has come to an end. Beeb just pulled that off again down in Sydney.'

He paused and looked intently at Roland. 'We'd like you to be part of it, Roland. But the question is, are you ready to take it on?'

Roland considered asking exactly what Dalton was talking about, but decided it wasn't the right moment. Staying deliberately vague, he replied, 'As long as it has nothing to do with the EJA, I could easily be tempted to say yes.' Changing the subject, he asked, 'Have you heard about the tape?'

'Yup. Looks like they're keeping their side of the bargain. At midday I'll be keeping ours. Reps from the green groups are coming here to receive their cheques. You'll be part of it too. A little reward for your role in making it happen. We're making up some three-foot-long cheques for an on-air presentation ceremony. All you've got to do is hand me the right cheque at the right moment. Sounds easy, huh?'

'It sounds like fun,' Roland replied, with heavy sarcasm. In truth his feelings were mixed. He felt he deserved to play at least a small part in the process, but wasn't sure about an on-air appearance.

'Beeb said you'd run for cover, but I told her I knew you better.'

Roland wanted her to be wrong so much that he felt a surge of enthusiasm. 'As usual, she's completely misjudged me. I'm really looking forward to it.'

'Glad to hear it. Now, I'm going to give you some news you'll like even better. After the presentation, I want you to go home and stay there for the next couple of days. If Balchin makes his payments too, his daughter will be free in the next 48 hours. The EJA are sure to release another communique and I want you at home in case they try to make contact. Go home and stay there. Okay?'

'Now that sounds like the kind of order I'm willing to obey

without question.'

'And keep my mobile phone with you at all times. Come back and see me at 11.30 and we'll go through the presentation script together.'

Roland was home in time for the one o'clock news. He watched himself, looking paler and more uncertain than he remembered, as he walked on set with three oversized cardboard cheques. He had no memory of stumbling slightly on a square of loose green carpet the floor crew had hastily laid on the studio floor. The slip was recorded forever along with Dalton's toothy chuckle as Roland jabbed him in the stomach with a cardboard cheque.

He knew Gwen would be on the phone instantly if she saw this stumbling performance and was grateful that she hardly ever watched television news. Phil did watch Channel 5 constantly and when he rushed up the front steps less than an hour later Roland expected a hard time.

'Roly, thank God you're in.'

Roland was in the kitchen, making a late lunch. Phil, looking flushed and excited, leaned on the counter near the sink and tried to catch his breath. Roland worried that he was about to collapse. 'You don't look so good, Phil. Maybe you should sit down.'

'Just give me a moment.' When his breathing was under control, he said, 'It's the police. They've found the house.'

'What are you talking about?'

'The house you and Suzie went to for the interview.'

'They've captured the EJA people?'

'Not yet. They've got the place surrounded. Asking for them to come out. So far, they've refused.'

Phil picked up a glass from the draining board and filled it with tap water. He started pacing as he drank, until Roland put out a hand to stop him. 'What is it, Phil? What's wrong?'

'I'm afraid of how this will end.' He sat across the kitchen table from Roland and reached distractedly for the cheese on Roland's plate. 'My friends are in there.'

'Your friends?'

'I thought you might have guessed by now.'

'Come on, mate. As usual with you lately, I have no idea what you're talking about.'

Phil ran his fingers through his hair. Almost casually, he said, 'I'm with the EJA.'

'You!' Roland started to laugh. But something in Phil's eyes stopped him. 'You can't be.'

'Why do you think I've been so bloody busy lately? All those *special events* that took me out of the office.'

Roland struggled to take it in. He thought about his own contact with the EJA. The most puzzling aspect, why they had chosen him, suddenly made sense. As he grasped at the consequences, he mechanically stood and crossed to the sink to fill the kettle. 'No, I don't believe it. You, of all people.'

'It's true, Roly.'

'But, why? What's the point?'

'The point is that in a matter of days we've done more for our cause than in ten years of attending meetings and fund-raisings and sit-ins. We captured the attention of Queensland and made a few people think about what they're doing to the environment. And we've done it without anyone getting hurt. Not so far, anyway.'

'So it was you who followed us the night we buried the gold.'

Phil nodded. 'I had to tell you I was too busy to help. I didn't want you to know I knew where the gold was.'

'Why did you want the gold anyway?'

'It was just a stupid publicity stunt. We thought it would keep the media momentum going when the box was eventually found. How was I to know you'd dig the stupid thing up again. Nobody buries treasure then digs it up and reburies it a few nights later.

It isn't logical.'

'What about Dalton's second bug? Was that you too?'

'I had nothing to do with that. It must have been a rival channel.'

'Now I know how you could predict the exact moment of the explosion the other night.'

'Mate, you don't know the half of it. I triggered it by radio signal from a device in my briefcase. I thought for a moment you actually heard the click of the switch.'

'Oh, God. I did.' Roland sank into a chair and stared at Phil. 'I feel like I hardly know you.'

'I haven't changed. I still believe in the same things I always did.'

'What sort of friend would use me the way you have?'

'You didn't have to do any of it. I gave you a choice right at the beginning. The rest was circumstance.'

'That just isn't true.'

'Think about it. Dalton, Beeb, Suzie have been driving you on this, not me. I've just been trying to play catch-up.'

'It was more than that. You sat down and coldly planned all of this: the kidnapping, stealing the gold, the firebombing of the house, all of it.'

Phil spread his arms. 'Planning isn't exactly how I'd describe it. The only thing we planned perfectly was the Balchin kidnapping. The rest has just been trying to keep one step ahead of disaster. It's been out of control right from the start.'

'So, how are you going to fix it?'

'I can't.' He paused and stared at Roland. 'But maybe you can.'

'No. Whatever it is, I won't do it. Leave me out of it.'

'It's too late. The EJA will demand that you act as a go-between to negotiate Ginny Balchin's release. You're an outsider, someone both parties trust. The police have probably already been told this at the house. They'll have to agree, or look like they're holding up negotiations. They'll make you do it, even if I can't.'

Roland shook his head. But he already knew he wouldn't refuse if the police asked for his help. 'What would I have to do?'

'Just sit tight and wait. Any time now the police will contact you and give you your instructions. When you speak to the EJA, give them a message for me. Tell them not to take any chances. The most important thing is that no one gets hurt.'

30

A fleet of news helicopters circled expectantly overhead as Roland crossed the open ground between the road and the farmhouse. It was two hours since Murphy had bundled him into a car and driven him to Police Headquarters for a meeting with Assistant Commissioner Lockhart. Now Lockhart and Murphy were 200 metres behind him at the police cordon, watching as he edged closer to the low-set brick farmhouse.

When he was a few metres from the bull-nosed verandah a loudspeaker above the front door crackled. 'That's far enough, Kendall. Stop where you are.'

The voice was tinny and hollow, like an old gramophone recording. There was something familiar in the tone and he decided it must have been one of the people he had spoken to on the night of the interview. He stopped on the withered lawn in front of the house and waited for the next instruction.

'Take your shirt off.'

'What?'

'Undo your shirt and take it off.'

He loosened his shirt and slipped it off, exposing the microphone and wires taped to his chest.

'The trousers too.'

He hesitated, aware that every movement he made was being broadcast live on national television. 'Look, is this really necessary? I'll pull the transmitter off.'

He ripped the surgical tape from his abdomen, wincing as it took hairs with it. He pulled the transmitter and its slim battery pack from his underwear and threw them onto the ground. 'That's everything,' he said. 'I promise.'

'Stop pissing around and drop your trousers.'

Roland unbuckled his belt and took off his trousers. He hoped he would be allowed to stop there.

'Okay. Now leave your clothes where they are and come into the house.'

He walked slowly onto the verandah and opened the front door. Inside, it took a moment for his eyes to adjust. He was in a wide, dimly lit hallway that ran the length of the house. The doors leading into the rooms had all been closed. On a narrow table halfway along the corridor, a telephone handset was sitting off the hook. He could just hear the same voice that had addressed him through the loudspeaker say, 'Kendall, pick up the handset.'

He put the receiver to his ear. 'Hello?'

'Okay, first some ground rules. For your own safety, don't go near outside doors until we tell you. We don't know what the people outside will try to do. And when you leave, open the door slowly. Don't make any sudden moves as you walk outside and keep your hands visible. They need to be sure it's you and not one of us. Understood?'

'Yes.'

'Now, what are your instructions from the police?'

'Only to receive your message and leave. And to add that you should give yourselves up immediately. I'm also to observe whatever I can.'

'Which is?'

'Nothing so far.' He scanned the gloomy featureless corridor. 'Look, this line is terrible. Can't we talk face to face?'

'Not this time. We want you to deliver a message. Tell the police we won't deal with them directly any more. You carry all messages from them to us. When you want to speak to us, telephone precisely on the hour.'

'Anything else?'

'Do you know if Balchin has made the payment yet?'

'Not when I last checked. Channel 5 has made its donation, though.'

'We know. We watched the ceremony. You did a great job with the cardboard cheques. But events have rather made that yesterday's news.'

'What do you want me to do next?'

'Nothing until Balchin makes the donation. Tell the police that Virginia Balchin is still being well cared for, but we can't guarantee her safety if they make any move against us.'

This spoiled the genial air of the conversation. 'I thought the arrangement was that she would come to no harm.'

'Just tell them we can't guarantee her safety. When you've spoken to the police, call a news conference and tell them what I've just said. We're monitoring television stations and will know when that's been done. We'll contact you when the Balchin payment has been confirmed on the news. Any questions?'

'No.'

'And tell them not to bother wiring you up next time. It's a cheap trick. Now, get going.'

Roland held his breath as he opened the front door. He knew that somewhere in the distance a marksman was watching every movement through a telescopic sight. He stepped into the light, aware that a single misunderstanding, an error on his part, could put him in danger. Forcing the idea from his mind, he walked slowly across the lawn and collected his clothes. He dressed carefully and continued down the driveway.

As he approached the perimeter fence, a swarm of reporters charged towards him. They swirled around him, bathing him in light from a half-dozen camera-mounted sun guns. Disoriented, he pressed on until the crowd parted and the familiar moustache of the policeman Cleary appeared in front of him. He extracted Roland from the scrum and guided him into the presence of Lockhart and Murphy.

A quarter-hour later, Roland stood before the media again in a hastily arranged news conference. As he squinted at the lights on the cameras, he gave the best answers he could to the dozens of questions thrown at him. It was soon clear that he had very little news to share. He was answering a third variation on the *How did it feel?* question when Murphy interrupted and brought the news conference to an end. He drew Roland aside and told him to stay close and to speak to no one from the media without permission.

Left alone, Roland did the opposite. He sought out Suzie and found her with her crew outside the Channel 5 live-eye van. As he approached, she broke off the conversation with her team and turned to greet him. 'So, how does it feel to be a star?'

'I'd rather be at home in bed with a good book.'

'Come on. This is your 15 minutes of fame. You'll be able to bore people at parties with this for years.'

'I've managed pretty well up to now to bore people at parties without resorting to this.'

She squinted into the setting sun and studied the farmhouse. 'What's the mood in there? What are they thinking?'

He shrugged. 'I only got as far as the hallway.'

'And no sign of Virginia Balchin?'

'None. I think it's going to be a quiet night. They won't want me back until Lloyd Balchin makes his move.'

'What will you do now?'

'Wait here, just like everybody else.'

She faced him again. Her chin lifted and her eyes locked on his. 'What is it, Roly? You're keeping something back.'

'It's nothing.' He looked away. 'I'm just not used to being the centre of attention, that's all.'

She gave his arm a reassuring squeeze. 'You're doing fine. And you're helping bring this safely to an end for everyone. Now, I have to get going. I'm co-anchoring the news from here. Let's talk later.'

The *Newscenter5* bulletin was dominated by the siege. It included film of Roland's entry to and exit from the farmhouse, and featured extended highlights from his news conference. He was fascinated by the coverage and felt, against his will, a growing engagement with the process.

Dalton called him on his mobile as the broadcast ended. 'Roland, you're doing great work for us. Remember to liaise closely with Suzanne. We have to stay one step ahead of the competition. Oh, and Phil wants you to call him. He's borrowed a cell phone too.'

Dalton dictated the number. Roland called it from his own mobile phone and reached Phil immediately. 'Roland! You've talked to the people in the farmhouse?'

'Yes. One of them, anyway.'

'What do they plan to do?'

'Hold out for a while, I think, in the hope that Lloyd Balchin will make the donations.'

'Maybe we should both save batteries. Hang up and turn around.'

Phil was standing about 20 metres away at the counter of a mobile hot dog stand. He waved and, as Roland joined him, collected a king-size hot dog with the works.

'I just couldn't stay away,' Phil said, when they had found a quiet corner of the media encampment.

'How can you possibly eat at a time like this?'

'When I'm stressed, I eat. You know that.'

It was true. Roland had seen him eat prodigious quantities of snack food at the most inappropriate times. Seeing the strain on Phil's face, he lowered his voice and asked, 'You're not thinking of giving yourself up, are you?'

'I considered it. But I can't see how that helps anyone right now. Someone's got to stay on the outside to pick up the pieces.' He paused to nibble at the hot dog. 'I could use some help to do that, Roly.'

'Me?' Roland was shocked. 'You think I could get involved in something like this?'

'You already are involved. I'm only suggesting the possibility of taking it a step further.'

'Well, don't. There's no denying I might feel some sympathy for the broad objectives. But I completely disagree with your methods. These are criminal acts you're committing. How could you even think of dragging me into it?'

They faced each other for a moment until Phil realised that mustard was leaking through the napkin wrapped around the hot dog. Licking it from his fingers, he said, 'I'm sorry, mate. I really am. The EJA must look pretty bad from where you're standing. But we're actually a group of pretty normal people who just took things a little further than we meant to. I'm just trying to get it back on an even keel before any harm comes to anyone.'

'Then use your influence. Get them to release Virginia Balchin tonight and give themselves up.'

'I wish it was that simple. But I'm out here and they are in there. There's a police cordon between us.'

Roland could see the implications of this. He was the only one who could cross that line. 'I'll pass your message on next time I'm in there.'

'Thanks, Roly. You're a real mate. Tell them it's over. They've done all they can.'

Roland nodded. 'You should go home. You're not going to achieve much hanging around here.'

'Short of getting indigestion.' Phil had just taken a large bite from the end of the hot dog. He screwed up his face. 'Maybe I am better off watching it all on Channel 5.'

As he watched Phil drive away, Roland felt a mixture of sadness and anger. The exchange had confirmed his determination to distance himself totally from Phil. It meant leaving Channel 5, a decision that filled him with unexpected sadness. It also meant finding somewhere new to live. He looked forward to it now, and promised himself he would grasp the first opportunity for change that came his way.

Overloaded, he bedded down in the back of a Channel 5 news car and tried to get some rest.

31

At dawn two helicopters appeared in the northern sky. They were from rival television stations, intent on recording the scene for breakfast news. The beat of their engines brought the media encampment to life. News teams emerged from the various makeshift shelters they had been using to snatch a few hours' sleep.

After circling low over the farmhouse, one of the helicopters came in to land on the grass halfway between the police cordon and the homestead. Roland watched as a camera crew jumped out and turned to cover a reporter who stepped down after them. With the camera running, he flamboyantly signalled to the pilot. The chopper rose and swept over the farmhouse again as it departed.

The reporter and camera crew walked towards the farmhouse. They managed a dozen paces before an alarm sounded on the verandah. It was deafening and wailed like an air raid siren for a full minute. It stopped the journalist and his camera crew in their tracks.

When the alarm ended, the voice of the EJA spokesperson came over the loudspeaker:

DO NOT APPROACH THE HOUSE. THIS IS A FINAL WARNING. TURN BACK AND RETURN TO THE POLICE PERIMETER.

A yawning Suzie joined Roland and they watched the camera crew trudge back to the police cordon. She slipped her sunglasses on and squinted into the rising sun. 'Bloody cowboys from *42 Minutes*. They'll try any stunt.'

'You're just jealous,' he replied as she straightened her hair. 'You'd have done it yourself if you'd thought of it.'

She looked at him sharply. 'I do have some principles, you know. I thought you might have realised that by now.'

He saw immediately how deeply he'd hurt her. She was so hard-nosed about her work, so competitive, that he had forgotten there was also a sensitive side to her. She forgave him when he put his arm around her and together they watched two police officers hurry over to the *42 Minutes* team. The confrontation that followed was captured on film and shown that night as part of an ABC panel discussion on media ethics. Eventually the reporter and his camera crew were escorted through the perimeter cordon for an encounter with a visibly shaken Lockhart.

The tension ebbed and the media village returned to normal. Suzanne and Roland bought meat pies from a vendor who had abandoned his usual haunt on the Gold Coast Highway for more lucrative pastures. As they ate, they walked across to the police media liaison van to check for news. They were listening to an ABC radio news bulletin when a message came for Roland from Lockhart. The EJA had asked for another meeting.

Fifteen minutes later he was once again walking up the driveway towards the house. This time there was none of the gut-wrenching tension of his first visit. He put this down to lack of sleep after a night in the back of a Channel 5 station wagon.

When he was a few paces from the verandah, the loudspeaker crackled to life again. 'Okay, Kendall. Come on in.'

After a glance at the security camera above the door, he entered the house. As before, the uncradled telephone was waiting for him in the hallway.

'Morning, Kendall,' the voice on the phone said. 'You look a little tired this morning. Didn't you sleep well?'

'I had a reasonable night, thanks. But you probably had the better rest. You're the only ones around here with proper beds.'

'We hadn't meant to call on you quite so early. But those idiots from *42 Minutes* brought things on a little sooner. We should be admiring it, I suppose. They really know how to use the media. But we want you to warn Lockhart not to let it happen again. We won't let anyone come that close next time.'

'You could have told him that on the phone without getting me up here.'

'You're a little testy, aren't you?'

'I have a message for you from people on the outside.'

'Our media man?'

'He said it's time to give yourselves up, before anyone gets hurt.'

'Tell him we're grateful for the concern, but he's out of the loop now. Is there any news from Balchin about the money?'

'Not yet. I checked with Suzie Denning this morning. She said Balchin is stalling now, waiting to see if you'll give up.'

'Balchin must pay the money before we will even think about releasing his daughter. You have to make people understand that.'

Roland returned to the police area with this information. Lockhart and his team seemed unsurprised. They told him they were settling in for a long siege.

Afterwards, he presented himself to the media again. The

press conference was shorter, with Roland delivering a summary of his conversation with the EJA. The media questions quickly descended into speculation. Roland was asked about the state of mind of the EJA and to give an opinion on how long the siege would last. He answered that he thought things would end well if the EJA were given what they wanted. On the other hand, he said, he wasn't a trained psychologist and couldn't read the minds of the people he was dealing with.

The press conference ended with Lockhart emphatically telling the gathered journalists that they were only this close to the action on sufferance. As the media dispersed, he reinforced the message by confronting the *42 Minutes* journalist. The cameras were still rolling and the altercation was captured for the lunchtime news bulletins.

Roland spent the rest of the morning in or near the Channel 5 live-link van. The number of vehicles in the vicinity of the farmhouse was growing rapidly, both in the media and official parks. A wider variety of caterers arrived and began selling a range of hot and cold snacks at inflated prices. Hired marquees also went up, sitting randomly among the vehicles.

One of the arrivals in the early afternoon was Dalton. Roland encountered him outside a marquee the Channel 5 crew were now using as an office. 'Hi there, Roly. You're becoming quite a celebrity. I had no idea our little offer to the EJA would result in all this.'

Roland smiled. He wanted to tell Dalton that Phil was actually responsible for Channel 5's special access to the EJA. But he knew that he never could.

'Beeb and I brought you a present,' Dalton told him. He waved to Beeb and she joined them, bringing with her a plastic suit bag. She undid the zipper and lifted out a charcoal *Newscenter5* blazer.

'Try it on,' Dalton said, holding it out for Roland.

Roland slipped the jacket on and turned to Suzie and the others for approval. 'Not a bad fit,' Dalton said. 'Beeb estimated it from the clothes you keep at work. Another of her many skills. Hop into the marquee and try the rest on.'

'But this is only for on-air staff.'

'So? You're a member of staff, and at the moment you're on air a lot. Even better, you're on air on every channel around Australia. Next time you walk up to the farmhouse I want people to know you're from the *Newscenter5* team, and that we go places where others just can't follow.'

32

Late in the afternoon, news reached the media encampment that Lloyd Balchin had established a $1 million trust fund for environmental causes. He had named Virginia Balchin as the head of the trust and on her behalf had already offered $100,000 to two causes. Both organisations refused at first, distancing themselves from any implied association with the EJA. But Balchin had insisted that it was now a matter of principle for him and in the end the donations were accepted.

'We're carrying the story on *Newscenter5* at six o'clock,' Suzie told Roland in a rare moment when she wasn't huddled with the growing Channel 5 team. They were all there, he learned, to produce the entire *Newscenter5* hour on location. A makeshift set was being constructed on a platform overlooking the house. Even the roving weatherman, Gus Paulson, who never broadcast indoors, would for once be reunited with his *Newscenter5* colleagues under the open evening sky.

Roland watched the construction of the set with growing dismay. He reminded himself that the EJA actually wanted a media feeding frenzy. But it still seemed wrong that a carnival atmosphere was building around a situation where people's lives were at stake. Dalton was the walking breathing embodiment of this. When Roland encountered him at the edge of the set, he had a wide grin on his face. 'We've had all sorts of problems getting this done in time,' he said. 'But it's afternoons like this that remind me how much I love television.'

'I'm sure it will all be perfect when show time comes around.'

'I hope so, but this is going right down to the wire. We had to reprogram the anchor buggies for the smaller footprint of the temporary set. The biggest challenge will be preventing one of them gliding off the platform. I shouldn't be telling you this, because you'll be up there in one of them.'

'Me?'

'Suzanne will be interviewing live. I want you to repeat the things you said at the press conference today, then she'll ask you a few questions about what it's like to be a go-between.'

'Can't you use the footage from the press conference?'

Dalton shook his head. 'Absolutely not. It's a basic rule of television news that you never ever use material everyone else has, not when the talent is available to you on an exclusive basis.'

Suzie rehearsed Roland shortly before *Newscenter5* began. As 6 p.m. approached, she left him with B.B., who took him through to the make-up area in the Channel 5 marquee. During the first commercial break, Beeb guided him up the steps onto the edge of the set. 'Just remember one thing, Roly. If you get into trouble, just keep smiling and look like you know what you're talking about.'

She helped him into an anchor buggy, threaded a cable up the back of his jacket, and pushed an earpiece into his ear. 'Ignore everything you hear through this unless it's coming from me or Dalton,' she said. 'He's just over there.'

Roland followed her outstretched finger and saw Dalton waving to him.

'Gidday, Roly!' The words came through the earpiece just below the threshold of pain. 'Can you hear me?'

Roland winced. 'Do you think you could dial yourself down a notch, Dalton. I'd like to come out of this with my hearing intact.'

'Sorry, Roly. I want you to forget that the rest of us are here. Imagine you're home alone with Suzanne and you're having a conversation with her in your kitchen, or bedroom, or wherever you two like to be alone together. I'm handing back to Beeb now. She'll guide you through this. Okay?'

'Okay.'

'Thirty seconds everybody,' someone said in his ear. His buggy jerked worryingly into motion and trundled slowly across the set.

'Listen up, Suzie and Roland,' the voice said again. 'Both of your buggies will be moving throughout the whole interview, turning so that the farmhouse comes into view behind you. The programmer is controlling them manually. He's doing his best, but it could be a bumpy ride.'

'Ten seconds, everyone.'

When Roland was about a metre away from Suzie, her buggy bucked and leapt across the gap, colliding with his. She kept a perfect smile in place throughout but, with her lips barely moving, she said, 'Will someone get this fucking milk crate under control.'

As the *On Air* light came on, she switched effortlessly into her on-air persona. 'And welcome back to this special *Newscenter5* broadcast, live from the EJA siege site. With me now is Roland Kendall, a member of the *Newscenter5* team, who is acting as a go-between during negotiations between the police and the EJA.'

As Suzie turned to him, Beeb said in his ear, 'Roly, you're not smiling ... No, that's too much, you look stupid ... Yeah, just right.'

'... the only person so far who has been inside the farmhouse,'

Suzie said. 'Roland, what went through your mind as you walked up the pathway to the door?'

Their buggies were on the move now, gliding in an arc until the floodlit house was behind them.

'Obviously it was pretty tense,' he began, uncomfortably aware that his buggy had stopped on the edge of the platform. 'I was conscious that everyone's eyes were on me. But inside the farmhouse it was just a matter of staying focused on the job I was doing.'

'Have you seen Virginia Balchin either time you've been inside?'

'No. I've asked to see her but, so far, the EJA have refused.'

'But you're sure she's there?'

'I don't think they would lie to me.'

'Why do you say that?'

'It's just an impression I have. They've always been straight with me in the dealings we've had so far.'

'The EJA showed some alarm this morning when reporters from another channel landed a helicopter close to the farmhouse. What did they tell you about this?'

'They were extremely concerned. They blamed the police for failing to control the perimeter. They're worried, I think, about losing the calm that has been a feature of negotiations so far ...'

As he spoke, Beeb's voice crackled in his ear. 'Roly, mention the opposition by name. You've got to be more negative about them.'

Roland decided this was his chance to offload his concerns about the media circus. 'I've got to say, the stunt pulled by the *42 Minutes* reporter this morning was pretty outrageous. Just another example of a disturbing lack of professional ethics displayed by today's media in general and by some news organisations in particular. Too often, reporters place their own goals above the safety of others ...'

'Wow, chill out there, Roland!' Beeb squawked in his ear. 'You'll start a media war! Get him under control, Suzanne.'

'When do you expect to go back into the farmhouse?' Suzie asked hastily.

'Soon, I think. The donations by Lloyd Balchin were a precondition for his daughter's release. I expect they'll want me back in there soon.'

'Do you think they'll release her now?'

'I don't know, Suzanne. I hope so. The important thing is that this ends without anyone getting hurt.'

'Roland Kendall, thank you.'

When the *Newscenter5* hour was over, Roland shared a pizza with Suzie. She ought to have been tired, having been on the go for more than a day and a half, but showed no hint of it. 'I feel great,' she said when Roland asked her. 'I love the buzz you get from a thing like this.'

'You're a junkie, Suzie.'

'I already told you, reporting is like a disease. You must be feeling something yourself, or you wouldn't be here. No one can make you do what you're doing.'

'Of course there's a buzz. Sitting up there on live television. Who wouldn't be excited. But the difference between us is that I don't have a choice.'

'You're kidding yourself. There's always a choice. If you don't want to be here, just walk away. Go home right now. It's as simple as that. They'll find someone else.'

As he reflected on this, he began to wonder if she had a point. Maybe he wanted this just a little, to feel needed or important, and somehow play his part. He replayed the events of the last few weeks, and re-examined his own motives. Slowly, he realised he had been making choices all along. The difference between being one of the players, and one of their toys, was simply a matter of attitude.

Two players with attitude to spare were Dalton and Fraser. He encountered them together near the Channel 5 stage late in the evening. They were huddled conspiratorially, Dalton with his hand on the older man's shoulder. Roland stared dumbly at them until Dalton saw him and called him over.

'I guess there's a secret I need to share with you, Roland,' Dalton said, grinning. 'Fraser has been looking after you for the last week.'

'Looking after me? He has a funny way of doing it.'

'He's unorthodox, sure, but that's why I like him.' Putting his arm around Roland, Dalton drew him aside and they walked away from the set. 'Shortly after your first contact with the EJA, I hired Fraser as your guardian angel.'

'You're kidding, aren't you? Of all the people I've come into contact with recently, he's the one I'm most afraid of.'

'Relax, Roly. He's one of the good guys. I had to convince him about you, though. At first, he thought you were up to no good. I still don't understand why.'

Roland was barely listening. His mind was working overtime to make sense of this new information. 'Dalton, I don't need a guardian angel.'

'I disagree. We didn't know what these people were capable of. I was responsible for your safety and I saw a free agent like Fraser as a sensible precaution.'

'But he made threats against me. He might even have knocked me off my bike.'

'You're way off base there, Roland. Fraser told me about those incidents. Go talk to him, if you want to know more. And when you're through, come back and find me and Beeb. We've got some exciting news we need to share with you.'

Fraser was still standing on the edge of the set, watching Suzie deliver an hourly news update. 'Dalton just said the funniest thing,' Roland said quietly when he joined him.

'What's that?'

'That you were my guardian angel.'

'It's true. He explained everything?'

'Dalton never explains everything. Pretty much like you, really.'

Fraser grunted. 'I don't mind confessing that I've changed my opinion of you. I thought at first you were playing a very clever game with all of us. Now I realise it wasn't the case.'

'I thought you were the one who was playing the game.'

'I was just doing a job. And gathering material for my next book.'

'It was you in Mrs Campbell's house the other night, wasn't it?'

'Of course. Dalton warned me to expect the EJA at your place. The old woman leaves her house unlocked, so it was the perfect place to wait.' Chuckling, he added, 'She would have slept right through it if she didn't have such a weak bladder.'

'You could have killed her with shock.'

'She's as strong as an ox. I dropped in on her yesterday and explained everything.' He laughed again. 'She made scones and tea and we had a good laugh about it together. She has a couple of my thrillers on her bookshelves, you know. And she thinks it was terribly exciting having the EJA popping up in her neighbourhood.'

'I wish I felt the same.'

'Well, you won't have to worry any more. They won't get out of this.'

They both glanced at the brightly lit farmhouse. One huge issue still troubled Roland. 'Were you driving a grey Commodore last week?'

'Now that's a leading question. You're really asking, who took a swipe at you and your bike last week?'

'Was it you?'

'Christ, Roland. Don't be ridiculous. I was there and saw it happen, but couldn't intervene in time. If you want to know who was responsible, start by asking that pair over there.'

Roland followed Fraser's gaze and saw the two policemen, Murphy and Cleary, coming his way. 'What do you mean? They did it, or they know who did it?'

'Did Suzie tell you why I came up to Brisbane?'

'Something about conducting a risk assessment.'

'And she really needed it, too. She has no idea the risks she was taking. Anyway, it turns out that her problem has now gone away.'

'The stalker?'

He nodded. 'Funny thing is, he turned out to be your problem too. And that was his downfall.'

'Are you saying Suzie's stalker knocked me down?'

Fraser nodded. 'I managed to get the Commodore's licence number and gave it to the police. They did the rest. His flat was a shrine to Suzanne Denning. They think he was actually pretty harmless, and would probably have stayed that way. Then you popped up in the newspapers, cheek to cheek with Suzie, and that somehow set him off.'

Roland was staring now at Murphy and Cleary. From the looks on their faces, something was up. 'Fraser, you'll have to tell me the rest later. I expect details.'

Fraser didn't reply. When Roland turned back to face him, he had melted away.

33

The news that Roland would soon be returning to the farmhouse spread quickly through the media encampment. He was instantly the centre of attention again, with a battery of questions flying at him from the growing pack of reporters. Lockhart, who was at his side, deflected every query. He guided Roland through the scrum to the security perimeter and accompanied him part of the way across the open ground.

When they were out of microphone range, he stopped and turned to Roland. Keeping his voice low, he leaned in and said, 'We need Virginia out of there tonight, Roland. This is a turning point. You have to make them see that.'

'I don't understand. Can't we let this thing come slowly to an end now that Balchin has paid the money?'

'He's only made a partial payment, a lot less than the EJA are demanding. Now he's digging his heels in and it's turning into a stalemate. The politicians are starting to get involved now and the pressure is on to hand the whole thing over to the Federal Police. The Counter Terrorism squad. And if that happens, they'll bring it to a pretty rapid conclusion. Flash, Bang, Wallop. Do you get my point?'

'I do now. I'll do everything I can.'

'I hope so. That Federal mob terrify me, good and proper. It's really important you're at your persuasive best in there. The clock is ticking.'

Roland nodded and started for the farmhouse. Lockhart had done a pretty effective job of frightening him. With the first of the Balchin payments confirmed, the tension should have been ebbing away from the siege. Suddenly everything had been turned on its head. Roland wanted the siege to be over as quickly as possible. But he couldn't see how he was going to persuade the EJA that this was the best course of action.

He reached the verandah without the usual challenge through the loudspeaker. It puzzled him and set him even more on edge. The red light on the security camera above the door was active and he waited for his presence to be acknowledged. One minute turned into two, then stretched to five, until he couldn't stand the wait any longer. He opened the front door and walked into the house.

The phone, as usual, was lying off the hook. When he picked it up and spoke into it, the line was dead. Worried now, he walked down the hall and knocked on the first door he came to. 'Hello. This is Roland. Is anyone there?'

There was no response. He knocked again and opened the door. In the gloom from the hall light, he saw that he was on the threshold of a normal suburban bedroom. It was sparsely furnished and devoid of terrorists.

Roland worked methodically along the hall, opening each door in turn. At the far end of the corridor, the last door opened into an open-plan living area at the back of the house. Here, he found evidence of recent habitation. Pizza boxes, takeaway containers and soft-drink bottles sat on the dining table. Dirty plates and cups were stacked in the sink and across the kitchen counter tops. It reminded him of the first student house he had lived in.

A door on the far side of the kitchen took him along another internal corridor to an empty garage. As he was returning to the kitchen, he tried the only other door in the corridor and found that it opened into a windowless storage room. Peering into the near darkness, he saw a figure lying on a mattress against the far wall. He couldn't be sure at first but, as his eyes adjusted, he realised it was Virginia Balchin. She had a light blanket over her, and was sound asleep. He watched for a moment then squatted beside her and gently shook her awake.

Virginia was groggy and only slowly became fully alert. She sat upright, keeping the blanket wrapped protectively around her. After running her fingers through her hair, she rubbed her eyes. As they adjusted to the dim light coming from the hallway, she realised she was looking at a familiar face. 'You're Roland, aren't you?'

He nodded. 'Are you all right?'

She took an age to answer. 'I think so. Can you get me some water. I finished the last of mine this morning.'

On the floor beside the mattress were a half-dozen empty plastic bottles. Beside them, in the corner of the room, was a covered bucket. The stench of urine hung around it. Evidently, she had been in the storeroom for some time.

'Come on,' he said, 'I'll help you through to the kitchen.'

'I wish it was that easy.'

She pulled back the blanket and he saw that a length of chain was attached to her left ankle. It snaked along the concrete floor to a metal bracket mounted on the wall behind her. He tried pulling on the bracket, but she stopped him. 'It's no use. I've been trying that for days. We'll need help. But can you get me the water first.'

He found an unopened bottle of mineral water in the kitchen. Virginia took a long drink from it, then poured a little into her hand and wiped her face. 'Thanks, Roly. You're a lifesaver.'

'How long have you been in here?'

She shrugged. 'A few days, maybe. I don't really know for sure. I've lost track of the time.'

'So what happened to them? How did they get away?'

'You haven't worked it out yet, have you? They were never here. Not while you and the police have been outside, anyway.'

'But …' He stood and paced across the room as he considered what she was telling him. It slowly dawned that she might be right. And he felt like a fool for not realising it sooner. 'The voice on the phone. It sounded like it was miles away. You're telling me that it actually was?'

'They left a few hours before the siege started. They often went off somewhere together like that and, when they did, they would lock me in here. The difference this time was that they didn't come back.' She was gushing now, a reaction, he guessed, to the hours she had spent alone. 'The phone and the loudspeaker outside were set up right from the start as a precaution. They've got some way of controlling it all remotely. They used to talk about it all the time when I was around them. It wasn't something they thought would ever be needed.'

'You must have been worried when they didn't come back.'

She nodded. 'At first. But they always left me a radio when they went out. I heard about the siege on the news and realised it was just a matter of time before someone came in to get me. The batteries on the radio died a while ago. Did Dad finally cough up the ransom?'

'The first $200,000 of it, anyway. It looks like he got cold feet about handing over the full million.'

Virginia smiled at this. 'So my father loves me enough to actually pay over some of his ill-gotten gains to set me free. Maybe that makes going through this worthwhile after all.'

'I'm sure there are better ways of finding that out.'

'You don't know my father, Roly, or you wouldn't say that.'

Roland didn't respond. He was still working through everything she had said. Something about her attitude bothered him. It was nothing he could put his finger on, just a feeling that she was delivering a well-rehearsed record of her incarceration. 'That's the second time in a couple of minutes you've called me Roly.'

Her face hardened slightly. Then she shrugged. 'That's what everyone calls you, isn't it? I'm sure I heard them say that on the radio.'

'My friends certainly call me that. Friends like Phil Porter.'

'I know Phil too. Maybe not as well as you do, but I'd still describe us as friends.' She was watching him carefully now and he couldn't tell if she was worried or simply puzzled that he had raised something so trivial. He felt foolish for even suspecting her. Maybe it was simply that he didn't know who to trust any more.

They continued to stare at each other until eventually she said, 'Maybe it's time you went and found some help, Roly. I think people on the outside will want to know it's all over.'

Thirty minutes later, Roland watched from the shadows of the verandah as Virginia Balchin left the house. She was flanked by the policemen, Murphy and Cleary. Lloyd Balchin met her halfway to the perimeter fence and, in front of the assembled media, made a show of embracing her.

As she spun around in her father's arms, Virginia realised that Roland was watching her. Their eyes locked briefly, and he knew that this was the moment when he had to speak out if he was going to. But he had nothing to go on, just a growing feeling that he had been comprehensively used. He looked away first.

He crossed the open ground from the house to the media area, and braced himself as a gaggle of reporters ran towards him. Suzie reached him first. For once, she said nothing, and he put his arms round her and rested his head against hers. Dalton and B.B. emerged from the crowd and placed themselves between him and the media. They shielded him from probing microphones and questions, but allowed the cameras to record Suzie's embrace. It would be good publicity for *Newscenter5*.

Eventually, Suzie asked, 'What happened in there, Roly?'

'I'm not sure, exactly. But it looks like they were gone long before the police arrived.'

'Gone. But how?'

He shrugged. 'I found Virginia in a locked storeroom. She must have been alone in there for days.'

They were surrounded now by camera crews and reporters. Dalton turned to Suzie and said, 'Come on. He's our exclusive. Let's find somewhere you can talk in private.'

They shepherded him across the open ground and into one of the Channel 5 marquees, brushing aside the attempts of a camera crew to follow. In the doorway, Dalton turned to address the reporters. 'We'll have a full statement for you shortly, once Roland's had a little time to recover. Don't go away.'

Inside, Roland said, 'Dalton, the police told me not to make any statements to the media tonight.'

'Have they finished debriefing you?'

'For now, yes. There really wasn't much I could tell them. And now they want to focus on Virginia Balchin. Do you think you can get me out of here on the quiet?'

'But you're news. You can't just turn your back and hope it all goes away. That's not how it works.'

Exasperated, Roland turned to Suzie for help. She was staring professionally at him, waiting for information. He knew then he would somehow have to get away from all of them until he had worked out what he was going to say. He slumped into a director's chair and put his head in his hands.

Beeb correctly interpreted this as a sign of stress. She squatted beside him, loosened his tie, and opened the top button of his shirt. Gently, she said, 'Roland, honey, just relax. We're not going to let anyone get to you tonight.'

This was the best news he had heard all day. When he smiled his thanks, she said, 'I want you to listen to me. This has been an extremely stressful few days for you. But you're in luck. I am a trained and qualified stress counsellor. If you put yourself completely in my hands, I can guide you through this. You'll feel stronger than ever by the time it's all over.'

It was too much, but he realised it was a potential escape route. He nodded gravely at her, then closed his eyes. He heard Dalton say, 'Suzie, I think you'd better take him home. He shouldn't talk to anyone tonight. Not when he's like this.'

Suzie was incredulous. 'Take him home! You're joking, aren't you? I'm due on air in 15 minutes with an extended bulletin on the end of the siege. I can't walk away from that.'

Dalton's voice hardened. 'Stop and think, Suzanne. We're a team, or we're nothing. That means we look after each other when the situation requires it. Roland needs you to take him home now. Lisa can handle the bulletin. There will be plenty more for you on this story tomorrow.'

Roland's eyes were open now and he was watching Suzie. Beeb and Dalton were staring at her too. It was clear that she wanted to argue, that she hated the idea of handing anything over to Lisa. Then she glanced at Roland, and he saw the guilt creep across her face. Eventually, she swallowed and said, 'Roly, I'm sorry. I don't know what came over me. I've been going at this for two days without a break. Of course I'll drive you home.'

Dalton smiled at her. 'Thanks, Suzie. Now, get out of here, both of you. I'll square it with the police.'

34

Roland and Suzanne hardly spoke during the journey home. He knew she was deliberately withholding the many questions she had about the end of the siege. And he was determined to volunteer nothing until the whole story was clear in his own mind.

The stalemate continued when she turned into the driveway. She switched the engine off and they stared through the windscreen at the darkened house. Eventually, pleading the need for a night's rest, he convinced her to go home. She seemed relieved to be going.

Alone, he put into action the escape plan he'd been working on during the endless hours of waiting at the siege site. He gathered camping equipment and food and packed them into his cycle's touring panniers. He dozed for a few hours, then around 5.30 manoeuvred his loaded bicycle onto the first train to Caboolture. As it stopped and started its way across the northern suburbs, he composed the letter he had decided to write to Sir Adrian Porter. He felt like a Judas, but knew that he had to tell the story of Phil's involvement with the EJA. The words came more easily than expected and by the time he left the train at Caboolture he felt purged of the burden he carried. He sealed the letter in an envelope and packed it in a pannier for posting when he found somewhere to buy a stamp.

For the rest of the morning, he cycled north towards Landsborough. His mind was quickly distracted by the pleasures of cycle touring: the physical effort and rhythm of the road; the little mechanical sounds from the moving parts of his cycle; watching the world as he passed it by. It was hypnotic, and he happily continued from Landsborough towards Kenilworth. Late in the afternoon he arrived at a state forest camping ground. He selected a quiet area near the creek bank away from other campers, pitched his tent and collapsed onto his sleeping bag.

Over the next few days, he relived the events of the siege. There was no doubt that he had been thoroughly used – by Phil, by the EJA, by Dalton and Beeb and everyone at Channel 5. But he blamed himself too. There were too many moments when he should have stepped back and thought more clearly about the choices he was making. And there were times when he should simply have said no. He realised he was in no position to judge others. Eventually he took out the letter he had written to Sir Adrian and burned it in the camp fire. Writing the letter had made him feel better at the time, burning it was another step in the process of freeing himself from Phil and moving on.

He knew he needed to talk about the siege and wanted it to be with Suzie. But only on his terms. After four days he felt ready to make contact. He cycled in the dark that evening to the nearest telephone box, hoping she would be at home when he called.

Her answering machine triggered after a few rings. After a moment's panic about what to say, he started to compose a message. She picked up her phone as he finished. 'Roland, don't hang up!'

'I won't. I won't.'

'Where are you? We're all worried. Dalton, Beeb, me

especially. Why did you push me away like the rest of them?'

She sounded genuinely hurt and he realised how harsh he had been with her. 'I'm sorry, but I just had to be on my own for a while. I couldn't think properly if I stayed where I was. I wanted to be with you, but you're too much a part of everything that happened.'

'I think I understand,' she said, but the tone told him otherwise. The conversation stalled until she asked, 'I don't suppose you've been watching *Newscenter5* this week?'

'Nothing could be further from my mind.'

'Someone found the treasure. Or at least the box. I presented them with the gold on air last night. I thought you'd like to know.'

He tried to calculate how many of his clues had eventually been broadcast, but had to give up. 'How did they find it?'

'It was a couple of students with a metal detector. They got a couple of your early clues and started a systematic search of the parks in their area. Luckily for them, they live in Auchenflower, so it was only a matter of time.'

'I'm very happy for them.' He had forgotten about the competition, and it no longer seemed important. 'I'm sure they can make good use of the money.'

They continued to make small talk for a while. He was enjoying just hearing her voice and let her do most of the talking. Eventually, she steered the conversation back to him. 'Roly, Dalton really wants to talk to you. He's started a new viewer competition.'

'Not another treasure hunt, I hope.'

'Not quite. Actually, it's a man hunt this time.'

Roland felt a sinking feeling in his gut. 'I'm not sure I want to know.'

'He's offered a $5,000 reward for information on your whereabouts. Any viewer who spots you can ring in to claim the cash. I think he's genuinely worried about you. And he seems quite desperate to talk.'

'That must be a dilemma for him. On the one hand he wants to know where I am. On the other he won't want the new competition to end prematurely.'

She laughed at this. 'Roly, I've missed you. More than I wanted to. Tell me where you are and I'll come to you tonight. There's so much to talk about.'

He almost gave in, but found the strength to stick to his plan. 'We need to agree on something first.'

'Anything. Name it.'

'I need to know who I'm talking to: Suzanne Denning the journalist, or Suzie Denning my friend.'

'That's ridiculous. I'm both of those things.'

'I want to talk about what happened, but first you have to promise you'll keep all of it to yourself. Can you promise that?'

'It has to depend on what exactly you're talking about.'

'Not good enough, Suzie. There must always be things in your job you know about but can't broadcast.'

'Of course. But I can't make a blanket promise. Be reasonable.'

'I'm sick of being reasonable. I want to be able to share this with someone and I'd like that person to be you. Think it over. I'll ring you back in a few days.'

He hung up before she could protest. Angry and disappointed, he cycled back to the campsite.

The knowledge that he was the subject of a television man hunt made him self-conscious around his fellow campers. When they approached him over the next 24 hours, he checked for dollar signs in their eyes and wondered who would be the one to disclose his whereabouts to Dalton. Everyone seemed to act oddly around him. Eventually, he realised it was his fault. He was behaving like a fugitive, turning away or averting his eyes when someone approached. It was only a matter of time before someone realised who he was.

He devoted the remainder of his time at the campground to deciding the next step in his life. He had to free himself from any dependence on Phil, and that meant moving house as soon as possible. It also meant leaving Channel 5. Once, he would have been only too eager to go, but his working life was suddenly full of possibilities. His instinct was, and always had been, to steer well clear of Beeb, but four days away from Dalton had made him realise he would miss the excitement of being around the Americans, both of them. There was Suzie too. A relationship with her had a better chance if he stayed on at Mount Coot-tha.

In the end, Phil was the deciding factor. Roland couldn't be around him any more, and that meant his time at Channel 5 Brisbane was over for good.

35

Two mornings after the call with Suzie, Roland sat beside his camp stove, cooking two ageing sausages and the last of his eggs. The early morning peace of the forest was broken by the familiar strained beat of an aero engine. Memories of his hill-top vigil during the film shoot flashed through his mind and he scanned the sky for the source of the disturbance.

There was only one helicopter this time. It took him a full minute to locate it away to the south. As it came closer, the morning sun glinted off its charcoal skin and he realised it was the Channel 5 chopper. It swooped low over the campsite and hovered over the trees, bringing campers out into the open to watch a scarlet-clad cameraman leaning through the open door to record the scene.

Roland did his best to ignore the commotion. He concentrated on the frying pan and transferred his breakfast to a plate as the chopper touched down on the open ground near the creek. He looked up as Dalton stepped down, followed a few seconds later by Suzie and a camera crew. She waved and started towards him, leaving Dalton and the crew to be mobbed by a crowd of fascinated kids and their mums and dads.

Suzie appeared hesitant when she first reached him. She

kissed him on the cheek, then stepped back and smiled. 'Roland Kendall, you're not an easy man to find.'

The mixed emotions whipped up by the chopper's arrival settled. He smiled and patted the log he was sitting on, inviting her to sit beside him. 'If I'd known you were going to drop in, I'd have put more food on.'

She looked suspiciously at the leathery egg and greasy sausages. 'It's a generous offer, but I'm going to say no. I get queasy at the best of times when I go up in the chopper.'

'So *Newscenter5*'s star reporter gets airsick. Imagine if the magazines got hold of that.'

'You wouldn't do a kiss-and-tell story, would you?'

'Give me another kiss and I'll let you know.'

She did, and he made a show of evaluating it. Still mulling it over, he bit into a sausage and burned his tongue. 'I think I've got the kind of story that might just sell to a glossy mag. People will pay big money to find out what it's like to go to bed with Suzanne Denning. Beeb will know the right magazine to place it in.'

'You wouldn't do it, Roly,' she said confidently. 'You value your anonymity too much.'

'You're right, I'm afraid. I just want a quiet life. One where helicopters don't drop in on me at breakfast time in the middle of a state forest.'

'You haven't asked yet how we managed to track you down.'

He pointed his fork at the gaggle of campers surrounding Dalton. 'I suppose it was one of them.'

'I'd guess it's the loud woman in the lime-green leggings. Dalton's giving her most of the attention.'

They watched as Dalton, with the camera rolling, presented the woman with a bundle of crisp $50 notes. When the act was recorded, he disengaged and crossed the campsite to Roland's tent.

Realising her time was limited, Suzie said, 'Roland, I just want you to know that I came with Dalton this morning to find you, not to track down another lead in the EJA story. I can't help wanting to know everything – that's part of my make-up – but I won't tell anyone else, not unless you decide it should go on the record. I suppose I'm trying to say that some things are bigger than the story.'

Dalton arrived before Roland could think of an appropriate response. The American grinned and slapped him on the back. 'Roly, we really surprised you, I bet.'

'I knew it was only a matter of time.' Roland lifted his camp kettle onto the gas stove. 'Coffee anyone? It's only instant I'm afraid.'

Dalton shook his head. 'I think I'll pass. Suzie will too. She has a living to earn. I didn't bring her up here to schmooze around with you.'

Suzie took the hint and rose from the log. 'I'll see you later, Roly. I have to go and ask that lucky winner a couple of breathless *How does it feel?* questions.'

As she crossed the campsite, Dalton said, 'I'm determined to surprise you today, Roland. Do you know why I came up here this morning?'

'Publicity, I reckon. You'd have to work pretty hard to convince me otherwise.'

'I admit that was a factor. But the prime reason was you. I was genuinely worried when you disappeared like that. Beeb told me it was a textbook reaction, but I feel bad I didn't see it coming.'

'I just needed some time on my own.'

'You should have been at home talking it through with someone. Beeb, preferably. That's the best way to get through a thing like this. And to get yourself ready for the next challenge.'

'The next challenge?'

'You're a valuable part of the team. I need you back at work with me.'

To Roland, this sounded genuine. He felt almost sorry it wasn't going to happen. 'Dalton, I can't go back to Channel 5. I actually wish I could, but I can't.'

'I'm not asking you to. I don't want you working there any more.'

'So what exactly is my next challenge?'

Dalton was laughing now, enjoying Roland's confusion. 'I told you days ago I had some exciting news about the future, but you skipped town before I could share it. It's over for us at Channel 5 Brisbane.'

'Sir Adrian sacked you?'

'Technically, Beeb and I quit. And we took the liberty of doing it on your behalf too. I guess you could withdraw that if you wanted.'

Roland tried to conceal his surprise. 'You saved me the trouble of doing it myself. But I'm curious about why you and Beeb are going too.'

'A better deal came along. I told you Beeb was up to something in Sydney and it paid off big.'

'The thing with Mal McDarrow?'

Dalton laughed. 'McDarrow was just a cover for her real mission.'

'Which was?'

'Meeting with the national executives of *Network 5*. They want to adopt the whole *Newscenter5* concept nationally. We had national attention during the siege and viewers across the country liked what they saw.' He broke into a grin. 'B.B. and I leave for Sydney next week. I want you there with us.'

'In Sydney? But why?'

'You know the *Newscenter5* concept, and Beeb and I know you. That makes you the right person to help us hit the ground running. The three of us have had our differences from time to time, but that only makes us stronger as a team. Roly, we like you. And we need you.'

Being needed at work was a completely new concept for Roland. A flattering one too. He was tempted to make a snap decision, but couldn't overcome the inertia of a mind that insisted on methodical rumination. To delay a little, he asked, 'What's in this for me?'

'A new start. There are new challenges, in a new town, with new people. Sure, there's a risk in that, but there's an even greater risk in standing still. It looks to me like you've done enough of that to last the rest of the century.' He paused long enough for his words to sink in. 'You can't turn back on yourself now, Roland. Standing still is for closed minds and stagnant ponds, and you are neither of those.'

Roland could only agree with the sentiment, even if he would have chosen different words. 'You're right about the dangers of standing still. I should know – I've been doing it for almost a decade. I've resisted nearly everything that's happened to me in the last month too, but I've come to realise that I'm enjoying at least some of the ride. I shouldn't tell you this, but I've actually missed the action in the last few days. Over the last few weeks, I haven't known what's coming next, and it's not altogether a bad feeling.'

Dalton sensed victory. Rising from the log, he said, 'I've already booked your air ticket and I've got your new apartment keys in my briefcase. I won't press you for an answer right away. Come back in the chopper and give me your decision when we get back to Mt Coot-tha.'

'Wait a minute, Dalton. There is something that would stop me coming with you. It's someone actually.'

'You mean Beeb? Listen Roland, you've got her all wrong. And I'm not just saying that because our pre-nup requires it.' He waited for Roland to laugh. 'Hey! That's supposed to be humour.'

Roland smiled weakly, and a satisfied Dalton continued, 'Beeb and I are a perfect match according to her computer modelling. You might think that's cause for concern, but it works great for both of us.'

This time Roland did manage to laugh, and so did Dalton. 'She's been operating here in a carefully chosen persona – I told you that right at the beginning – but down in Sydney, she'll be a different woman entirely. She'll treat you differently too. It's a whole new situation, and this time you'll be an insider. Now, come on. I need to be back in Brisbane. I'll help you get your gear together.'

36

Roland quickly discovered that the Channel 5 chopper was no place for quiet reflection. The vibration, combined with the after-effects of a hurried greasy breakfast and the proximity to a blanched Suzie, inhibited decision-making dramatically.

Dalton, who was sitting up front with the pilot, turned regularly and smiled knowingly at him. It made him want to surprise the American with a rejection of the job offer. But it was too compelling. It offered an instant and relatively painless escape. His only concern was Suzie. He wanted to believe they could somehow stay together and he told himself that, even from a distance, they would find a way.

When they touched down at Channel 5, he was ready to commit. 'I've made up my mind,' he shouted at Dalton as they walked in a crouch away from the chopper's decelerating rotors.

'Come over to my office in ten minutes. I'll make sure Beeb's there to hear it too.'

Roland was left alone with Suzie. They walked into the building and along the corridor as far as his office. Unable to keep the decision to himself, he said, 'Suzie, I'm leaving Brisbane for a while. I wanted you to know before anyone else.'

She stopped and stared at him. He waited for a reaction, but she managed only to shake her head slowly.

'Is it possible that I've finally managed to silence Suzanne Denning?'

'I'm stunned. I never guessed for a minute you'd actually leave. Have you been considering this for long?'

'No. And that's what feels so good about it. I've been worrying all week about what to do next. I decided I really had to move house, and to change my job. This morning, an opportunity arose for something more comprehensive.'

'Are you sure you want to hurry into it? A lot happened in the days leading up to the siege. Maybe you need time to get over it.'

'I've been marking time in my life and I just don't want to waste any more. Besides, I have to put some distance between myself and Phil for a while.'

'Haven't you heard? He's gone up north to work on a resort project with Porter Construction. Sir Adrian announced it at a staff gathering a few days ago.'

'A construction project? Phil? That doesn't make sense.'

'No one explained it. It just happened. He saw me before he left and gave me a letter for you. He said he didn't want it lying around where someone else might see it.'

She retrieved it from her bag and passed it to him. 'So, tell me,' she asked, 'have you decided where you're going?'

'Sydney. I'm going to work for Dalton down there.'

This time her jaw dropped. 'You are?'

'For a while, anyway. Until I work out my own next step.'

'Sydney,' she said, and began to laugh.

'What's so funny about that?'

'I somehow thought you'd always be here, that I'd be the one to say I was leaving for Sydney.'

'You will come down to visit me, won't you? I mean, I do want you to.'

She cocked her head at him and grinned. 'I expect we'll

somehow get together. If that's what you'd like.'

'I'd like it a lot. And the sooner the better too.'

He left Suzie and walked along the corridor to Dalton's office. Beeb was already on the sofa and Dalton poured each of them a mug of decaf. 'So,' Dalton said, 'are you still on the team?'

'I sure am.'

Beeb and Dalton looked at each other. 'We knew you'd accept,' Beeb said. 'It's the right thing to do.'

'It's going to be different this time,' Dalton added. 'You're one of us now. No more exclusion from our thoughts. It also means total commitment from you. Are you up for that?'

Remembering his first encounter with Dalton, Roland replied, 'I think, Mr Hinsley, you'll find me surprisingly useful.'

While Dalton laughed at this, Beeb said, 'That's good enough for us, honey. Dalton shared your concerns with me, and I respect them. We're two very different people, you and me. You need your space, and you like to internalise your thoughts. I'm cool with that. All you have to do is learn to push back a little, switch me off, put me back in my box when I get to be too much for you. It's as easy as that, Roly.'

Roland couldn't think of a response. They all knew that handling Beeb would never be that easy. He managed to say, 'Thanks Beeb. I appreciate the advice. I'll do my best.'

Unperturbed, she sailed on. 'We have a lot of work to do. Starting now. You're going to launch a string of nationwide treasure hunts, and coordinate a team of Newsrappers in every state. We're taking Dwayne down south with us too. He'll select and train a national *Newsrap* team. But you'll be in charge of it – development, promotions, merchandising.'

'And that's just for starters,' Dalton said. 'There's also a local issue to deal with first. Maybe you'd like to share your thoughts on it. Beeb, run the demo tape, will you.'

B.B. pressed the play button on the remote control. The centre monitor burst into life, replaying a taped edition of *Newscenter5*. The familiar strident theme played over the promo film shot weeks ago in the quarry. Then the *Newscenter5* set appeared and two anchor buggies trundled onto the stage. Roland leaned forward when he realised that David Burton's anchor partner was Lisa Demchek. 'What's Lisa doing there? Where's Suzie?'

'We're making a few changes to the line-up,' Dalton said, as they watched an obviously thrilled Demchek play to the camera. 'It's not final yet, but she'll probably replace Suzanne in a couple of weeks.'

'But why?' Roland asked, dismayed. 'I thought Suzie was what people wanted.'

'Oh, she's what people want, all right,' Beeb said. 'She's got solid and rising figures from the audience focus groups, especially since you officially came into her life. The thing is, we're planning on taking her down to Sydney with us. She'll be part of the new national anchor team. And on top of that, we'll be offering her a new on-location interview programme called *Crossing Live*. We want to know your thoughts on this.'

Roland shook his head, amazed at how easily they were still able to spring surprises on him. 'Does she know yet?'

'No,' Dalton replied. 'And it's highly confidential. You're sworn to secrecy. So don't look so happy when you're around her.'

'But it is decided, isn't it?'

'It's about as sure as anything can be in the world of television.'

'Then I think you've made the right choice with her successor. I used to think Lisa was a little inexperienced for a top job, but I've recently changed my mind. I know you'll already have gathered a ton of data, but sometimes you've got to go with your gut instinct. I vote yes.'

Dalton patted him on the shoulder. 'Couldn't agree more. Now let's get back to you. You are officially our advance man in Sydney. That means going down there tonight and working through the weekend to set things up for us. We'll get someone to meet you at the airport. Are you up for it?'

'I think so, but what about all my things here?'

'You can come back and settle everything once we're down there. I guess you'd better go pack, huh?'

37

After a frantic day of preparation with Dalton and Beeb, Roland boarded a mid-evening Ansett flight to Sydney.

Shortly after take-off, his neighbour, who was something in computers, decided that Roland was also interested in PC operating systems. He talked excitedly through the light dinner about the soon-to-be-released Windows 3.0 environment. It was only after the man's second cup of coffee, which brought on a trip to the toilet, that Roland had a chance to tear open the letter from Phil.

He unfolded the single sheet of paper and read:

Roland,

By now, you'll know I've gone up north for a while. I thought it best to clear out of Brisbane until the situation settles down. Dad talked me into taking over the project management of a resort he's building on the edge of a rainforest up here. He insisted on me doing it, actually. Which makes me wonder how much he knows about what I've been up to recently. I know you'd never tell him anything. I guess he must have worked it out on his own.

I owe you an explanation about the end of the siege. I had no idea Ginny Balchin was alone in the farmhouse. I'd lost contact with the rest of the group and thought they were trapped in there too. I feel bad about the way I used you. When things got out of control I stopped thinking straight. Which is not an excuse, I know. But you really were the best hope as a go-between, a neutral party, someone that both sides would always trust.

Ginny has been persuaded by her father to recuperate on a Barrier Reef island he owns. She's coming over to see me in a few days. I couldn't tell you before that Ginny and I will be announcing our engagement later in the year. Officially, we've only met a few times at social functions. The story is that we're about to fall head over heels for each other. The truth is, we've been close for more than a year. She says thank you, by the way, for helping her at the end of the siege.

I want you to know I'm through with the whole EJA thing. I can see now how wrong (and crazy) it was. That doesn't mean I'm giving up on the cause, just that I'll be trying to achieve it through more orthodox methods from now on. Gwen would be proud of me if she knew. She might even start talking to me again.

I'm sorry, Roly, for everything. None of this was fair on you. On the other hand, it did give you the chance to be with Suzie Denning a fair bit of the time. So, depending on how that works out, you might want to thank me for that sometime.

I won't be down in Brisbane for the rest of the year, but if you decide to come up north for a holiday, be sure to drop in.

See you mate.

Phil

As he finished reading, the computer expert settled back into his seat. Roland quickly opened his book and pretended to read about the final days of Charlemagne's reign. He realised he no longer bore Phil any malice for involving him in the whole EJA mess. It didn't mean he was anywhere near forgiving him. But in time, perhaps, they might be on speaking terms again. Until then, one thing was sure – north Queensland was definitely off the holiday list.

Dalton had been deliberately vague about who would collect Roland at Sydney airport. He soon realised why. As he lifted his suitcase from the luggage carousel in the arrivals area, he heard a familiar voice say, 'I'll take that if you like.'

He turned and saw Fraser standing a few feet away. Roland glanced down at his suitcase, thinking that Fraser was offering to carry it. But when he looked up again, Fraser was shaking his head. 'I meant the book. I didn't get a chance to finish the introductory chapter at your house that night.'

Roland was using Phil's letter as a bookmark. To prevent Fraser from seeing it, he pushed the book into the side pocket of his suitcase and zipped it shut. 'Did Dalton send you to collect me?'

'I was coming out this way anyway, so it was no trouble to meet your flight too.'

They stared awkwardly at each other until Fraser let his face soften into a smile. 'I expect we'll be seeing each other around from time to time. If not for work, then for social reasons.'

'Social?'

'In the meantime, maybe we should agree on a fresh start.'

Fraser held out his hand. After a moment's hesitation, Roland shook it. He said, 'I have a hundred questions for you about the last few weeks. I don't suppose you'll answer any of them.'

'I very much doubt it. But feel free to ask whatever you like.'

Fraser turned for the exit. 'Come on. My other passenger is waiting.'

When they reached the car, Roland understood what Fraser had meant by *social.* Suzie was leaning against the vintage Jaguar's passenger door. He had last seen her late in the afternoon at Channel 5 when she was rushing off to cover a breaking story. During their hurried goodbye, she had given him a peremptory peck on the cheek and left him with a breezy *See you soon, I guess!* It had seemed odd at the time. Now it made perfect sense.

She hugged him, then stepped back and grinned. 'Welcome to Sydney, Roland.'

'Did Dalton send you down early?'

'Early?' She adopted her interview face, the road-tested expression for extracting maximum information. He almost cracked, but managed to resist. 'Believe it or not,' she continued, 'they don't control all of my activities. I happen to have a weekend off and I decided to spend it with you.'

'There's nothing I'd like more. But I have a full weekend of work ahead of me at Channel 5.'

'Then I'd say you are on the horns of a dilemma.' She fingered the open neck of his shirt as she spoke. 'On the one hand, you could spend the whole weekend working. Or, you could explore Sydney with me, and cobble an excuse together when Dalton gets here. It's up to you, but I know which I'd prefer.'

Roland quickly decided on the latter. His new life, in a new town, was beginning exactly where the old one had left off. He had no idea how it would unfold, but that was precisely the point. He settled into the soft leather on the Jaguar's back seat and, with Suzanne beside him, enjoyed the sensation of being transported willingly to a completely unknown destination.

More about *Crossing Live*

If you enjoyed *Crossing Live* and would like to read more about the story, visit: www.andrewbowie.net

www.ingramcontent.com/pod-product-compliance
Ingram Content Group UK Ltd.
Pitfield, Milton Keynes, MK11 3LW, UK
UKHW040603210726
13854UKWH00009B/2151

9 780995 649019